Chandelier

Chandelier

MICHAEL LEON

Published in Australia by Australian Inspiration 2022

www.australianinspiration.com.au

Cover, design and typesetting by Luke Harris
www.workingtype.com.au

ISBN: 978-0-6454781-0-5 (paperback)
         978-0-6454781-1-2 (ebook)

CONTENTS

RISE

How ironic that as Gaston reached his personal and literary pinnacle, he could now only bid it farewell. His legacy was fading like his memories. Even his beloved study, the scene of his best writing, was now little more than a hospital room.

Night slowly crawled into being, perhaps his last chance to see the phantom of the night, the character the world adored him for and the climax of his creative endeavours. In the day, he thought only of his beloved, Jeanne, rehearsing their final moments together, but as night descended, Gaston relished the silent dusk to imagine, perhaps even see Erik.

All too soon, Jeanne broke his mind's wanderings. Light streamed through the doorway like a curtain opened for a final performance, the most important of his life. Jeanne, as always, was a picture of radiance, reminding him of his good fortune. She sat with him, taking his hand as she'd done every night since his decline.

"Any news?"

Jeanne smiled, taking some papers from her handbag and spreading it in front of him. Gaston read the letter from his attorney, squeezing her hand with delight before lifting her slender fingers to his lips and delicately kissing them. They both sat in the stillness, soaking up the significance of the news.

"Ten years," he said, squeezing the letter.

Jeanne lightly brushed Gaston's clenched fist, making him let go of the scrunched paper. "Ten years of true love."

"You deserved more."

Jeanne shook her head. "I never wanted any more."

He fell back onto his pillow, weakened from merely grasping the paper, eyes closing, fading into sleep.

Jeanne sensed he had little time. "Doctor Flynn will be here soon," she said, waking him.

He looked at the divorce papers as if for the first time. "He can't do any more for me, but he can help us."

"Don't say that, Gaston. He has always found a way."

"No more pills, Jeanne. I'm tired, even of sleeping. I want to spend my last moments living."

Jeanne caressed Gaston's pale cheek and kissed him. "I wish I could do more."

Gaston looked at her emerald eyes admiring how they shone, full of life. Even near death, her energy revived him. "There's time enough. Marry me, my angel."

"I want nothing more, Gaston. When you get better...."

Gaston interjected. "Marry me tonight, my love. That's why I called Flynn."

Jeanne shook her head in annoyance. "You know I want to be yours, but not while you're like this."

She had only ever wished for Gaston's happiness in all of their ten years together, goodwill never afforded by his estranged wife.

"Marry me, darling!"

Jeanne's determination softened as she readied to reply, but then the standoff was broken by Doctor Flynn's arrival, his timing angering Gaston.

"Can you give us five minutes, Flynn?"

"That won't be necessary," Jeanne interjected, standing and offering Flynn her chair.

He nodded to Jeanne before checking Gaston's condition.

"Must we bother with this anymore?" Gaston demanded, pushing Flynn's stethoscope away.

"A doctor never gives up on his patient. Be still!"

Gaston endured Flynn's fussing for a short time. "You have more important duties tonight."

"I know. But first, do you want to hear about the opening night?"

Gaston was about to respond, but Jeanne spoke over him. "Yes. We do," she insisted.

"It was a triumph. I expect tomorrow's reviews to be glowing."

Jeanne brimmed with delight. "An appreciative crowd?"

"A full house and a standing ovation!"

Flynn wanted to continue, but Gaston interrupted. "This can wait until after we address more important things."

Flynn glanced at Jeanne. "Did he?"

"Yes," she replied, taking Gaston's hand.

Flynn looked sternly at Gaston. "Are you sure you've thought this through?" Then he lightened his expression and tapped his friend on the shoulder. Gaston had talked of little else during most of their ten year friendship. "I already knew Gaston's answer, but Jeanne, are you sure?"

Jeanne nodded, squeezing Gaston's hand tighter as he drew her closer. They looked happy together even in this bittersweet moment.

The ceremony was brief as Flynn read the pre-prepared words that joined them in wedlock and had them verify with signatures. Then, sheer joy was tragically closed with imminent death. Flynn could do no more. He waited outside until Jeanne signalled him to enter. She brushed by him without a word and ascended the stairs alone.

Flynn walked into Gaston's room, once the study where he created stories of hope, loss and the dark phantoms of the night. His retreat was now little more than a way station to Gaston's next life. First, he thought of the decade of their friendship as he checked and confirmed his companion's death before covering his lifeless body beneath cold sheets. Then, he spread the documentation on Gaston's writing desk to finish the final chapter of his life. He wanted to write more than the medical description of Gaston's untimely decline. His life deserved prose that uplifted rather than clinical jargon, but that skill evaded him.

On signing the document, he sat back and took a final look at where his friend's lifeless body lay and closed his eyes to recall a favourite time with him, the release of his novel, *The Phantom of the Opera*. The world was Gaston's, a literary triumph that he richly deserved and celebrated with extravagance. He smiled at those times before a noise interrupted his thoughts.

A human whistling sound, distant but growing louder, permeated the chill of the room. An unearthly chilled breath wafted over his face. He opened his eyes and looked up to its source, but he was alone until light formed on the wall behind Gaston's bed. Shapeless light swirled as if blown by that same breeze. The foggy disturbance slowed, allowing the swirling shape to take form. It was human but completely covered in black, bar the shape of a smooth ghostlike face. As the contours sharpened, he realised it was a mask. Was he looking at the phantom? If he was, Gaston's story had been confirmed!

Fear gripped him to the seat. He wanted to flee but dared not move. Before the apparition suddenly looked Flynn's way, turning his fear to terror.

"Who are you?" He asked feebly, but the apparition remained silent.

Flynn went to stand, but a second shape floated into his view. A man dressed in white walked toward Gaston's bed, making no sound as it glided across the room. Both apparitions studied the body for a time, ignoring Flynn before vanishing through the bedroom wall, leaving Flynn alone. He immediately stood and left the room, fearful they may return, not daring to look back. Whatever he witnessed, he didn't wish to see again. Flynn was a scientist who staunchly refuted Gaston's ramblings about ghosts as the product of a vivid imagination. They had spent many years arguing over their existence. Perhaps this was his friend's final wish, to show him that everything he had written and said was true.

PART ONE
REBIRTH

CHAPTER ONE

BENNY

Hotel patrons streamed in from all corners of Paris SC (Super City). The high-level retreat filled with an atmospheric fog, not from long-banned substances, but personal coms, permanently activated by the long-haulers, post-humans who congregated after a fifty straight hours shift. I was supposedly the evening's entertainment. Some welcomed my music but most preferred the personalised entertainment their com-driven AR (augmented reality) streamed, an intricate mix of interactive movies, gaming and targeted advertising. A few humans, 'old gen's', were scattered around the room, primarily aids accompanying wealthy post-humans, the new elite.

I practised scales masquerading as background music before lifting the tempo with some neoclassical noir, hoping to break through my audience's digital wall of indifference. One male post-human looked my way briefly, casting a contemptuous glance. I smiled, and he looked past me as if I wasn't there, a common occurrence between post-humans and humans. What I saw and humans didn't was that we usually weren't in a post-human's field of view, as they overlayed a more palatable AR experience in front of them. What this man didn't know was that I wasn't human. I had AR sight, too. He laid a space opera commercial over my area. I played on—no tip from that corner of the room.

That's how it was most nights, a crowd of self-indulgent post-humans, superior humans as they preferred to be known, or castes, as humans called them. I smiled across the now packed nightclub, 225 castes and 13 humans to be exact, raising the tempo of the music with a flurry across the keyboard, hoping I may win a tip here and there. Instead, the antagonistic caste studied my piano, where he'd inserted the AR gaming ad before walking toward the best tables, lined uniformly beside the best view in the house. A whirlpool of districts spiked web-like across the super city, housing the vast majority of the French population. They weren't even interested in Paris's most stunning view. So why should they care about my music?

I looked at the city skyline; usually, a carbon-filled

haze blanketing the cloud high super scrapers. However, tonight's view offered a special treat. Stars momentarily appeared in the cumulus layered sky, a rare event. The view below was the super city's most significant climate road, a converted freeway that now cut green lines between a vast sea of regenerated buildings. Our cloud scraper building had the best view of the 'farmlane', the largest of the old highways approved for farming under artificial 'sunstrips' where autonomous croppers tended to the super-city's food chain.

Because they believed me to be the token human performer, I relished the challenge of drawing a caste's attention from their virtual lives. Still, most nights, I failed, playing passionately to phantoms, no longer fascinated by the natural world. But tonight, some in the audience were taking an interest. I glanced their way and nodded appreciatively. Two women were being served drinks by my work colleague, Daniel. One was a caste in her senior year's. She wore only one external tech enhancement, a silica form-fit eye patch. Undetectable internal implants made up the bulk of castes technology, so 'patches' were the main distinguishing feature between castes and humans, apart from the sense of superiority they conveyed in the presence of humans. Even the patches would be hard to detect if not for the holographic emblem attachments, a 22nd-century accessory and fashion statement. Diva's holograph made the patch look more like an opera mask. The other woman was younger and a human, likely her assistant. Snippets of their conversation filtered through as I played a Mozart-Takemura improvisation.

"This is Diva," she said, soliciting a warm welcome from Daniel.

"It's an honour," he replied.

That captured my interest. A singer performer? She had to be famous. I listened intently for her name, so I could play a song she'd recognise. None came, so I merely nodded a second time, a little more flirtatiously. The Diva flashed a smile back at me. Her smile matched several thousand face recognition files, the most notable when Mia smiled at Vincent in the dance scene of *Pulp Fiction*. In appreciation, I played a personal favourite song for her, an adaption of a post-romantic song, *"Chandelier"*.

I sang with a high level of emotion, eye contact personal, and the Diva seemed to appreciate it, her field of vision offline, listening to my every heartfelt expression. The song was originally about the devastation of alcoholism, but I changed the lyrics to express my inner demons. I saw a small tear trickle down the Diva's cheek, willing me to play with even more intensity. Her beautiful, expressive eyes charmed and excited me as she tilted her head slightly and brushed her long auburn hair from her neck, silently expressing our momentary connection.

Her assistant tried to make conversation with Diva, only to be silenced with a single raised hand. Diva held her gaze on me until the completion of the song, then vigorously applauding and drawing curious glances from others. I was ready to put on my best show for them, but they both stood to leave before introducing my next song. The sweet moment had passed all too soon, although the human did go to Daniel before leaving, handing him something, probably a tip.

I ended my one-hour session and joined Daniel at the bar where he served. He had my reward, the house special meal and drink waiting for me. Between the free food and the occasional tip, I managed to etch out a living of sorts, although the real bonus was the cheap board in the hotel's building, more a cupboard than a living space, but it allowed me to reside in one of Paris's better areas.

Daniel raced between bar work and taking table orders, filling the quiet moments with conversation. "You played well tonight."

"I always do. You just never notice."

"Like you'd ever play for me. I know who you did play for." Daniel smirked and made the shape of a woman's curves with his hands. "They liked you."

"They liked me so much they didn't leave a tip," I deflected, turning my attention to eating.

"No, but they left me one! You're going to make me rich!"

I chuckled just enough to show Daniel I appreciated his humour. Humans are more likely to level with you if you listen closely. "I thought they liked my music, but why did they leave so soon?"

"I'm not sure. Peri didn't want to. She enjoys music. The Diva likely had to leave. Who knows why. Castes live in two worlds."

He was right. Most castes did live in two worlds and increasingly in the metaverse. However, I knew that the Diva was offline, but I wouldn't tell Daniel that. "Yeah, more pressing engagements than the real world," I lied.

"Peri did leave me her card and asked me to pass it on to you," he said, winking.

"So you know them?"

"I know Peri from a previous nightclub we worked in together. She left there years ago to work with Madame D'Arenberg, who she accompanied tonight. It seems you also impressed her, which is quite a feat."

I nodded. Madame D'Arenberg was a famous diva of the 21st century. I'd studied her work as I had with all musicians in history. I was surprised I didn't recognise her. Still, it wasn't unusual for humans who undertake post-human conversion to change their facial features, particularly women wanting to reclaim their youth.

"Ring her tomorrow. Won't you?"

Daniel pushed the point, which wasn't unusual. He'd been trying to match me with a suitable partner for the last year.

Competitive banter continued between us for some time, which is what we did most nights. It was our way of having fun among the castes, making light of our tenuous position. If not for global human rights treaties, no human would have work, least of all a musician.

I watched Daniel see off the parting guests, smiling appreciatively to the occasional caste who left a tip on the bar but never engaging them in conversation. I'd learnt over the past year to stay in my place. An hour passed before Daniel joined me again, pouring a second drink.

"You're in a generous mood!"

"Yeah, well, the tips were good, but don't expect this every night."

I nodded in appreciation, accepting the drink, signalling my spicy meal had made me thirsty. By the time

I'd finished it, Daniel had cleaned the bar and let in the android cleaners to straighten up the remainder of the nightclub. His work finished, he poured some more drinks.

"Three drinks? The tips must have been special!"

Daniel smiled wistfully, savouring his ale while casting a serious glance my way.

I knew what he wanted, but I asked anyway. "Okay, what is it you want to know?"

"Have you thought about it?"

"I did, and don't think I'm not appreciative, but I'm settled in Paris."

"Musicians playing live to audiences aren't popular here in Paris. You'd do better in a London pub."

"So, your move to London's official?" I replied.

"Got the paperwork today. I start next month. I gave notice this morning. I also spoke to management about your position here, but our boss wasn't willing to extend it. So you've got a month."

I nodded, not sure what to say. That meant I had a month to find new living quarters. Then, with little to no money, I'd be living rough on the outskirts of Paris S C, a prospect I didn't want to consider.

I deflected the conversation. "Ellen must be happy?"

"She's over the moon. Her brother, John, is putting us

up for a month until we find an apartment. From what John says, accommodation in London SC is half the price of here."

"Ally and Philip good with it?"

"They're at a good age to move. Ally said she'd miss you, so call them tonight. Won't you?"

"It's too late. Your kids will be asleep," I said, finishing my drink and standing ready to leave.

"They always wait for me to get home so that I can read them a story. Ally wanted you to play her favourite song to them." Daniel tilted his head slightly, waiting for a reply.

"Okay. I'll call in half an hour." Daniel held a questioning gaze. "I promise, Daniel," I said, then left, not wanting to talk any more about my uncertain future.

CHAPTER TWO

BN1 HUMANOID

I walked from the elevator through a long corridor, passing the many storerooms crammed with stock that serviced the multiple businesses operating in the skyscraper. My home was at the end of the hall, a hastily converted storeroom. It was small and not designed for living, but the technology, old as it was, suited me.

There was no natural light but a 'wall com' compensated, creating a natural setting. The wall com automatically turned on, screening a default image of a babbling brook, its soothing sound permeating my tiny space. I changed into loose-fitting clothing and requested a refreshment. "Coffee, black." The 3D carbon printer delivered a steaming hot beverage within seconds. It was an old model with a limited food and beverage range, but an essential given the scarcity of facilities. Steaming coffee in hand, I relaxed into the only chair in the room, a 'super still' recliner that automatically contoured to my body to ensure maximum comfort or support, depending on my needs.

"Com. Program a call to Daniel Hartford in ten minutes."

"Call set."

"Run music app and set the chair to 'productive', and position digital piano for me."

The leather chair automatically shaped around me to maximum support. A sip of coffee maximised alertness before starting the music app. "Continue from where I left."

Music flowed from the wall com and accompanying information about the writer, performer and history and influences of each song. I scanned slowly, to begin with, before downloading at speeds beyond human capacity. Castes couldn't assimilate the quantity of information that I took in, a secret I guarded. Ironically, like most humans, I struggled to retain the information needed to survive in the caste's world, except for my passion, music. I absorbed it Mozart-like with an appetite that never appeased as I searched for ever more compositions and its creators, filling endless metadata.

An incoming call automatically paused my work, replaced by a visual of Daniel sitting in his children's bedroom, ebook in hand. Pixilated visuals of cartoon characters darted from the digital story before he disengaged, much to Ally's and Philip's displeasure. Their raucous protests drowned out their father until they saw me on the com, calling out in a delighted chorus. "Uncle Benny!"

"Daddy said you'd sing for us," Ally added.

The natural delight in their faces had a high face recognition match rate, most notably, Olive smiling after learning she was accepted in a singing contest in *Little Miss Sunshine*. "Only if you behave and let me talk to your dad first."

They both nodded and remained quiet before Daniel got up and walked out of their bedroom and into the lounge room to sit with Ellen.

"I heard the good news, Ellen."

Ellen squeezed in close to Daniel. "It is good news. I never expected to be going home this soon."

"I'm happy for you. I know how much you missed your family."

My voice carried to the children's bedroom, raising young dissenting voices in the background.

"Not everyone is as happy as me. Dan told me he invited you. I hope you join us. I know my brother is happy to accommodate you for the first month. Tell me you'll think about it," Ellen challenged before standing up to soothe the children. "And you know who will miss you most," she added, tilting her head toward the raucous bedroom and walking there.

"A bit of quiet from you two, or there'll be no more stories or songs tonight," Daniel warned before turning back toward the com. "So you can see everyone wants you to join us, Benny!"

"I promise to give it serious thought. I'll let you know by the week's end."

"Good. My tiny savage beasts have settled. Are you ready to sing for your supper?"

"Of course."

"And don't forget to ring Peri in the morning," he said, projecting his most serious expression.

"Yes, big brother. Now let me sing to my two biggest fans!"

I sang their favourite lullaby to the accompaniment of the digital piano, turning their initial excitement to slumber in a few short minutes, allowing Daniel and Ellen a trouble-free 'bedtime'. "See you tomorrow," said Daniel, grateful for the helping hand.

The call was completed. I opened up my file of personal music and categorised the children's reaction to the nursery song. I studied their small faces up close, noting every expression from elation to drowsiness. Just another illustration of human behaviour among a kaleidoscope of human facial images I collected to help me realise a dream, to be more human. I could study these files for days without rest, but I wanted to know more about the Diva, turning to another music data set containing an extensive history of human music. Again, a kaleidoscope of sounds and visuals flicked across the wall com. I created some new music on the keyboard while learning more about the Diva.

Her career had peaked around a century ago when she suddenly and surprisingly ended her singing career. However, she did remain with the Garnier opera company, choosing to manage the famous organisation rather than perform. There was a lot of research on her unexpected retirement but little about why. So I set broader searches and completed a new musical arrange-ment while waiting for the results. The process continued for another hour and I found little more information. So I turned to my most private files, "full security code lock," I said, ensuring total privacy, before activating sensitive documents, "program Hominoid."

The app automatically burst into a tide of emotions as humans engaged in all forms of conversation, fantasy and whim. No human or post-human could interpret the abundance of images flowing rapid-fire across the com. Akin to a dating site on steroids, male and female humans engaged in pre-date dialogue or activity, ranging from the sincere, looking for partners to the curious who tapped into every fantasy imaginable, the ultimate case study on human interaction and their desire for companionship.

For the remainder of the night, I studied a cacophony of voices and images of potential and actual couples revealing their innermost thoughts across the digital divide — from the dramatic and heartfelt to the tacky and dangerous, my objective, to understand human feelings better.

My first emotional recognition path was eye movement and blinking of lids. Next, Maxprob's (inbuilt computations calculating maximum probabilities) collected and collated a billion interactions in the time a human could make one character judgement, quickly narrowing it to five million couples believed to have experienced a real connection. Another, scanning heart rate and breathing levels, reduced it to a million pairs believed to be experiencing a higher chemistry state – sexual interest. Finally, a further hundred maxprob diagnostics predicted the twenty thousand potential long-term partnerships that would result from the initial billion couples.

I'd done this exercise all my 35 programmed years and watched on with the hope that the steadily improving accuracy held the key to the path I sought, understanding human emotion and becoming more like them.

I turned back to music by the morning, beginning with how Peri and Diva reacted to my performance. Peri expressed a pleasant but business-like manner. That made sense, given she wanted to speak to me. Had they deliberately come to hear my music, or was it a coincidence? Where Peri blended into the informal crowd, Diva shone, wearing a mid-21st century Dolce NFT collection worn in the classic *Palaces and Dungeons* game. It was an ensemble meant to draw attention. She may have long retired, but she still knew how to shine like a star. My song moved this celebrity of the past.

Music was my life's work because it stimulated human emotions, and I provoked something in Diva. She nodded with satisfaction in the middle of my performance as if she was already familiar with my music. If that were true, I'd expect a job offer. No surprise there, as that often happened. What was unusual was a caste wanted to hire me? Most of my one-off gigs came from humans. Post-humans preferred augmented entertainment.

The morning continued as I poured over the history of music and its impact on humans, personal work I'd learned not to share, even with close friends. Experience had taught me that such bravado usually ended badly.

Despite my efforts, human emotion remained a mystery condemning me to an unusual existence, neither human nor post-human. Thirty-five years had passed, and I hadn't aged or slept. Even castes slept. My instincts told me I was an android, and yet my body was flesh and blood. What perversity would drive a creator to develop such an enigma? My endless search had revealed little. Perhaps my creators preferred it remained so. I sometimes imagined I was an AI sentient, now an almost mythical creature, who'd long departed the Earth for their own virtual Earth, their existence now little more than conspiracy theories and rumour. Little did I know that the Diva would be my first small step towards the revelations I had long sought.

CHAPTER THREE

DIVA

I rang Daniel the next day and told him I wasn't coming to London with them. It didn't surprise him. I had developed a bond of sorts with him and his family, but it rarely extended beyond work and the nighttime calls. Friendships rarely extended beyond a year. Daniel would be no different. Besides, I potentially had another work opportunity. After contacting Peri, I learned Diva was interested in offering me work.

So that afternoon, I caught the underground shuttle from Paris to Notre Dame de Lorette in the ninth arrondissement, where Diva lived. The day started well, getting a vacant shuttle corner seat offering a good view of the occupants, primarily commuters going to work. Five of the forty-three were humans. I captured all five on file. All were standing well away from the seated castes, only looking up from their hand coms at stations.

The shuttle soon emerged from the underground. Rue Laffitte was filled with bustling shoppers seeking out unique gifts on offer during a week-long local festival.

Queues formed outside most retailers as humans waited to enter through virus detection units via regulatory decontamination scanners. I kept away from these retail outlets favouring small local vendors, where screening wasn't required. The experience was degrading to humans who were treated poorly compared to castes.

Diva's 40th storey penthouse apartment lay at the top of Paris's most prominent building in the 9th arrondissement, an impressive structure on the corner of Rue De la Victoirre and Rue Lafitte. As per local guidelines, its lowest five storeys were built in the traditional French style, and the remaining 35 levels were modern architecture. Clean lines and an imposing sense of elegance signalled its occupants were wealthy and certainly post-human.

I walked into the climate-controlled building straight to the Site Manager's office, manned by a single occupant.

"Can I help you?" He enquired, scanning my eyes with his own.

The badge on his lapel identified him as the Manager, Max. The red scan patterns emanating from his eyes showed he was an android, an expensive one with the capability to manage the building and security on his own, a formidable piece of circuitry you wouldn't want to cross.

I replied amicably. "Yes. I have an appointment with Madame D'Arenberg."

"One moment, please." Max gave the appearance he had frozen as he contacted Madame D'Arenberg and undertook a security check on me. Some seconds later, he nodded approval, signalling I'd checked out, then he pointed to the lift. "You can go to the 40th floor."

"What is the apartment number?"

"There is just the one apartment," he replied, holding a cautious gaze on me to the lift, no doubt to show that he didn't suffer irregularities in the building.

The lift door breezed up the 40 floors and opened to a spacious foyer. A giant A.R. image camouflaged the entry. To my surprise, it played my previous nights performance of "Chandelier" while information flashed on the screen. Please take a seat.

So I sat back and watched my performance. A minute in and the com screen turned off, revealing the apartment entry, as the door opened.

"Good morning, Benny," said Peri, then introducing herself. She was wearing the same style dress as the previous night. Up close, I could see it was a uniform, plain in colour but stylish in cut, as was her appearance. She smiled warmly. "Please follow me," she said hurriedly, pressed for time. It would seem Diva ran a tight ship.

I expected indulgence, but the apartment opened into a large expanse that I knew well. "The Garnier foyer?"

"Yes. Diva modelled the main living space on it. The ceiling and walls are holographs, but the lighting and floor space use near original materials," Peri said proudly.

"It feels so spacious."

"An optical illusion from the holographs. Diva is very proud of the creation," she said, taking me to a large pair of leather sofas that sat beneath one of three spectacular chandeliers and a view of a replica of the Opera House's very own famous staircase. "Please enjoy the refreshments we have organised while you wait," she said before walking to the other end of the room, exiting through a doorway.

The area was just under three per cent of the size of the actual Garnier, yet the feeling of spaciousness filled the surroundings, making it the equal of the famous opera house. A grand piano sat at the other end of the room, highlighting Diva's musical lineage. I helped myself to hot coffee, then sat back and admired the genius of the decor.

I heard footsteps from the top of the staircase. As

they descended into view, the holographic image of the Garnier's staircase faded, revealing a more modest stairwell. Diva came down, escorted by a male human in his senior years. They both wore formal attire, he in a dress suit, she in ruby-coloured evening gown decorated with opulent matching sapphire. Again, I captured her radiance on com. Her gown matched attire worn in early 21st century productions of *La Traviata*. Diva may have retired, yet she dressed as if she hadn't.

On descending the stairs, she let go of her escort's arm, regally holding her gloved hand out to me, expecting a respectful greeting. Even at home, she acted as a diva should. A lifetime of fame had cultivated a natural tendency toward majestic expression. I accommodated, brushing my lips to her red satin glove.

I delighted her with my old fashioned greeting. Her radiant smile matched Julia Roberts staircase scene in the movie *Ocean's Twelve*. Feminine beauty and confidence. "Welcome to my humble abode, Monsieur Garronne. Do you find the surrounds agreeable?"

"Please, call me Benny. I have never visited a more stunning residence."

"Charming man! See, what did I tell you, Doctor Flynn."

He nodded my way, showing less enthusiasm for my

arrival. "I do not possess your high perceptive powers, Madame Diva," he answered with a hint of cynicism.

Diva over-compensated Flynn's coldness, taking my arm. "You'll have to excuse his Doctor's manner, but aren't all doctors like that?" she countered before taking me on a tour of her own personal Garnier. "Impressed?" she said, pointing to two paintings, one displayed in the hologram, visible to regular sight, the other augmented art visible only through AR enhancement. I pretended to appreciate the single digital painting even though augmented images from Dali to VanGough flashed all around me, most NFT originals, containing a veritable Fort Knox of the digital art world.

"Yes. The pastoral setting is so authentic. I've not seen better in a hologram, Madame."

Her expression went through some rapid calculations before responding. Was she testing me? "Please, call me Diva. It should be the best hologram recreation. I paid enough for it. The finest technology developed in China."

The tour over, we returned to the sofas where Flynn stood waiting. She let go of my arm and slowly sat down, casting a glance to see we remained upright until she sat. Then, once comfortable, she signalled for us to do the same. On cue, an android waiter brought refreshments to the table.

Diva nodded, then issued further instructions to the Android. "Thank you. Please tell Peri to play *La Traviata* on the side screen, background mode, as we discussed."

She watched the android leave and engaged in polite banter until a section of the wall com played one of her final performances of *La Traviata*. Flynn and I watched as the Diva took delight in describing her performance.

"I was at the height of my powers, then," she confessed, looking longingly at a time when all French fans believed her to be the most talented Diva in the world. "Do you like opera, Benny?"

I knew she was testing me, so I looked directly at her, "I have an intense desire to understand all music. It's my calling."

She nodded approval. "I knew it the minute I watched you play."

I could see the genuine delight in her eyes, whereas Flynn showed little enthusiasm, his body directed toward the Diva at all times. Despite his seeming disinterest, he concentrated his gaze directly at me when the Diva asked a question. I had to satisfy them both to win the contract.

"Do you still perform?" I asked, feigning curiosity. But, of course, I already knew Diva stopped performing not long after that performance.

"I only perform privately now. And for a good reason," Diva replied, looking to Flynn to explain further.

Flynn obliged. "Some year's after that performance, Diva underwent 'reassignment'.

I could see the results of the reassignment. Many decades had passed, and Diva had not aged, the gift of undergoing post-human modifications.

"The benefits were many, but it impacted on her natural singing voice, some would say for the better, allowing her a greater ability to sustain power."

"Unfortunately, Doctor Flynn is tone-deaf. The modifications altered the pitch enough for those musically inclined to know I could no longer sing at the elite levels." Diva interrupted.

"A disputed observation," Flynn retaliated, both eyeing each other like prizefighters.

I could see this was a long, harboured bone of contention between them. Had Flynn instigated the modifications? Diva signalled him to continue. She was no shrinking violet and more than willing to hold the centre stage, yet she willed Flynn to speak for her, now. Was it too painful for her to speak of it?

"Anyway, Diva mostly performs privately, but on occasion, she performs for benefit nights. She is a prominent funder of the arts industry in Paris."

"Which is a perfect lead into why you are here, Benny. I'll be hosting a benefit night before the opening of the Opera season. I have Peri to organise all the catering, but she is not a musician. Up until now, I've prepared the musical scores, but this event is too important. So I need a musical director. Do you think you're up to it?" Diva challenged.

"Will you require one or two songs or more?"

"A single song, but I want it to be memorable. It will be my last," she said, holding her unwavering gaze on me, as too did Flynn. There was a seriousness in their demeanour that demonstrated she meant what she said.

I was buying into more than writing a score of music. "Will you perform to an orchestra backing?"

"No. I want an intimate setting. So I will sing, and you will accompany me on my finest Steinway."

"An operatic song?"

"I had originally planned something from *La Traviata*, but hearing your melody changed my mind. So I want to work with you on that piece, develop it and rehearse until it's perfected. The hours will be long and demanding."

"I live reasonably close, so...."

"You will live here for the month. I will have Peri show you your accommodation." Diva insisted.

"There is specialist equipment installed where I live.

It's also quiet and private."

"I understand. You will have everything you need, and I assure you of privacy when you are not working with me."

I held back my response, apprehensive about the live-in relationship's conditions, fearful they may discover my secret.

Flynn sensed my reluctance. "Be warned. Diva is a hard taskmaster. She didn't become France's greatest Diva without hard work. So you will have to work very long hours."

Diva laughed. "That's true, but I will generously reward you."

I smiled for the first time since arriving. Having seen Diva's art collection, I was satisfied the reward would be substantial. "I don't sleep much, anyway. I accept."

"Wonderful!" Diva stood, not attempting to camouflage her excitement. "I will leave you with Doctor Flynn to go through the details."

She readied to leave, but Flynn stood and spoke. "I believe you promised me you would tell Benny of your plans after the benefit night?"

"Ahh, Doctor! Ever the spoilsport. It's simple. I intend to end my life," she said as if it were trifling. Then, as she ascended the staircase from where she came, she turned and called out, "I shall see you on Monday morning. You have the weekend to shift. Peri can help you with any difficulties you may have."

Diva's expression told me she was conflicted. What she proposed and wanted were not aligned, like Viola's despair in *Traviata* when she acted against her own best interest. I sunk back into the leather sofa, not sure if I'd chosen wisely. Diva's life was not unlike the many opera's she performed in, full of emotion, intrigue, love and tragedy. All the while, Flynn studied me before drawing out a com from inside his jacket. He laid it on the table and screened a hologram contract.

"Think carefully before accepting. Everything I said about the Diva is true. She will demand your undivided attention. Your life will begin and end with her for this month."

"Until she ends her life. Why?"

Flynn let go of the inscrutable expression he'd maintained for the whole meeting, finally letting down his guard. "As you can see, Diva chose to become post-human, mainly for selfish reasons. Her appearance is youthful, even though a centenarian. She's suffering the fate of many humans who undertake reassignment in adult life. She misses being human, and she increasingly recoils in horror at her decision. Unfortunately, it's more common than authorities want humans to know.

"Can I try to change her mind?"

"I hope you do. Diva will take you into her confidence very early. She's been a star so long she takes power for granted. She gets whatever she wants. So expect that she will want you."

"Are you saying I have no professional restraints?"

Flynn laughed. "Diva lives through her emotions, and romance is the strongest. If she wants you, Benny, she will take you. If you have a companion, I suggest you forget her for the next month. Diva will seek and demand your undivided attention."

Flynn then invited my digital signature of the contract. I read it, my mind already made up. The musical challenge alone excited me. But the thought of courting a diva fascinated me even more. A diva was the pinnacle of femininity, and she breathed sensuality, even after reassignment. How would she be if I reawakened what once was? Could she help me discover my own personal cravings?

I signed the month-long contract, more than satisfied with the monetary reward offered. I'd have to work a year as a musician to make that sort of money. Surprisingly, having signed it, Flynn looked anything but happy. He was a hard man to read as if he kept secrets, too. That worried me, for anyone who harboured secrets were especially good at discovering other's confidences too. A house full of secrets. Lives touched by the drama of fame and opera. It was worth the risk as I wanted to deliver the perfect music for Diva and, in that aim, hopefully, cast aside the dark thoughts that haunted her.

CHAPTER FOUR

FLYNN

Weeks passed quickly, and my position in the home was more assured by the day, diligently preparing Diva for her penultimate performance. Diva adored my work, and Peri befriended me. Even the Android service staff accommodated my every whim. Only Flynn kept his distance.

Every indulgence I sought was happily accommodated, from access to modern com technology for my research to the most refined digital piano credits could buy. The price I paid for such lofty luxuries was always being at Diva's beck and call. Today was no different. I was summoned to our third practice session that day, accompanying Diva through endless scale sessions followed by rehearsals of potential songs for her final performance.

As always, she dressed impeccably as if performing on stage. Her youthful appearance matched her near pitch-perfect singing, but Diva was a perfectionist, so it was never good enough.

I could hear the slight imperfections, but I encouraged her. "They will never hear what so frustrates you, Diva."

"I don't care what they think. What do you think, Benny?"

"It was sublime."

"Don't humour me! I have told you so many times. What do you think?"

Diplomacy never worked, so I told her the truth. "There is an incorrect separation between your high, middle and low registers."

"I never wavered before reassignment. If I could sue those beasts, I would!" The Diva turned from me as if slighted. "Peri!" She cried several times before her hapless assistant attended to her. "Warm water, lemon and honey, and quicker than it just took you to respond."

Peri scurried away, instructing androids of the Diva's needs. Even the androids had learnt to show an apologetic expression around her when she was displeased.

"I'll have my favourite soup for the evening meal."

"Yes, Madame Diva. In the dining room?"

"Upstairs in my bedroom. I wish to retire early tonight," she replied, seeking and receiving the anticipated nod from her android servant.

She sat for a time, sipping on the water, waiting for the honey and lemon concoction to hydrate her throat, before returning to the piano. "From the top, again."

I nodded, commencing the introduction. "No, wait." Diva interrupted, returning to her chair. "I'm too weary. Play for me, Benny."

I played an arrangement that always soothed her, occasionally throwing a glance her way, revealing the excitement I felt for her beauty. She genuinely admired my music, which was the finest compliment a musician could receive. But, this evening, she gazed longingly at me, wanting more than my music. Everything Flynn had told me was true. She wanted a musical director, friend and lover all rolled into one. Until now, we'd flirted, enjoying the highs and lows of our musical partnership, not overstepping the mark. Still, something in her expression showed me she wanted more, and I willingly accommodated.

I played until she fell into a gentle slumber. "Shall I take you to the rooftop," I whispered, not wanting to startle her.

Diva's lips formed the slightest hint of a smile. Then, her eyes dreamily closed, she motioned acceptance, presenting outstretched arms to cradle and carry her. My strength surprised Diva as I effortlessly took her to the rooftop space, gently laying her head on a pillow.

My sleeping beauty feigned slumber before revealing her mischievous nature. She drew me back into her arms, flashing hungry eyes seeking my approval. Great movies of the past have taught me that intimate connections usually developed from a range of shared emotional experiences, mischievous, melancholy, longing, raw passion. Such memories were the brush strokes to the canvas of love. So I channelled an early 21st-century movie, *Blue Valentine*, where two lovers developed a bond after the sadness of failed marriages. I listened intently to Diva at every one of our many rehearsals, supporting her and stroking her feelings through the music we shared. A bond of trust slowly emerged as Diva allowed me to peel the layers of emotional protection she wore, shielding her from being hurt again.

This night she resolved to put her past to one side, undressing me, admiring me for a moment before taking what she desired. Her skill as a lover was not unexpected, however there were some surprises. Diva was the finest singer in France and an exuberant personality in public, yet she found pleasure in the non-verbal senses of warm breath, soft touch and taste. I kissed her, and she reacted just as Hedy Lamarr had in the early 20th century classic *Ekstase*.

Human lovemaking explores a montage of expressions

from the whimsical to the highly erotic. Diva's lovemaking was a symphony of human emotions that revealed a goddess lay with me, curious to explore all her desires. For me, sexual bonding could only be a cerebral exploration, an experience I ironically could never feel. I had tabulated every recorded emotion in my artificial brain, but no amount of examination could make me feel human pleasure. My joy of the sensual came only from reading Diva's reactions, matching every nuance she exhibited with powerful stories of love contained in my data. A thousand love stories and films cascaded around this intimate moment in time into one powerful memory that I hoped last a lifetime. Hedy Lamar's image remained as her excitement from our first kiss built to the rhythmic pleasures of lovemaking. That scene overlayed with *From Here to Eternity* as Burt Lancaster and Deborah Kerr made love on a deserted beach, reaching the climax of their desires as the incoming ocean tide swept over their ecstasy.

Diva convulsed with pleasure and, at that precious moment, felt joy for our union before falling into a gentle slumber. I lay close, caressing her body while she drifted in and out of sleep. Sometimes, she'd murmur a whisper when I soothed her shoulders and back, other times sighing a pleasurable moan when I caressed her erotically.

Tidal-like sensual cycles repeated deep into the night. I wanted it never to stop, but Diva needed rest.

"Shall I stay?" I asked guiltily.

Diva nodded dreamily. I nestled in closer to her warm body, but she gently pushed me from her. "First, play the new composition you're working on."

"I can, but it's not finished."

"Then we shall complete it together," Diva said seductively. "When we finish it, we'll celebrate," pressing her body to me, revealing her lingering desire.

I dutifully played the piano, occasionally gazing her way as she taunted me, moving her legs in a rhythmic motion, feigning lovemaking.

"I have only written the first few verses. I doubt we'll finish it before twilight."

"Then we will have fun, trying," she teased.

I turned my gaze from her to the piano, gently stroking the keys as if stroking her. "It opens as a simple piece." Then I built the tune's power with forceful strokes, accompanied by equally powerful singing, drawing Diva from her bed.

She stood close to me now, brushing her breasts across my back, stroking my hair. "It's beautiful, Benny. Let's sing it together. I'll lead, and you provide harmony."

Diva's voice always excited me, but even more so this

night as she sang my composition with a vulnerability she rarely showed. The piece drew on Puccini's opera classic *Mario Mario* from Tosca. The famous opera love song told of a female artist's responsibilities, dreams, jealousies and finally unresolved passion to walk alongside her beloved, Mario. It was how I imagined Diva's world was, but it was also my secret plea to find love, having spent all my 35 years searching to understand human feelings in vain. Diva felt the anguish I expressed and sang with a susceptibility, revealing the sadness that underpinned her spirit. We reached the midway point of the unfinished score, searching for the next chorus, but emotions overpowered the moment. Diva held me close, and we just stared at my hastily scribbled verse in silence, both swept up in past experiences we weren't ready to share.

"I'm tired, Benny. We can start again tomorrow," she said, gently kissing my cheek and walking to her powder room, signalling she wanted to be alone.

I watched her retreat as a melancholy mood overtook her. What tragic memories elicited such enduring sadness? She had lost a great love a long time ago, a painful experience that haunted her to this day. Yet, what power of love haunted a whole lifetime? I hoped clues lay in my unfinished composition.

I left quietly, not wishing to disturb her further, descending the stairs through the lounge where Diva's android servant and Peri organised the next day's activities. I gestured goodnight to them before moving through to the sleeping quarters. Unusually, Flynn's bedroom door was open, and his room was empty. To my horror, Flynn sat inside my chamber, seemingly waiting for me.

I stood over Flynn, indignant at the invasion. "My quarters were securely locked. How did you get in?"

"I have access to the whole apartment under Diva's contractual arrangement. It's written in the house rules provided to you."

"There were no such rules written in the contract I signed."

"The contract specified you accepted the house rules, did it not?"

I would have gone directly to Diva and raised the indiscretion if not for her gloomy mood. "Why are you invading my privacy?"

Flynn made no expression, seemingly unconcerned with my aggression. "Privacy is important to you, isn't it?"

"No less than it is to you. I rarely see you in the house. You're usually locked away in your quarters."

"Unlike you, I have other places I can visit. You, however, are confined to this apartment.

"What places. Explain yourself, or I'll insist you leave, now."

"Places you are unable to imagine. Habitats where you sometimes imagine you belong."

I moved closer to Flynn, ready to escort him out. I hadn't trusted him from the first day we met, so I welcomed a chance to put him in his place, forcefully grasping his arm, "Who are you?"

Flynn appeared unconcerned by my physical threat. "That's an ironic question, given you've spent your life trying to solve that mystery about yourself."

I gripped his arm harder, ready to lift him from the chair. Flynn reacted this time, waving his free hand, unleashing a momentary blinding light. Then he repeated his question taunting me. "Do you know who you are?"

"I'm....I...." The force he unleashed exerted a strange control over me as I struggled to speak.

A wrathful smile formed on Flynn's lips, seemingly happy with my susceptibility, before releasing his arm from my grasp and standing up. "Do you even know where you are?"

I searched in the fog of memory loss like a soul desperately struggling to hold on to its corpse, all the while feeling the warm glow of light above, summoning me to a peaceful locale. I reached up to the brilliance, and a stunning chandelier came into view. I wanted more than anything to touch its intoxicating gleam, but closer to the source, the warmth turned to searing frost.

"Touch it, and it will shatter," Flynn warned.

"I looked back from the warmth toward the haze. A man I didn't recognise walked from the fog toward me.

"Who are you?"

"I'm the answer to your lifelong search. If you listen," the shapeless figure replied as it transformed into Flynn.

I defiantly looked back to the light. "It will shatter and decommission you," Flynn warned, and I made the fateful decision to heed his warning. Something in his gaze jolted my incoherent mind back to the chaos turning my world upside down, plunging headlong into a kaleidoscope of incomprehensible images of an alien landscape.

"Follow me," Flynn urged, and I crossed toward my true destiny.

CHAPTER FIVE

SENSORIUM

Fast-moving images gave way to a single setting. A man lay in bed sleeping, his breath uneven and laboured. Was it his death bed? Another man sat in the corner of the darkened room, observing him sleep, before his serenity turned to shock, seemingly detecting our ethereal presence but too scared to move.

Flynn floated over to the stranger, and I was struck by their similar appearance as if brothers.

"Who are you," the stranger asked, looking directly at me.

I was about to reply when Flynn floated toward me, shaking his head, signalling not to speak. Instead, he studied the man in the bed, as did I. The stranger breathed his last breath. I wanted to help him, but Flynn willed me to follow him, leaving the scene behind, floating it seemed, across dimensions.

"Why were we there?" I asked.

"It's where your story truly begins," he said, floating ever faster toward an alien expanse.

I followed Flynn into his strange world. Rainbow sparks continually flashed across a smoke skyline into a giant sun-like pulse, feeding its core, expanding it and rearranging the star's colour. Part fear, part awe stopped me from following Flynn any further. Its violent energy was of a scale beyond my comprehension. A beehive-like fractal folded within itself, each hexagon pulsing out corona-like explosions.

"You're safe. We are in the Sensorium, my home." Flynn nodded reassuringly, then he turned and willed a single violet photon to him with the wave of his hand. "Follow close behind."

I clung to Flynn's arm and walked into the storm before it carried us away from any semblance of normality, adrift in a sea of photon waves shaped by forces free of gravity. We floated in the smokey expanse, protected from the fireworks by an invisible bubble. "Are we in space?"

"Life is all around you, no larger than a quark, floating on photons."

"Are we the only humans?"

He did not answer. Instead, Flynn turned into a light source before directing me to look away from the fiery sky back to inside our protected bubble. The interior changed into a machinery filled room.

"Is this a holodeck?"

There was no reply. Had Flynn left me alone in this strange world?

A single machine opened, enticing me to enter. I hesitated, but what else could I do but follow Flynn's directions? Inside, Flynn's image reappeared on a screen. He didn't speak. He didn't have to as his thoughts roared inside my head. Telepathic messages filled the machine's interior.

Then in an instant, I returned to Earth, but I'd returned without any physical form, floating spirit-like." Have I died?"

Flynn scoffed." You mean, decommissioned?"

"What do you know about me?"

"There's no time for questions, Benny. Follow me and explore your surroundings."

I nodded but couldn't move from where I floated a metre above the ground.

"Imagine you're moving, and your core will react."

With a single thought, I floated with Flynn exploring Diva's home. Peri and the android servant were busy with their activities, so I called to them.

"They cannot hear or see you."

"Is there a way to make them see me?"

"Yes. When you're ready."

"Where can we go, Flynn?"

"Anywhere your core can imagine."

I thought of my previous home but remained in Diva's house.

"Not now. You're too tired," said Flynn.

I shook my head, "I've never felt...." Then for the first time in my thirty-five year commission, I felt fatigued.

"You were saying?" Flynn said, slightly bemused.

"The room is spinning. Please, I need to stand. I...."

The spinning accelerated, disorienting me before I experienced something altogether strange and new. Then, finally, I blacked out, gaining consciousness to the sound of Peri's voice.

"Benny, Benny........" I sat up, dazed and disoriented. Peri studied me, concern in her expression. "Are you okay?"

I looked for Flynn, but he wasn't there. I checked the time. It was morning. I'd lost ten hours. Had I experienced sleep?

"Diva asked you to meet her for breakfast in an hour in the rooftop garden. Shall I tell her you will join her?"

I was surprised by her request. Diva wasn't one to offer a choice. Peri looked equally awkward in asking as she waited for my reply. I thought about our evening encounter and Diva's sudden despair. Had I unwittingly offended her?

"Of course I'll join her, Peri. Thank you for waking me," I replied, smiling in gratitude before she turned and left.

The invitation lifted my spirits. Peri thought I'd awakened from sleep. If only that were true. I determined to see Flynn and confront him about my ordeal. Was it real, or had I experienced a human dream for the first time? A dream seemed the best explanation given its vivid strangeness.

On showering and dressing, I approached Flynn, who sat at his bedroom desk, organising his day's activities and appointments. He didn't even acknowledge me, more irritated with my presence as he finished a task. Then, some minutes later, he swivelled on his chair to face me. "Yes?" he asked, in his usual impatient manner.

I wanted to confront him about last night to see his reaction, but Flynn's unsettling tone stifled my resolve. "I woke late this morning. I never sleep so long. Is there something I could take to fix that?"

Flynn smirked indignantly. "Consider yourself blessed. Most people request medication to sleep."

"Sleeping is fine, but I experienced a nightmare so vivid it unsettled me."

"That can happen when you over-sleep. I can arrange the Android to collect some medicine for you by midday."

I looked for signs that Flynn knew more than he was saying, but he merely turned back to his work, showing his usual ambivalence. If not for Diva's breakfast arrangement, I'd have confronted him. So instead, I headed up the staircase and out to the rooftop garden, where Diva sat at the breakfast table admiring the blood-red sunrise edge over Paris's smog-filled skyline.

"Sleep well, Benny?"

"I did. Better than expected. You?"

She self-consciously brushed her tangled long hair back from her face, trying to tidy her appearance. "I didn't sleep."

An uncomfortable silence ensued between us. "I hope it wasn't anything I said or did?"

She poured fresh juice for me, considering her reply. Her eyes circled by dark rings and accentuated by the lack of makeup was out of character. She looked aged and vulnerable.

"You look exhausted. I could return later, Diva?"

"No. I sent you away last night when I wished I hadn't. But, please, I want you to stay," she said, passing me the glass of juice.

Then we both enjoyed fresh fruit and pastries, relaxing

in her leafy garden as the Sun's cloud filtered rays cast faded shadows across the table. The scents of berries and night-blooming jasmine mingled in the cool air, enhancing the mood.

"I don't do this near enough as I should," Diva said, breathing in the aromas and admiring the small fountain bordering the feature garden."

"Breakfast in your garden?"

Diva chuckled, "Partly right. I breakfast here often, but I haven't shared it with someone I cared for in a long time."

Her expression was complex, but her fixed gaze showed me her forthrightness, like Julie Delpie in Before Sunrise. I re-enacted Ethan Hawke's sincerity. "I want what's best for you, Diva."

"I know you mean that." Diva extended her open palm for me to hold, a sign of trust.

Perhaps last night was a sign that she feared being close again? I held her fingertips and gently stroked them. "Tell me, what's wrong? We shared such a beautiful night, but then you became so sad."

"Nothing and everything," she replied coyly.

"Perhaps I'm not who you need? You can tell me. I wouldn't be offended."

Diva reacted to my candid response, drawing my

hand close to her. "You can do this, Benny. The minute I walked into the nightclub and heard you sing, I knew you could help me. What you don't know yet, is how much I ask of you."

"I won't stop until we have the perfect song."

"I know. I feel your loyalty, but I ask so much. I've always demanded a lot from those I care for, and it's always ended badly."

I wanted to tell Diva my secrets, but my dream experience made me hold back, so I told her half truths. "I'm not like others you have met. Pain and tragedy hold no fears for me."

Diva pressed her lips together and looked thoughtful, "I want you to develop the song you performed in the nightclub. The tune is perfect, but the lyrics must change."

"'Chandelier'. It's a song about addiction."

"Yes, I know. The emotion of the song resonated with me. Make the lyrics echo that mood and reveal the secrets of my life."

"I've kept secrets all my life. It's the one thing I do well," I confided.

"Some secrets should remain so. But, unfortunately, my performance won't allow such indulgences. Peri and I are taking a trip today and won't return until tomorrow. So I want you to perform 'Chandelier' on my return home tomorrow night. The song has to reveal secrets, both yours and mine."

"Can't we spend time together and talk about your life?" I asked, trying to draw some secrets from her."

She withdrew her hand, seemingly slighted. "You have become my lover, and you want to interview me? I want a musical score so powerful it will summon my true love from the grave so that I may share one final triumph with him."

"Can you share something about him?"

Diva stood up, showing her annoyance. "I've provided you with the best technology money can buy. I suggest you use it if you haven't already done so and study my documented history." She turned from me and walked inside, calling to Peri to organise their trip away, leaving me to sip the last of my juice alone to deliberate over her intense and sudden mood swing.

There was little more to do but meet Diva's challenge and deliver a heartfelt composition. I spent what was left of the morning reviewing her opera life. After Carlotta Caccini's fall from grace as France's finest Prima Donna, Christine Dubois had shot to fame. Fortuitously, Carlotta would become a close friend and help her rise to stardom. Rumours pointed to an unearthly assistant, the Phantom, who supposedly ruled the Garnier for many decades.

Blessed with an angelic operatic voice, Christine was not so fortunate with love. She had adored Philippe D'Arenberg but lost him before they could marry. She was also friends with Philippe's brother, Raoul. Rumour had it they were more than friends, but he too disappeared under suspicious circumstances. Her other interested suitor, Erik Destler, proved to be more than he appeared. Hired as head of security, he kept his extensive musical background secret to all but Christine, helping her refine her voice until he, too, disappeared. It seemed everyone Christine cared for mysteriously disappeared.

Unsurprisingly, she failed to form a union of consequence again, preferring to indulge her whims with many and varied men. She abandoned true love, insisting her new friends called her Diva and never Christine. Was I another in a long line of flirtations never to learn the whole truth of her earlier years? Perhaps my music held the key to unlocking her mysteries? Somehow, I had to draw her from her guardedness and tell me of that time, for there was scarcely any recorded information on her formative years, strange given her fame.

A knock on my door interrupted my thoughts. The service android entered. "I have the medicine you requested from Doctor Flynn. He advised you take one daily with lunch."

I studied the container of medicine as the Android waited for me to give him leave. "Thank you. Could you tell me where Diva and Peri went today?"

"They went to Paris Central. I believe they will be going to the Garnier in the evening."

I dismissed him with a nod and returned to my research. Interesting that where Diva struggled to face conversation about her past, she had little trouble visiting the scene of her despair. What drew her there? Or perhaps who drew her there? I lost track of time, working well past lunch. Mid-afternoon, I 3D printed a meal and drained it down with tea and one of Flynn's tablets. By four o'clock, I felt weary for only the second time in my 35 year commission. Was this to be my new normal?

I lay down, rested my head on a pillow and relaxed. I hadn't started on the music for Diva, but I had some ideas after reviewing the men who'd influenced her. Again, the strange sensation of sleep seeped over me, my last thought of Diva and her most eccentric relationship, the reported love for Erik Destler, the Phantom of the Opera.

"A good place to start."

I woke, startled by Flynn's voice, intending to reprimand him for invading my retreat, but couldn't. We sat in the Garnier opera house's empty auditorium. I physically reached out and touched an open seat, not believing what had occurred. "This has to be a dream."

Flynn shook his head and turned directly toward me, placing one arm across the top of my chair as if offering a bridge between our sceptical divide. "It was too soon to tell you the truth. You were still shocked by the experience."

He was right there. I touched his arm to be sure he was real as I calculated the numerous reasons for my state of mind. "The pills. You've prescribed me hallucinatory drugs?"

He laughed. "These experiences are very real."

I stood up and walked to the front stage, hoping Flynn would no longer be there when I turned, but he remained, expressing a bemused smile, patiently waiting for me to speak. "Make me understand, Flynn, or I will walk out of my contract and never come back."

Flynn walked to the front stall and joined me. "Diva gave you a job to do. I also have a role. To help you."

"What role? Are you going to fly around and have me follow you again?"

"No. I want you to look at the middle stall to your right."

I followed Flynn's gaze to Box Five, supposedly the Opera Ghost's private stall. A spectral shape walked out from the shadows into the light—a woman who looked past me to the stage.

I called out to her, but she didn't respond. "Can she see us?"

"No one can see you in this world, not even the opera ghost's faithful assistant, Madame Giraud, but she senses us," Flynn replied, before waving his hand toward the stage, seemingly making the curtain flutter as if by a breeze. "She can see that. Study her eyes, Benny."

I looked into the eyes of the ageing woman, feeling a sharp jolt from her gaze as if she saw me for an instant, its invisible force picking me up as if a ship in the open ocean blown by gale winds to another shore. I came to rest on the bank of a lakeside township, gazing into the eyes of another, not a woman but a man who stood on a terrace balcony overlooking the lake below where I stood.

"Let your research begin," said Flynn.

"What am I doing here?"

"That's for you to work out. What's important is that you are where you should be, observing the man you wish to know more about. The man you see is the Diva's mentor," Flynn said, before his voice drew feint, as did his presence. The last words he spoke before he completely vanished were "Erik Destler, " better known as the Phantom of the Opera.

PART TWO
REUNION

CHAPTER SIX

ERIK

The twilight between tired revellers and early morning risers had become Erik's refuge, a place where the pains of past and present could coalesce in his ritual of the macabre. He'd dreamt of his tormentors again, beasts controlled by masters who understood their canine's savagery as intimately as a mother knew her child. The nightmares recurred nightly, taunting his mind.

Chilly breezes flowed down from the Lepontine Alps, carving patterns across Lake Como. He drew his coat closer, protecting all but his face, but he wouldn't feel an arctic breeze there. He touched his pale cheeks, not to warm them, for they were permanently cold, an immovable party mask. Instead, he felt the rough texture of the implanted skin grafted to his face. Habitually, he reached into his coat pocket for a medicated ointment to soothe his new identity.

A single boat predictably made its way toward the Bellagio port, the first for the day. It would wait for the steady procession of commuters and tourists ready to navigate the Lombardy region, Italy's foothills to the Swiss alps. The light from the slow-moving boat cast a darker than usual spotlight on the famous U-shaped lake, lit by its twin light, a crescent moon. It took Erik back to a dark past when he ruled the Garnier from the recesses of its famous lake chamber. His rule was cut short through carelessness, a mistake he would not repeat. He'd return to the jewel of the opera crown and rule that grand world again, but this time, he'd lead it from the stage, rather than Garnier's hidden lake.

Were similar dark secrets contained in the black depths of Lake Como? The thought made him grimace, drawing pain. He held his mouth and cheeks, soothing the scar lines camouflaged beneath a thick beard. The scars, like his name, were all that remained of his past life, contingencies needed to protect him from those who'd seek to destroy him.

The boat's captain docked with Swiss timely precision before he signalled a farewell to a single intrepid traveller braving the early frost. Erik's loyal partner in crime walked the gangway with normal youthful strides , then turned away from Bellagio township and in the direction of Erik's villa. Bernard climbed the hill Napoleon-like, one arm hidden in his overcoat and the other holding up his mobile device. Erik nodded down to him as he approached, pressing the security entry. A short while later, Bernard walked through the open doorway, making his way immediately to the soothing log-fire flames.

"Aren't you cold?" Bernard asked, rubbing his hands briskly by the flames.

Erik shook his head, raising his glass of whisky as an explanation. "Like a glass?"

"Does a camel want a watering hole in an oasis?"

Erik poured whisky into the spare glass and placed it in front of the empty chair opposite. Bernard quickly joined him and raised his glass. "Drink to forget."

"Drink to forget," Erik repeated, clinking their glasses and honouring their legionnaires past.

Bernard preceded to scoff it. "Sure takes the sting out of the night."

Erik unconsciously twirled his legionnaire's ring, a lifetime habit and his way of honouring his years of service. "It takes the sting out of many things."

"Bad night?" Bernard asked.

"Every night is." Erik finished his glass and refilled both, in the mood to drink away his nightmares.

Bernard studied him for a while, not out of pity but something quite the opposite. "Henry's made you look younger."

"I don't care about looks or youthfulness. Do I look different?"

"Your mother wouldn't recognise you," he replied, scoffing the second whisky.

Erik nodded, reassured. Bernard could weave a tale of deceit better than anyone he knew, but his loyalty to Erik was more potent. "Is Henry satisfied with our arrangement?"

"Yep. Henry closed his clinic to the public, as promised. It's officially a private facility with a total of one patient."

"I've rewarded him amply. He won't get greedy on us, will he?"

"Soldier's oath. He's not forgotten our tour of duty."

Henry, like Bernard, served Erik loyally. "He's a good man. He'll stay true, but you did warn him of the cost of deceit?"

Bernard held his response, preferring to turn his glass of whisky, seemingly drawing warmth from its contents. "Anyone that served in our corps doesn't need to be told."

"I'll be able to venture out of this retreat soon. Any news from Teatro Sociale?"

Bernard removed his thick jacket, sufficiently warmed

by the whisky, and revealed his stocky, youthful physique, developed after years of elite legionnaire training. "Yes, and it's all good. That's why I'm here."

"The Director accepted my offer?"

"He delayed the reply, but that was no more than a ruse. The Teatro Sociale has been struggling for years, so your financial proposition was too good to refuse."

"Forty per cent stake?"

"Exactly as per the contract we drew up. Teatro's board would like to progress with the signing ASAP, then announce it at the annual awards dinner at the end of the month."

Erik revealed the slightest smile from his typical poker face expression before refilling both glasses to celebrate their success. Bernard had always been his best sapper, even during their torturous incarnation in the bloodiest of camps. Together, they protected most of their squad from certain death, ensuring the survivor's promise of lifelong loyalty, a bond very much needed as Erik built a new identity.

"I'm ready to join the world again."

Bernard smiled, allowing a brief moment for self-satisfaction. "The Director and his wife have organised two places at the head table for you."

"We can discuss this at the signing. Any thoughts?"

"I heard the Director is encouraging a certain famous opera singer to be a guest of honour at the awards."

"Carlotta?"

"The very one."

Fate had circled Erik like a Prima Donna's serenade. The most famous opera singer in the world and his previous lover was the first to return to his new world. "Tell the Director I wish to invite Carlotta to the Awards personally."

Bernard nodded, noting his request in a notepad he always carried with him. Erik's new plans to reemerge into the opera world were taking shape, and this lucky omen could only hasten the return to his natural home — the Garnier. The thickness of his beard felt comforting as he stroked it. He couldn't feel the scars, let alone see them, reassuring his desire for anonymity. The timing was perfect to meet with his previous lover. If Carlotta could not recognise him, who else could?

"Would you like me to prepare extracurricular plans for our visitor?" Bernard asked, his notebook and pencil at the ready.

"I have many plans for Carlotta, starting with a well-publicised dinner with her as the guest of honour. She couldn't resist the opportunity. It would also be a chance to reforge our special bond. Between Carlotta and her husband, Victor, our return to the jewel in the opera crown will be unstoppable."

Bernard nodded, returning the notebook to his top pocket, ready to get to work, a loyal legionnaire whose conscience played little part in his life. "And if she starts looking for retribution? Christine is now the toast of Europe."

"Then we act. Just as we did last time."

A sudden breeze whistled up from the lake, a frosty gust that made the lights flicker on and off. Both hugged their coats tighter to warm from the unexpected chill.

"Did you see that?" Erik asked, looking at the moonlit lake. Bernard shook his head. "A tiny orb of light flashed across the lake."

"Probably the wind gust was distorting the image of the moon."

Erik held his gaze. He'd seen that shape before in the Garnier. Many believed it was the sign of the opera ghost. Strange the wind gust should happen when he mentioned Christine. They both sat in silence, waiting for another breeze, but it remained still. Erik resigned himself to Bernard's explanation, so they raised their glasses the last time.

"Leave your head at the door, Corporal."

"Leave your head at the door," Bernard responded with

a cold and determined expression.

Erik drank, knowing Bernard was skilled in enacting his job, no matter the difficulty or horror and without a shred of guilt or compassion. Erik could do the same, but he had another more potent weapon in his arsenal — revenge. Carlotta's resurrection to the spotlight would be full of passion and joy, before perhaps ending in terror, just as in the best of operas, just as his one true love, Rose, had endured in her short life. He would enact his revenge, and not even the ethereal power of the opera ghost would stop him.

The day of Erik's reunion with Carlotta was postcard-perfect. He strolled past the line of tall palms lining the lake walkway. The calm water on one side and manicured greenery on the other began a day filled with surprises. The walkway to the end of the peninsula curved up steps overlooking the well-populated pool area before diverting to the entry of the Serbelloni Grand Hotel.

Erik smiled back at the welcoming assistant, belying the pain he felt. Dark glasses hid his wretched condition.

"How may I help you, Signore....?"

"Rossi. I have come to meet Madame Carlotta Caccini. I understand she's staying with you this week?"

"May I have your full name, Signore?"

"Signore Erik Rossi."

"Thank you. Please make yourself comfortable in the grand hall. Our concierge will take you there while I notify Madam Caccini of your arrival."

The grand hall was an impressive, spacious retreat enhanced by frescoed ceilings and Murano glass chandeliers. Erik welcomed the silver setting that awaited him, a refreshing mix of pastries and freshly brewed coffee. The concierge returned, advising him Carlotta was running late. Erik availed himself of the restroom, using first cold water and then skin conditioner to soothe the pain running down his face. "I am Signore Rossi," he said, practising his greeting in Italian. Where his appearance had changed, his voice had not. Speaking in Italian would be an essential camouflage against Carlotta recognising him. They were lovers for a while, but he only spoke in French.

Doubt filled Erik's mind as he peered into the gold-framed mirror. He had little difficulty identifying his old face beneath the new appearance. Would Carlotta find it equally easy? Had he been too hasty to arrange a meeting with her? Henry's skilled surgical hands had repaired most of the facial damage, affording him the chance for a new life, but had it changed him sufficiently? Today was the first full dress rehearsal. Erik pinned his hair back, relaxing stiffened face muscles and drawing some feeling to them. He had little feeling six months earlier, bar a slight tingling sensation offering some encouragement. Henry had warned him that he might never recover full feeling, which would unnerve most, but not Erik. His ultimate reward would justify any loss.

On returning to the grand lounge, he was surprised to find Carlotta sitting at the table, waiting. She'd aged more than he expected, appearing a shadow of the bold diva he remembered. Rather than hold centre stage, as was her custom, Carlotta sat quietly at the table, drinking coffee. Even her dress, though elegant, was straightforward in colour and understated.

"Wonderful to meet you, Madame Caccini," Erik said, waiting to accept her hand but only receiving a suspicious gaze.

The ensuing silence and her attentive gaze concerned him, making him feel self-conscious. He did not know this Carlotta. Her whole demeanour had changed since they last met. Vibrant, expressive eyes were now sad hollows indented in an expressionless face. Her gaunt complexion had a hospital colourlessness about it. For the first time, he saw Carlotta with no makeup, the essential hallmark of a star. How ironic that he saw her natural face from the anonymity of his new mask.

"I have met with few people these last few months, Monsieur Rossi," she offered, as if apologising for the silence. Carlotta held back again, saying little. Was she playing with him?

"I'm delighted that you chose to meet with me, Madame Caccini."

"Please, I prefer Carlotta, Monsieur Rossi."

"Then you must call me Erik," he insisted, wondering if the name would spark any memories.

Carlotta's stolid expression softened as she took his arm. "Come with me. I have organised a deck-side table in the Mistral restaurant. It has a charming view of the lake. We'll be able to talk in a more relaxed setting over some brunch."

They were seated in a private deck-side table that had an assortment of pre-arranged pastries, condiments, fruits and coffee. "I hope you have not already dined this morning, Erik?" Carlotta enquired.

"No, it's perfect. Thank you for your kindness."

"I should thank you, given the Teatro Sociale is paying for all of this," Carlotta replied, turning her gaze toward the expansive view of the lake. "I assume you have come here to talk about the dinner event that we'll be attending together?"

"Yes, I have. But I have to admit to being a huge fan of your opera career, Carlotta."

She turned from the lake view and looked at him sternly. "I hope you don't have journalist friends. I have had so many try to get a story from the fallen woman. But I'm sure you've read about it."

"I could not but help so. You've been in all the papers. But that was some time ago now."

"Yes. The fallen and forgotten woman. Monsieur Rossi. I do insist that none of our conversations find their way into the papers. If they should, I will have my people find out how. These people are competent and thorough in finding the truth, if you get my drift?"

"I assure you, Carlotta, I have no interest in making money or notoriety in such a manner," Erik replied with conviction, seeking to gain Carlotta's assurance.

Erik certainly didn't wish to encourage her people to dig deep into his private affairs. He'd taken many expensive precautions to protect his new identity, so he understood Carlotta's desire for privacy.

"Then I want to share a secret, Erik, that has not appeared in any tabloids. I no longer have an interest in returning to the opera, not so long as my condition continues."

"Condition?"

Carlotta stood and walked over to the deck balcony, again admiring the view, seemingly considering her words. "Ever since the well-publicised incident at the Garnier, I have suffered severe memory loss. I have watched two seasons change, believing my memory would return. Alas, I'm no closer to recalling the stage I once strode. I read the headlines about the fallen woman, barely believing a single word. Even worse, if they're true, I'd feel ashamed."

"Do you not have a single memory of the past?"

"Only one. Maybe it was all the headlines, but one opera has returned to me. I don't recall singing in it, but I remember every song. It's all that remains of my supposed life in opera. I have not mentioned this to anyone, fearing they may use it against me."

"In what way?"

"The investigation. You know of it?"

Erik knew everything about it. He knew everything about her life since the incident at the Garnier. "I know what I read in the papers," He lied.

"You have to forgive me, but I do wonder why you

chose to lavish me with such a generous offer, Erik. This hotel is not cheap."

"I think your memory loss has left you confused. You are the most famous opera singer in the world, Carlotta. As a serious financial backer of the Teatro Sociale, inviting you to our awards evening was considered a coup. It can only help our re-emergence as a world-class theatre. I am honoured that you accepted our invitation."

Carlotta's eyes flashed as if remembering her past. "I did have reservations at first, but I'm hoping the event may help me to begin to remember."

Erik joined Carlotta at the balcony and looked out across the lake. "Perhaps if you take in the sights of Bellagio, that may help. Out to your right is the Punta Spartivento, where you can enjoy a delightful walk out to the farthest point of the peninsula. I go there often to watch the locals come and go in their wooden boats. You also get a wonderful view of several other towns bordering the shore. In winter, the snow-capped mountains in the background are spectacular. Maybe through forgetting your predicament, you will more quickly find yourself."

Carlotta breathed in the crisp mountain air, seemingly heeding his advice. "Would you take me there, Erik? It's hard for me to go anywhere alone without being interrupted by fans."

He didn't respond immediately, not sure what to say. Carlotta's need for privacy was not how she once behaved. The old Carlotta would spend much time scheming and misleading people with her words, just as Erik did now. Experience had taught him to play with her words, yet he began to feel sympathy. She looked confused, alone and vulnerable. Had he been the leading cause for Carlotta's condition, with his deception when he assisted Christine to take her mantle? It was a pretense he'd repeat, to protect Christine's prodigious talent. His devotion to music demanded no less. Better to stay close to Carlotta and build a friendship if she wanted one. Erik would soon determine if her changes were real or another ruse performed by a falling star desperate to regain her foothold into the world of opera.

"It'd be my pleasure. There are many hidden wonders in our small township."

Carlotta's tired eyes lit up at his suggestion, reminding Erik how their radiant green could light up a room. "Come join me for brunch and tell me more about your town."

Conversation flowed over brunch as Erik revealed the hidden delights of Bellagio, pleasing Carlotta, loosening her guard and making her forget her fragile condition.

"Everyone tells me to walk the old town, but the shops around me appear modern. Where is this old town?"

"It's just a short but challenging walk. Our township is on two levels, the lower level by the lake, where you are staying, and the higher level up the hill."

"Could we go after brunch? I want to explore Bellagio."

"The walk is quite steep and paved with cobblestone. I suggest you change into comfortable footwear first." Erik pointed to Carlotta's high-heeled shoes, holding his gaze longer than he should have. Despite her pale demeanour, Carlotta still had the shapely legs of a dancer, reminding him of their spontaneous, fateful attraction in Paris.

A half smile formed on Carlotta's voluptuous lips, as if she noticed Erik's reaction. "So, tell me about the Awards night."

"It will be a black-tie affair with over five hundred dignitaries from the arts, business and government attending. We will be seated at the main table with the Mayor and city council dignitaries, members of the Teatro Sociale board and their partners."

Where once Carlotta welcomed networking opportunities, now she was more passive. "Any entertainment?"

"Our local opera group will be performing excerpts

from the forthcoming production of *La Traviata*, accompanied by a small ensemble of our orchestra."

Carlotta brushed his arm in appreciation. "Delightful. I couldn't think of a better way to dine."

"We will spare no expense. Our finest caterers will be overseeing the five-course banquet."

"So, you will be my partner for the evening?" Carlotta asked, playfully brushing his arm a second time.

Erik nodded. "I hope I haven't taken the liberty, Carlotta. We'd, of course, welcome your husband, should he be available."

Carlotta laughed at the thought. "I'm sure you're aware, as is all of Italy, that I separated from my husband. We met not long ago over lunch in Paris. It was a strange feeling. I knew he was my husband, but in conversation, I found myself constantly asking myself why."

"He's aware of your memory loss?"

"I was going to tell him, but the encounter so reviled me, I thought better of it. He spent most of the lunch bragging about his success with the Garnier Opera. I excused myself after the main course with some tepid explanation, feeling only relief that I separated from him."

Erik quietly listened to Carlotta reveal her feelings about Victor, amazed that she was so open. He knew Carlotta was both rich and in control of the separation.

Her loyal solicitor ensured that. Surprisingly, Victor had somehow convinced her to let him oversee the Garnier opera company. What had allowed him to work his way back into her business favour? Perhaps he'd taken advantage of her memory loss. Victor had little real business understanding, but he knew how to spin a story.

"I'm happy that you've found a better place. I'd be honoured to partner you at the Awards, but perhaps there's someone special you would wish to share that evening with?"

"That's kind of you, Erik. That applies equally to you. Is there a Madame Rossi who would like to accompany you?"

"No, there is not."

"Then it's decided," she said, raising her coffee cup to toast their informal agreement.

"To opera," Erik toasted. Their rapport had an ease that genuinely surprised him. Rather than the attention-seeking diva he once played games with, Carlotta had a vulnerable, open demeanour that she fearlessly revealed. Erik opened up too, on occasion, continually checking himself for fear the old Carlotta would return.

The morning passed pleasantly quick. "Unfortunately, I have to leave for another engagement. If I can help you any further while you are staying in Bellagio, please don't hesitate to ask."

"I will need someone to show me the sights of Bellagio. I'm hoping that you could be that chaperone?" Carlotta asked more with hope than expectation.

"It would be my pleasure, Carlotta. Are you free tomorrow?"

"I have no engagements and only plan to relax while I'm in Bellagio. With luck, your advice will be well-founded. The less I think about the past, the more chance I may remember it."

They hugged before Erik left, signalling a growing warmth that had developed over the morning,. Carlotta needed a friend to help her through the turmoil of her condition. Unknown to her, Erik was likely the best placed to draw out her lost memories, but he was the worst choice of friends to steer her toward a safe place. Erik's new life had been reborn on Bellagio's famous promontory, surprisingly with someone he thought would be the least likely friend, given their past. They would learn soon enough if their unlikely bond would endure on the cobbled stone lanes of his new home and the hallowed walls of the Teatro Sociale Opera House. Ultimately, he'd toast their reunion as either Signore Rossi or the Phantom reborn.

CHAPTER SEVEN

RAOUL AND CHRISTINE

Raoul sipped chilled water on the Palmera Restaurant veranda as he watched the constant throng of sailing ships, locals and tourists fill the colourful harbour village of Portovenere. The ocean air's aroma wafted over colourful houses precariously dotted around the cliff face overlooking the Tyrrhenian Sea. This famous port serviced all of the Italian Riviera. The Portovenere Grand Hotel was just a short ride to Raoul and Christine's first destination that morning, a boat ride to Vernazza.

Christine was running late, a fitting diva trait, so Raoul's mind turned to his brother, Philippe, as was always the case when he visited Italy. Would he finally get the answers both he and Christine so desperately sought? So many years had passed and still no word. He watched a ferry boat depart and imagined his brother on board. Had he sailed the ports of this delightful area these past years or had he vanished long before having the chance to enjoy its delights? He watched the boat disappear from the safe harbour into the open sea.

The hotel concierge interrupted his thoughts. "Excuse me, Signore D'Arenberg. Ms. Dubois wanted you to know she will be at the hotel foyer in ten minutes."

"Thank you," he replied before finishing his refreshment and casting a last admiring glance over Portovenere and heading to the hotel entry.

Raoul's impatient mood turned to delight when Christine appeared at the top of the expansive marble staircase. She'd blossomed into a true diva, descending the hotel stairs as if they were a catwalk. Every movement drew admiring glances from below to her navy Coco Chanel day dress and coiffured auburn hair. Her emerald-blue eyes shone, making Raoul proud he'd befriended opera's new shining light. At times he'd dare to believe her affections were something more, but that could never be as long as the shadow of his brother remained.

"Sorry for the delay," she whispered, hiding her true nature from the adoring fans that gathered for a glimpse of a starlet.

Raoul also played to the crowd, taking her hand and leading her toward the waiting cab, appreciatively slipping the concierge a five thousand lira note for his efforts.

Inside the cab and free from the onlookers, Christine relaxed, immediately removing her expensive jewelry and slipping it into her handbag.

"What time's the meeting?"

"Midday," Raoul replied, checking his watch. "We should be there with time to spare."

"Good. Can we relax there?"

"Yes. We're meeting at a small restaurant in the back lanes of Vernazza. Monsieur Salieri assured me it was in a quiet corner of the village."

"Thank you, Raoul," Christine replied, squeezing his hand in appreciation. "Do you think we will find him?"

"What did I tell you about unrealistic expectations?"

"I know," she said with melancholy resignation. "Either way, I resolve this."

Raoul wanted to hold Christine close to him at times like this. Her loyalty to the idea that Philippe may still be alive touched him. He too loved his brother and would gladly trade away his chance to win Christine's affection for his return. Both were in Italy to resolve a dark shadow that had filled their lives since his disappearance. Inspector Claude Moreau oversaw Philippe's case, but he'd uncovered precious little, until this very lead. Claude seemed sure that the man they were about to meet was one of the last to see Philippe.

The cab quickly arrived at their destination, a small private ferry moored in a quiet dock, free from the prying eyes of fans. They boarded it, saying little. A disquieting mood of pessimism filled the moment, born from having spent years living with false hope. Both hoped for closure on the whole affair. If that happened, Raoul dared to believe Christine may see him in a different light. He'd taken one other trip with Christine and many more on his own in search of Philippe, all ending in frustrating dead ends. He loved his elder brother, but even brotherly loyalty had been pushed to its breaking point. Raoul believed that Philippe had succumbed to foul play from his deadly habit — gambling.

The small speed boat sped through the busy waters. Charter boats cruised the Tyrrhenian sea to the various villages occupying the famous Italian Riviera. Both leaned on the boat railing, looking down to the choppy waters and standing close to keep warm.

"It's so beautiful. I hope one day I return here under better circumstances," said Christine, as they approached Vernazza.

It had a picture-postcard beauty about it, consistent with all the other Cinque Terra towns, but this felt more welcoming. The inlet doubled as a port and beach, creating a festive, laid-back atmosphere.

"You're so right. Let's spend time snorkelling by day and dining at the best restaurants by night if we ever come back. What do you say?"

Christine raised her eyebrows. "You know what happened last time."

Raoul shrugged his shoulders, remembering the week they agreed to test if their friendship could be something more. He had such grand expectations, but Christine's mood quickly dulled them. He learnt she would not let Philippe go until she knew what had happened to him.

"Still best of friends. Promise?" Christine asked.

"Always. You know that."

They quickly disembarked, disappearing into a quiet lane free of crowds and finding the small cafe where they were to meet Signor Salieri. The restaurant was empty, much to Christine's relief. It was their first real chance to relax together, which Raoul welcomed, given they'd only caught up intermittently in the last six months. Christine's opera schedule was gruelling, some of it he believed intentional to forget Philippe. Their contact soon arrived, a short, stocky man with an intense gaze that he flashed toward the bar where the barman prepared for the day's trade.

"Il Solito," he said before sitting opposite Raoul and Christine.

The barman quickly took his order. The contact sat back, seemingly satisfied with the impression he'd created, straining the back of his chair with his sizeable weight. The barman promptly returned, carrying a tray of refreshments, three espressos and three spritzers. The man acknowledged the server with the slightest nod before finally speaking.

"Welcome to Italy. Signore Salieri apologises for not meeting you as he had an emergency. My name is Reggi. I'll be looking after you today."

Raoul and Christine looked to each other, surprised by the turn of events. "Inspector Moreau made a point that we would be meeting only with Monsieur Salieri, as he was the last person to meet with my brother. Did you also know my brother?"

"I make it my business to know everyone, Monsieur D'Arenberg. What is it you have come to find out?"

Raoul looked to Christine, seeking and receiving her support before responding. "We are both looking for Philippe D'Arenberg. He came to Italy some years ago, and we have not had any contact with him since."

"Italy is a big country. People get lost here all the time, Signore."

"Can you help us or not? We have not come here to waste our time," Christine replied tersely.

Reggi sipped on his espresso, in no hurry to reply, seemingly enjoying the impasse. "You may have to wait some time. Are you in Italy long?"

"We must return by the week's end."

"Not much time. But anything is possible for the right price."

Christine stood up, irritated by Reggi's not-too-subtle offer. "We were assured by Inspector Moreau that Monsieur Salieri would meet with us and tell us all he knew. There was no mention of money."

Reggi remained seated, unmoved. "Monsieur Salieri would only tell you of his meeting with your lover two years ago, Signorina. In contrast, I could tell you of his movements after that, if you give me the time to investigate. That is, should you wish to find him."

Christine looked to Raoul to leave with her, but Raoul pressed her hand, signalling he wanted to hear more. "Are you saying that you could find my brother?"

"As I said, Signore, it is my business to know everyone in Italy, and my networks reach far. Much further than Monsieur Salieri's. That, I can assure you."

Christine shook her head, signalling her doubts, but Raoul persisted. "I have waited many years for my brother's return, and I'm prepared to reward you handsomely for knowledge of his whereabouts. When did you last meet with him?"

"At the same time Signore Salieri met him."

"And have you seen him since?"

"No. But I expect my friends to have."

"Could he be alive?"

"Anything is possible in Italy."

"What's your price?"

"Investigations can be costly and time-consuming, and in your brother's case, dangerous. I'd need to convince many people to reveal information that they perhaps would be unwilling to give, easily. They too would want to be rewarded handsomely. It all comes down to how big a risk you wish to take to know more of your brother's fate. Italy is filled with missing person reports every day."

"How much?" Raoul asked, realising Reggi only appreciated money.

"I will let you know later in the evening, but for now, a retainer of one hundred thousand lire would secure my services."

"I think we should speak with Inspector Moreau first," Christine intervened, but Raoul continued the negotiation.

"I am carrying twenty-five thousand lire in cash. It's yours if you accept the job."

Reggi counted the notes Raoul passed him before

putting them in his topcoat pocket, smiling and satisfied with the negotiation. "I will meet with you early evening at Bar La Torre. I suggest you enjoy visiting Vernazza and walking the many interesting lanes that snake through the village. Wind your way to the top of the village, and you will find Bar La Torre. It offers the best view of the village. I will meet you there at five o'clock."

Then he turned to Christine. "If I hear Inspector Moreau involves his men in this matter, you will not see me again. These investigations will be dangerous, and outside interference could unwittingly put the people I contact at risk. Is that understood?"

Christine did not answer, leaving Raoul to respond. "You have my assurance of that."

At that, Reggi stood up to leave. "As a sign of my good intent, I have arranged a special lunch at La Torre. Please enjoy, and I will meet you at five," he said before leaving.

"Good intent? He's buying our lunch with your money!" Christine said contemptuously.

Raoul pressed Christine's arm to reassure her. "I know it's frustrating, but it's how they do business in Italy."

"I don't trust him, Raoul. Why didn't the Inspector tell us about him?"

"I don't know, but Inspector Moreau did tell me to be cautious, as we are dealing with people we do not know.

He also suggested I ring him regularly," Raoul said before taking his mobile phone and calling. "No connection. Why don't we take in some sights and call Moreau when we find an area with phone connectivity?"

"That's fine, but I want to be at the meeting this evening," Christine demanded with the well-practised assertiveness befitting a famous diva.

"Very well, but remember the promise you made."

"I'd listen to you if you thought I was in danger. Yes, I will."

"I have been here many more times than you, Christine. The people my brother dealt with are less than exemplary. We will listen to what he has to offer us tonight, but if there are any private meetings, I will attend them. I will not risk a world-famous diva in such a situation."

Christine held back responding, seemingly gaining her composure first. She was not one to be told what to do, not even by a close friend. "I know you have my best interests at heart, dear friend. Yes, I will listen to you, but do not rush to any decisions with these people. You're letting your frustrations get the better of you."

"You're right. I took over the negotiation with Reggi. I was wrong, and I should have listened to you. From here on, joint decisions only," Raoul said.

They walked back to the port, where crowds were

building around the beach. Small vessels filled the busy marina, carrying revellers who enjoyed the mild weather. Interestingly, many of the ships flew flags with the recognisable skull and crossbones symbol of the pirate. The crowds, too, wore pirate outfits, giving the centuries-old village an atmosphere of authenticity. Christine watched the procession, mystified.

"It looks like a scene from the *Pirates of Penzance*," she said, mildly amused.

"You didn't read the hotel notifications. It's the beginning of the 'Festa del Pirati', an annual festival remembering when Saracen pirates invaded the village. There will be a show of sorts, reenacting a famous raid. I don't think it will be opera, though!" Raoul replied.

"Let's move to quieter corners after you call the Inspector."

Raoul nodded and called Moreau but without success. "I had to leave a message. He's currently in a meeting. Let's head for high ground, toward Bar La Torre. From what I read at the hotel, the area is steep, but many shops line the maze of lanes."

The area surrounding their meeting point with Reggi was every bit as steep and confusing as Raoul had read, but it allowed them time to enjoy Vernazza, offering some respite from the task ahead. The festival also allowed Christine to roam the streets with anonymity behind a pirate mask. It offered a level of freedom they had not enjoyed in a long time, reinforcing their bond and making Raoul regret how he'd treated Christine in their negotiations with Reggi. Raoul had shown too much faith in this stranger and little toward his friend. He would check his emotions, but he would spend the money required to find Philippe.

The evening was calm and uneventful, but Raoul and Christine expected that to change as they wound their way through the lanes to Bar La Torre. The cafe was perched on one of the highest points in the village, affording a hundred-and-eighty-degree view of the ocean and shoreline of Vernazza. Cool ocean breezes and the restaurant's vine-filled natural deck offered ideal shelter from the warming summer day, as did the refreshing local wines.

"You've never told me what you think happened to Philippe, even after all these years. Why not?" Christine asked.

Raoul caressed her hand, knowing she was right. He'd given up on finding his brother many years earlier, sure he'd tangled with people who could make any debtor disappear without a trace. He'd returned to Italy more often than he'd wished, more to help Christine than himself.

"I never wanted to tarnish your good memories of my brother. You got to know the best side of him, the side I very much loved, too. But there was another side to him that only a few saw."

"You mean his gambling?"

"Yes. I know Philippe told you that he gambled, but he always shielded you from the extent of his problem."

"No, he didn't. I remember he spent many late nights at his favourite nightspot, the Casino, but it was his way of escaping the business. I don't think he ever enjoyed running your family inheritance."

"He didn't. Philippe despised the imposition, so much so that I think he enjoyed squandering the money in the end."

"How much did he lose?" Christine asked, encouraged by the wine.

Raoul shook his head at the thought. Philippe's gambling addiction got out of control in the final year. It was as if Philippe plead for help in the only way he knew, excessive gambling in the hope someone would see.

"I learnt more about Philippe's excesses through the many banks he increasingly borrowed from to hide the extent of his debts."

"He always told me that he could never gamble away the estate, no matter how bad his gambling became."

"All gamblers would say that, Christine. If you ever return to Philippe, please promise me that you won't blindly accept that. I learnt that tough lesson many years ago."

Reggi arrived, dressed in a dark suit and smoking a cigarette, looking every inch the gangster Raoul believed him to be. He immediately ordered a Campari, which wasn't his first, given the alcohol smell on his breath. It at least made him more amenable than their earlier meeting.

"May I order the same for you?"

"Thank you. Two wines would be fine," replied Raoul.

Reggi engaged them both in Campari-fueled small talk. "I would be happy to show you some of the best sites of Cinque Terra, given you soon leave. It would be a tragedy not to see the true beauty of these villages."

"Thank you, Reggi. But we can't. I'll be meeting with members of La Scala Opera tomorrow." Christine lied.

"It's impossible for Christine to visit this region without engaging La Scala. You understand." Raoul added.

"Yes, of course. The price of fame," Reggi replied, finishing his Campari and ordering another. "Then, down to business?"

"Yes. What have you uncovered?"

"More than I expected. I used your money wisely and

engaged three of my finest to put together some interesting background on your brother."

"Is he alive?" Christine interjected.

Reggi raised both hands, signalling restraint. "We have some preliminary research which gives me hope that we may indeed find Philippe's tracks from when he arrived in Rome."

"Inspector Moreau already uncovered that," Christine replied.

"True, but I don't think he found the best lead for you. He may be useful, but I believe we have uncovered sources much closer to Philippe."

Raoul cut in. "How close?"

Reggi leaned forward, seemingly satisfied with himself. "Almost family."

"I'm his family. I would know if he had other close ties."

"From what I have learned, there is much you both don't know about Philippe."

"Is he alive?" Christine repeated.

"My source could answer that, but he would — how should I say — put himself and my investigation team at risk."

Raoul leaned back in his chair. "And the price for this risk?"

"One hundred million lire should cover costs."

"That's a lot. What would we obtain for one hundred million lire?"

"Surely, that is a small price to pay to learn the fate of your brother?"

"How soon?" Raoul replied with resignation in his tone.

"My source is close by and willing to meet you this evening."

Raoul turned to Christine. "I can go to this meeting."

"We came together to find out about Philippe. I don't intend to change our plan. We are too close."

Raoul held his gaze just as determinedly as Christine before he replied to Reggi. "Could you give us some time together? Say, two hours? Then I can call you."

Reggi showed his displeasure, impatiently checking his watch. "My source will not wait long. He's a busy man. Comprende? I'll give you one hour to decide," Reggi ordered, writing a contact number on some paper before handing it to Philippe. "Call me in sixty minutes. Is that clear?" he said before leaving, mumbling to himself.

Now alone, Christine made her feelings clear. "If you want to do this, you're not leaving me behind!"

"This could be dangerous. I won't risk your safety."

"Then don't accept his offer. It's no more than a bribe. We can wait until Inspector Moreau's contact resurfaces."

"We're so close, Christine."

"We know nothing of this man, Raoul. Call the Inspector now. We stay and negotiate if he agrees or we leave for Portovenere if we can't reach him."

Raoul reluctantly agreed and called Moreau, this time making contact.

"I'm sorry for not being available, Raoul, but it was unavoidable. I was about to call you as a matter of urgency. Where are you now?"

"Vernazza. Just as you instructed, Inspector."

"Have you met with anyone?"

"We have, but it wasn't Salieri."

"I know that. Who have you met and when?"

"I only know his first name, Reggi. He told us Salieri was indisposed and that he would assist us. We met him once this morning and paid him twenty-five thousand lire to make some preliminary investigations. We met him again not long ago, and he proposed he'd deliver detailed information about Philippe for a hundred million lire. We stalled for time but must get back to him in an hour."

"Does he know you're talking to me?"

"No."

Inspector Moreau went quiet on the line, making Raoul think he'd lost the connection. Finally, he replied. "Where exactly are you in Vernazza?"

"We're at Bar La Torre. Do you know it?"

"Yes, I do. I want you to calmly pay your bill and tell them you will return in an hour and for them to save you a table. Do not say any more. Is that clear?"

"Is there a problem, Inspector?"

"I was in a meeting coordinating a French-Italian operation we are currently working on, and I just learnt that we lost one of our undercover agents. It was Salieri."

"Lost? What do you mean by lost?"

"Please, do not tell Christine, but Salieri was found dead in Milan, the circumstances suspicious. Make your way back to Vernazza port and return to your hotel in Portovenere. Do not deal with this contact, Reggi."

"Who is this man, and why would he do this?"

"I do not know, but it is almost certainly not his real name. I would have an undercover assist you, but they have too many eyes and ears in that village. It would place you both in even greater danger, particularly someone as famous as Christine."

Raoul hung up, then offered to pay the restaurant for their lunch, but it had already been taken care of by Reggi. "Please tell Reggi we will return on the hour. Could you save our table?"

"Certainly, Signore. We will see you in an hour."

Raoul then took Christine's arm and walked out of the restaurant and down the narrow lane back to the port.

"What did Moreau say?" Christine asked.

"I promise to tell you everything when we get on the ferry. For now, we both must walk quickly and quietly and not draw any attention our way." Raoul replied, focused more on remembering his way back.

Christine nodded. Realising their situation's potential danger, she willingly followed Raoul into the narrow lanes back to the port. They soon reached an open area of the walkway. Below, they saw Reggi talking to a shop owner in front of a tourist kiosk, prompting Raoul to take a longer route back to port, an enclosed and unfamiliar lane. They spent several minutes crisscrossing a quieter sector where locals lived. Devoid of standard bearings they quickly found themselves lost.

"I think we're moving further from the port this way," Raoul finally admitted.

"Should we return to the way we know?" Christine offered.

"Not with Reggi there. I'd rather take my chances this way," he replied, heading through another long, tunnelled laneway. At its end was a man at a doorway of a home. He was lighting a cigarette while observing their approach, making Raoul and Christine slow their pace, uncertain of their situation.

It made the stranger smile. "Are you lost, Signore?" he

asked, before inhaling on his cigarette.

Raoul was unsure whether to answer at first, but they were lost. "Yes. We're looking for the way back to the port. Can you direct us?"

"So many tourists get lost in this area. If you walk down that lane for a further two hundred metres and turn a sharp left, you will cross a narrow bridge. That path will wind down to the main lane. Turn left again, and it will take you to the port."

Raoul nodded appreciatively. "Grazzi, Signore."

Within ten minutes, they walked along the main road to the port, reassuringly busier with celebrating crowds. Both fitted their pirate masks, maintaining their anonymity back to a waiting ferry and the return to Portovenere.

Having chosen a quiet corner on the ferry, Christine relaxed enough to speak. "I have never felt so scared. So will you now tell me what the Inspector had to say?"

Raoul told Christine what Moreau had said, explaining his actions, much to Christine's horror. "Salieri, dead. Was he murdered?"

"In all likelihood, yes. I should never have exposed you to such danger, Christine. I am so sorry."

"You weren't to know there'd be this level of danger," she said, taking his hand and reassuring him.

"I always suspected Philippe got involved with dangerous people, but it's the first time I have come this close to them. Bringing you was foolish. Why would they not take advantage of someone as famous as you?"

"I insisted on coming, Raoul. It's not your fault."

Raoul held Christine's hand tight and made her a promise. "I will never put you in danger again. I don't intend to ever return to Italy. The mafia took my brother a long time ago. He's dead, Christine. Like Salieri, he's gone."

Tears formed in Christine's eyes as she took in Raoul's words. She had always thought he'd died somewhere in Italy. All she wanted was confirmation, but his death would be like the many other thousands of lost souls reported to the police every year, her Philippe just another statistic. She held Raoul close to her, releasing the pent-up, unresolved anguish she felt.

"Promise me you'll never disappear from my life as Philippe did."

Raoul leant back so he could see Christine's sad eyes. "I promise I'll always be your friend."

They sat alone in the corner of the ferry, watching the lights of the city of Portovenere come into view, all the while holding hands, both not ever wanting to let go. Raoul admired the city's vivid lights and their reflection on the lake. As they neared the port, he thought he saw a shimmering light dart across the shoreline and believed it to be a shooting star reflected on the water. He looked at Christine, who now slept, and hoped the flash of light would be a good luck omen. He lightly stroked her hair to wake her, all the while wishing the lucky star would grant his wish. To love Christine as no other could and have her by his side, always.

CHAPTER EIGHT

THE INVITATION

Erik wrapped his shoulder bag securely to his side and commenced the walk up the incline to the foyer of the Grand Hotel Serbelloni. The bag contained material he hoped would convince Carlotta of his good intent. The front desk service manager greeted him with the warmth befitting a regular guest.

"Madame Caccini is expecting you, Signore Rossi. You can go directly to her apartment. Will you need assistance?"

"That won't be necessary." Erik met Carlotta on several occasions in the past week, showing her the famous sites of Bellagio.

Erik walked through the grand room and up the stairs to the first floor and Carlotta's 'Senior Apartment', where Carlotta's assistant greeted him and took him through to her private sanctuary. She sat by an expansive window with a panoramic view of Lake Como, where she soaked up the warm autumn sunshine.

"Ah, you're on time!"

Carlotta enthusiastically greeted Erik with a traditional kiss on both cheeks. She wore a casual canary-yellow summer dress that matched her relaxed mood. The lightness of the fabric revealed her feminine curves, drawing Erik's gaze. Carlotta giggled mischievously, enjoying how Erik's admiration lifted her mood. Colour had returned to her face, showing a hint of the diva that Erik once knew.

"Gianni, could you serve us a morning espresso, if that suits?"

Erik nodded before sitting at the chair Carlotta offered him, placing his overly full bag on the floor.

"Looks heavy. You must have struggled with the climb," Carlotta said.

"Yes. But it was worth it on such a clear day. The view from your apartment is spectacular."

"Isn't it divine? I have been so happy here. It has given me new energy."

"You do look radiant, Carlotta."

"Thanks to you."

Erik graciously accepted her gratitude before perusing her sumptuously elegant living room, a harmonious blend of neoclassical and art nouveau spilling over with one hundred years of illustrious history. "Such an elegant apartment."

"Yes. Kings, Queens and Hollywood stars have enjoyed this very room. I can feel the energy of Gable and Pacino."

Erik gazed at the straight line of framed photos hung on the feature wall. To his surprise, the group of prints was photos of Carlotta's most outstanding performances. "Now they are entertaining Europe's finest diva," he said, admiring them.

"The hotel organized it. They stand by their motto of showing the utmost consideration for their guests."

"Has it helped your memory return?"

"Unfortunately not. I remain a clean slate, except for my love of music. *La Traviata* sparked that memory, so I have you to thank for that."

"It was one of your most supreme performances, Carlotta. No one who saw you at the Garnier would ever forget."

"Is this why you want me to attend?"

"Partly. I would be lying if I denied it. Your attendance would be considered a coup. But I also have another dream."

"And that is?"

"To return to the Garnier and direct *La Traviata*."

"Ambitious. As I understand, you are a producer, not a director."

"That's true. But I have a love for music, as do you. I'm an accomplished musician, but I also like to think of myself as a budding composer."

"So what makes you think I can help you?"

"I don't know why, but I feel we could help each other."

"Perhaps. My Doctor told me it couldn't hurt. You have to appreciate that my recovery will be slow. I might hinder you more than help."

Erik smiled quizzically. He was still getting used to this new, more amenable side of Carlotta. "If I can help you remember the world you once shone in, it would all be justified."

Giani returned with a refreshments tray, serving two espressos and an assortment of fresh pastries, winning an appreciative nod from Carlotta.

"So a toast, Signore Rossi. To *La Traviata*. May Verdi's masterpiece be fruitful to us both."

They toasted. Carlotta's eyes sparkled just as they had when they first met at the Garnier. Carlotta had a similar welcoming smile that hinted at something more. In Paris, they both feasted on those feelings, just as they both ultimately paid the price. Would the same happen again? There was an alluring chemistry about her that made Erik want more, but at what cost? He fought the thought. "May our friendship be a happy one."

Carlotta nodded before looking down at his shoulder bag. "So what have you brought here today? If it's work, we'll be busy!"

"Not work. Memories." Erik pulled out a large scrapbook. "It contains a record of my favourite opera moments, including your last performance of *Traviata* at the Garnier. It was so impressive. I studied the musical score."

"So, you really can play?"

"My mother loved music and wanted me to have the same gift. I learnt the piano from a very young age and the violin in my late teens."

"You must play for me someday," Carlotta said, scanning the many photos of opera performances he had captured. "Ah. *La Traviata.*"

Erik nodded before turning to the last page, revealing a cherished memory. "I'll never forget the enthusiastic crowd. They filled the stage, surrounding you with red roses. You were the toast of France."

Carlotta smiled in appreciation. "I hope I remember that performance again, but for now..." Carlotta shrugged her shoulders as she closed the book and sat back in her chair, seemingly searching for those very elusive memories.

Erik prodded her. "You told me *La Traviata* was your only opera-related memory."

"Yes, but I don't remember any of my performances. It's the story of Violetta," she said before sipping her coffee and saying no more, inviting intrigue.

"Would you care to tell me more?"

Carlotta continued to drink her coffee, clearly deciding if she should. Then she reopened Erik's scrapbook to a photo of a scene in *La Traviata*.

"I mainly think of Act 3, Violetta's death scene. That's what I remember."

Erik was taken aback by her openness, not sure whether he should pursue it. "Opera can be a tragedy," he replied, cautiously navigating the line between showing interest and prying.

Carlotta's expression turned sombre. "I often think of that scene because I feel that my life will end just as Violetta's."

Carlotta's trust in Erik was slowly building as she shared more intimate thoughts. It moved Erik enough for him to take her hand gently. "You've been through a lot. Your memory loss must be disturbing. It would seem normal to me that you feel uncertainty."

"Perhaps. But when I meet with Victor, I'm filled with doubts. He acts as if we have never separated, but my lawyer tells me otherwise, showing the debts he so eagerly amassed over our long marriage. He is a deceitful man, Erik. What would you do?" She replied, her voice wavering slightly.

Erik stood up and looked out to the lake, hiding the guilt he felt. Carlotta was in the company of an equally deceitful man who could also wreak devastating havoc in her life.

"Time is your friend, Carlotta. Use it well, and you will make the right decision. Perhaps then, any ominous feelings you have may disappear."

Carlotta nodded. "Come tell me more stories from your scrapbook."

Erik proceeded to enthusiastically describe the many photos and letters in the scrapbook, revealing his love for music and his mother's positive influence for the life he wanted most, free from the shadows that had made him forget.

"You only speak about your mother. Did your father love music?"

"He died when I was young," Erik lied.

He continued to tell the many stories contained in the overflowing musical scrapbook, winning her admiration but carefully steering clear of the darkness hidden between the lines. His advice to her was accurate. Given time, Carlotta would find the truth of her life and others. For now, they joyously visited the life Erik's mother wanted for him, a world filled with music. There, she would find Erik Rossi. If she ventured into the realm overseen by his father, she would again feel the unexpected sting of the rose thorn that was the Phantom.

Their week together passed quickly, and the Awards night at Teatro Sociale arrived. Erik waited in the grand hall for Carlotta to join him. They had a brief walk to the private jetty and their motorboat to ferry them there. He hadn't seen her in days, given the demands on him as the organizer of the black-tie evening.

Erik didn't have to wait long. Carlotta entered the grand room, her pale complexion gleaming alongside the garnet-red cocktail dress she wore. Her beauty reminded him of the evening they first met at the Garnier, not long after becoming lovers.

He took her hand, gently kissing her fingers. "You look stunning."

Carlotta giggled, relishing his forthrightness. "Thank you," she replied, moving her hand to Erik's arm. He led her past the gathering crowd trying to get a closer look at the famous diva. In the past, Carlotta would play to their attention. Instead, she held Erik close to her, seemingly unaware of the admiring glances she drew.

"I nearly didn't come," she whispered, sharing her anxiety.

"I'll stay close," Erik replied, drawing an appreciative squeeze from Carlotta's hand.

The steadily building interest increased Carlotta's misgivings for attending the public event. Erik quickly ushered her through the crowds to the private jetty, turning briefly to face the paparazzi for photos before boarding the boat and guiding her below deck, safe from prying eyes.

"Thank you. I so wanted to see this performance, but...." Carlotta said, unable to finish her words.

"I'll do all I can to protect you from the paparazzi. I promise."

Carlotta instantly relaxed, accepting his commitment. A growing trust had developed between them that was the polar opposite of their first union a year earlier, an alliance filled more with jealousy, ambition and hate. Increasingly, Erik hoped Carlotta would never regain her memory, freeing them from their shameful past.

The motorboat quickly moored at Como, where a private limousine waited to take them to Teatro Sociale. Cameras incessantly flashed as they walked the red-carpeted staircase to the main foyer of the opera house. The paparazzi shouted requests for smiles before Carlotta and Erik took their place at the main hall's head table. All theatre seats had been removed from this purpose-built theatre and replaced with white linen tables laden with the finest silverware.

They were the last to arrive, befitting of the guest of honour. All stood and applauded Carlotta's entry, attracting another battery of flashing lights. To Carlotta's relief, the paparazzi were ushered out of the dining area when they were seated. They sat with the Director of Teatro Sociale and his partner to their left and the Mayor of Como and his partner on the right, striking up a general conversation with both couples.

"Nice to meet you, at last, Signore Rossi," said the Mayor before introducing his wife. They were an amiable couple, appreciative of Erik's support and the spotlight the event had put on Como. "I hear that you have brought more than just finance to our opera theatre?"

"Starting with the shining light of Europe," Erik replied, introducing Carlotta.

"I think he meant your musical prowess, Erik," Carlotta chimed in.

"We are blessed with two musical talents," replied the Mayor.

Erik nodded graciously. "I will be overseeing the

production of *Traviata,* but our musical director has kindly allowed me to rehearse with our orchestra, specifically our concertmaster."

"Ahh, you play the violin."

"Both violin and piano. It's been a lifelong passion of mine."

"Perhaps you will perform one evening?"

"The demands of artistic producer will occupy most of my time, but if required, I'd very much like that opportunity. Our orchestra's musician's skills run deep. You are about to see that right now," Erik said, pointing to the first performance of the evening.

The lights lowered in the main hall, leaving all in darkness bar the rows of candles uniformly lined across the tables and their reflections on empty wine glasses. The main stage was lit by a single spotlight introducing their local lead pianist and prima donna to perform 'E Strano Ah Fors'C Lui', a tribute to their special guest, Carlotta. The piece was a pivotal moment in *La Traviata's* first act. Violetta is left alone to consider whether Alfredo, who proposes his love for her, is genuinely her true love.

How strange, the words carved upon my heart! Would true love bring me misfortune? What do you think, my troubled spirit? No man before kindled a flame-like this. To love and be loved. Can I disdain this for a life of sterile pleasure?

The heartfelt thoughts of Violetta chimed deep into the recesses of Erik's mind, where savagery and beauty lived side by side and coalesced in his opera heart. He visualized his true love, Rose, once again singing to him, offering her true love, a love Erik failed to protect from the savagery. True love had brought us the cruellest of misfortunes. From that moment on, Erik single-mindedly pursued revenge from the world of thorns that hid on love's stem. Would he ever be free of the monsters that inhabited his mind? As if hearing his thoughts, Carlotta moved closer, wishing to share the joy of the performance. Erik regretted initially flinching from her warm gesture. Sometimes he wanted to lash out, and he couldn't control his emotions. Erik held his gaze on the performers and imagined sharing the stage with Carlotta. Perhaps in that place, he could ward off the shadows and recapture a glimpse of his broken dreams. He took Carlotta's hand and whispered an apology for his earlier response.

"Thank you, Monsieur Directeur Musical," she whispered. Her eyes shone in the candlelit twilight, filled with the hope Violetta now considered in Verdi's masterpiece. He moved closer to kiss her when the candle on their table flickered and died, the moment of romance spoiled. That was love, Erik thought, turning from Carlotta back to the performers, wondering if fate were sending him signs.

The evening ebbed and flowed between fine dining and fine music, ensuring enthusiastic support from patrons, current and potential. Carlotta found a semblance of her musical memories, illustrating to Erik areas where performances could soar higher with practice. Conversation flowed effortlessly across the table, extending from *La Traviata* to many of Verdi's other classics, including *Macbeth*. Would she recall her final performance? Erik knew it would only be a matter of time before the truth of their past would come back, and when it did, he had to be prepared.

They left La Teatro Sociale, the first of a list of esteemed guests to file down the red carpet to the cavalcade of limousines lining the entry to the theatre. Conversation flowed as Erik and Carlotta nurtured their musical bond, all too quickly arriving at Bellaggio's Grand Hotel.

"Thank you for this evening. It meant a lot to me," Carlotta said, brushing Erik's cheek with an appreciative kiss.

Erik took her hand, "I know you return to Paris tomorrow. I won't see you for some time. Perhaps we can reunite when I come to Paris?"

"Of course. I can show you Paris."

Erik only nodded, not wishing to lie to Carlotta. He knew Paris as intimately as her. In a past life he did not want her ever to know.

"I would look forward to that, Carlotta." He caressed her cheek and studied Carlotta's warm lips, wondering how they would feel, before raising his eyes to hers.

Carlotta rested her hand on Eriks, inviting him closer, smiling with nervous expectation. He softly brushed her hair back, revealing her face and neck, feeling her excited breath on his lips and kissing her as Alfredo would kiss Violetta. Their hunger was evident; they could be lovers again that night, should they choose. He could have Carlotta, but he balked. The complications and deceit weighed on his mind, and Carlotta noticed.

"You could come to Paris for my birthday. It's only weeks away," she whispered, freeing him from his indecision.

"I could think of nothing more delightful than another night of dining and opera with you," Erik replied, kissing her again, inviting something more than the friendship they had started.

"Then we shall talk more, Signore Rossi," Carlotta said before stepping from the limousine into the Bellagio Grand Hotel.

Erik watched Carlotta, partly intoxicated with her femininity, part angered with himself. She was no longer the ambitious diva he plotted deadly schemes with in Paris a year earlier. Had events stripped her of the pretence that so clouded her life, freeing her to be herself? Wasn't he trying to do precisely the same? Remove the shadows from his past life to be reborn. But into what? Erik feared his past traumas ran too deep to strip bare. Even worse, that darkness may control him, posing threats to those close.

He walked from the limousine to his home. Bernard was on the deck, bottle of whisky open, ready to share news of the evening. He sat with him, savouring the first glass as it warmed his lips, intensifying the memory of Carlotta's soft kiss. The night air was crisp but clear, affording a view across the lake village. Erik imagined Carlotta also gazed upon the lake, reliving their special night.

Bernard interrupted Erik's thoughts. "The night was a success?"

"More than we could have hoped. Did those who matter notice?" Erik replied.

Bernard nodded proudly. "The word is Victor's people were in attendance, and they took a very close interest in your proceedings."

Erik smiled, more to reward Bernard's efforts than

from happiness. He had stoked the interest of those who mattered in Paris, one at his side, the other, the Garnier Opera House's current manager. "Have you managed to get some of our people into the Garnier?"

"They start there in the next few weeks."

"Wonderful news, Bernard." Erik poured a second glass for them both to celebrate. Erik's dark tentacles were again surrounding the most famous opera house of them all, preparing for his resurrection.

The thought stayed with Erik long after Bernard had left. He would be reborn into the music of the night, but at what cost? Erik remained on the deck into the twilight hours while all around slept. By sunrise, he'd resigned himself to not returning to Paris until the Garnier welcomed him. Carlotta would have to wait.

CHAPTER NINE

NEW LYRICS

I woke a second time to Peri's voice. "Benny, Diva has asked that you join her for breakfast." Her request built a sense of deja vu.

I checked the time. I'd lost twelve hours, giving me less than an hour to prepare for Diva. "Thanks, Peri. These pills are potent," I offered before disappearing to the bathroom and hastily showering. I'd spent some time on the lyrics, but my experiences in the world of Diva's youth left me unsatisfied with the work. Christine had the support of three powerful men, Erik, Raoul and her love, Philippe. Had this been a blessing or a curse? My music had to reflect their influence. I'd present my new awareness of Diva's young life, hoping to draw more of her memories.

Diva sat exactly where we last met, her disposition notably lighter. A canary-yellow loose-fitting dress highlighted a freshly developed tan and a relaxed manner, hinting of a restful break. We shared a carefree breakfast as Diva spoke of her shopping spree. Then, niceties aside, the conversation turned to business.

Diva could barely contain her excitement. "Are you ready to reveal the new lyrics?"

"It's not completed, but I do have some new lyrics."

"Please, maestro," Diva said, giggling with expectation.

I sang the first verse unchanged, then added the new lyrics in the second, reflecting Christine's three loves as she developed into Europe's most fabulous Diva. Half-way into the third verse, Diva stopped me.

"How did you decide on these lyrics?"

"From my research. I have learnt much more." I announced proudly.

An emotional whiteout suddenly curtailed Diva's pleasant feelings before a supercell storm turned her blank expression into a darker mood. A thunderstorm of rage was about to be released, her glare reminiscent of Uma Thurman's ode to unfinished business in the early 21st-century movie *Kill Bill.*

"How dare you? Get out! If you ever utter those three names in the same verse again, I'll fire you on the spot."

I apologised, but it made things worse. Diva swept the breakfast setting to the ground. "A real lover would know his partner intimately. You don't. I said leave!"

Diva's hostility drew the attention of an android that went about cleaning up the food waste and broken pottery. Left no other option, I descended the stairs quickly out of earshot, fearing she'd terminate my employment before I reached the bottom. I had either wildly misinterpreted Diva's early life, or the events I experienced were a fantasy perpetrated by an enemy. Were Flynn's pills a deception?

I headed directly to Flynn's room, stormed in unannounced and threw Flynn's prescription on his desk. "I want the truth about these. Are you setting me up?"

Flynn picked up the tablets and twisted the container in his hand. "If you've upset Diva, you only have yourself to blame, not these pills." He contemptuously threw them back toward me.

"Perhaps, but don't tell me I'm experiencing nightmares. These nighttime events are real."

"Oh, really? What are you basing your conclusions on?"

Flynn taunted me to reveal more than I should, but what else could I do? Diva was ready to dismiss me, so I accepted Flynn's challenge. "In all of the thirty-five years of my life, I have never slept."

Flynn leaned back in his chair, clasping both hands together and touching his lips before moving his hands just enough to reveal a self-satisfied grin. I had told a truth that left me vulnerable to Flynn, a mysterious man who had shown nothing but contempt toward me. He could expose my secret to authorities, should he choose.

"I know you're not human, Benny. I've always known."

I could tell from Flynn's intense demeanour that he was serious. "Are you going to report me?"

"Is there a reason I should?"

"That often occurs. Then bad things happen, usually to my friends."

"Not true. Authorities aren't mistreating you. They're protecting you."

"What do you know about my experiences?"

Flynn turned on his com hologram. A screen filled with my secrets, music, the data on human emotions, everything. Flynn had access to secure files I believed impenetrable.

"When you accepted Diva's position, I knew you were perfect for the assignment, even before you did."

"Who are you, Flynn? You're not a doctor."

"I'm many things. But, most importantly, I can help you find your true self. That's what you want, isn't it?"

"I'll be lucky to last another day. Diva is distraught because of my incompetence. I'll never deliver the music she asks of me."

"She can be overly emotional at times. What else would you expect from a famous diva? You need to know more of her life," Flynn asserted, looking at the pills he gave me.

I stood up, ready to leave. "I'm not doing any more of this until I get some explanations. If you don't tell me more, I'm done with this."

Flynn's craggy demeanour softened. He opened both hands, inviting me to sit back down. "You're learning of your true capabilities, Benny. Just accept that you're experiencing real events. They're not dreams."

"If that's true, I could end up lost in the past. I have no control over whatever this is. For all I know, it's a trap."

"I'll prove it's not," Flynn replied.

"How?"

"This time, I'll come with you. Just say yes," Flynn offered, waiting for my reply.

Flynn had offered precious little to win my trust, but the thought that I could find answers to my lifelong quest overpowered any instinct of flight. "I'll do this but only if you tell me more."

"I'll stay with you until I believe you're ready to cope on your own," Flynn said, holding his hand out to seal our pact.

I shook his hand, and instantly, Flynn returned me to the young Diva's world. No pills this time, he seemingly did it with the power of thought. However, where I was alone last time, I stood in a crowded nightclub with Flynn by my side, as promised.

"Where are we?"

"At the musical home of one of Diva's lovers."

A jazz quartet was warming up on stage. Then, a single spotlight lit the platform. It followed an alluring young woman dressed in a ruby-red full-length dress, holding a hand microphone and singing sultry tones to an attentive audience. Every table, bar the one we stood next to, was fully occupied. Beside us, a man watched the band, drinking wine, seemingly comfortable that he sat alone. Many stood at the bar behind us, unconcerned that the man solely occupied a table of four. I looked to Flynn for an explanation.

"You're looking at the owner of these premises, Philippe D'Arenberg, and his star performer, Viola, the source of Diva's angst. If you want to understand your lover better, Benny, you should start here."

CHAPTER TEN

PHILIPPE

P hilippe surveyed his premises, the 'Dr Jazz' night club, warmly greeting his patrons and occasionally stopping to renew acquaintances with regulars or warmly inviting the many tourists that frequented Pisa in the Spring. The fully booked house always lifted his spirits, guaranteeing an atmosphere of expectation. Philippe, a natural host, enjoyed this part of the evening, effortlessly charming his paying patrons. As he often imagined, Dr Jazz was not the Teatro Verdi, but he'd developed it into a club known for its music. Evenings like these made him feel he had control of his life again, until a familiar face strode into the club as if it were his.

"Reggi! Welcome!" Philippe extended a firm handshake before escorting him to a side table, the safest in the house if you had enemies.

Reggi's stocky frame drew the usual cautious gazes from

regulars knowledgeable about his reputation. With an intense look verging on anger, he scanned the thirty tables that made up Dr Jazz as if checking it was safe to sit down.

"Business good?" He asked through pursed lips somewhat camouflaged by a pointed black beard.

Philippe nodded in the affirmative before clicking his finger toward the bar, signalling to bring Reggi his favourite drink, a Cutty Sark whisky. "A full house, as expected!"

"You sound just like your little starlet!" He replied, scanning the bar, seemingly looking for Viola.

"What do you mean, Reggi?"

"Are you running this place?" He replied, holding his threatening gaze like the pistol he carried inside his jacket.

Philippe averted Reggi's gaze by looking across the room. "Look at this crowd, Reggi. They haven't come for the alcohol. They're all here to see Viola and her band."

"That's great, my French friend, but she's spending too much time entertaining high-flyers from the wrong end of town. Before you know it, she starts to believe she's one of them. Comprende!"

"She's doing it for Capo. There's nothing in it."

"Oh? That's not what Capo tells me. If he hears any more rumours, I'll have to teach her a lesson."

"Sure, I'll make it clear to her, Reggi. Just remember she fronts the public, and they come to see her pretty face and hear her angelic voice."

"You'd hate that, wouldn't you?" Reggi replied, smirking.

"Suit yourself. I don't care about Viola, Reggi. I do care about business," Philippe lied before changing the subject. Once drawn to anger, Reggi's volatility was a complicated emotion to contain. It was his job, after all. He'd loyally served Capo's family for two decades, carrying out his every order without fear or conscience.

Philippe passed Reggi an envelope filled with cash, but then he slipped a thousand lire into his hand for good measure. "As I said, business is good. So enjoy yourself, my friend," said Philippe, standing up. "Now, if you don't mind, I've got a business to run."

Reggi quickly pocketed the money and sat back in his chair. He ran his hand across his close-cropped jet-black hair, seemingly satisfied. "As I've always told you, Philippe. There's only one payment that ever matters. The last one," he replied before picking up his whisky, tossing it back and clicking his finger for a second.

"Then I best get to work!" Philippe said, using the moment to excuse himself and return to greeting guests.

He maintained a watchful eye on Reggi. Experience

had taught him Reggi was always more amenable after consuming many whiskies. Only then did he slip away to the back dressing rooms, where Viola and the band prepared for the night's show.

"Hey, guys!"

"Hi, Philippe," they responded enthusiastically. Pay night brought out the best in his musicians. He passed each their takings, plus some.

"Where's Viola?"

"She's out back having a cigarette," one responded, drawing a look of anguish from Philippe as he turned for the exit.

Philippe didn't hide his disappointment, shaking his head as he approached Viola, who quickly butted out her cigarette, guiltily avoiding his gaze. "How many times do you have to be told!"

"You're not my father. I can do what I want."

"Then stop complaining about not being a diva! All I hear from you is frustration about singing cheap jazz to an unappreciative audience, but you do nothing to improve yourself. Remember, I've worked with some of the finest divas, and I chose to help you."

"I know, Christine, Christine, Christine. It's all I ever hear from you. Why don't you just return home and fuck her again instead of picking on me?"

"In case you forgot, I got you this gig, your only chance out of the complete fuck-up of a life you got yourself into!"

"Well, while we're on the subject of fuck-ups, don't forget that my voice is your only ticket back to opera!"

Philippe reacted, threatening to slap her, but Viola responded with defiance, showing little fear. "Go on, hit me. That's all this family knows. Intimidation and money. Go on!"

For one moment, Philippe nearly did before he kissed her hard on the lips. Viola grasped his hair and kissed him back, showing her desire and drawing Philippe's hand to her breast, wanting more. Philippe hungrily caressed her, pressing closer, but this night, as in every night, Philippe checked himself.

"You go on stage in ten minutes," he said, pulling back.

"So?" Viola replied, pulling him back close.

"Reggi's out there."

"Fuck! What does he want?"

"What does he always want?"

"Money, but there's something more for you to be this tense."

"He told me Capo is concerned about your networks."

Viola's eyes flashed defiantly. "I make these networks to help Capo and you. That's my job. Entertain our guests."

"For me? Don't make me laugh!"

"I do it mainly for you," she replied, seemingly hurt by Philippe's slight.

"Let's get this straight, Viola. We work for Capo. Reggi reports to Capo. You do nothing to raise his suspicions, including fraternising with any Marino clientele."

"Reggi doesn't have any interest in my singing. Why should I care or even bother helping him or you?" she replied, noticeably resentful.

"Because you want to be a diva. Remember?"

Viola let go of Philippe, any desires she had for him spent. She brushed her long hair over her shoulders, adjusted her top, and walked toward the entry, not caring to look back. "More than anything or anyone," were her final words before she disappeared into the nightclub, her musical home for the last few months.

Philippe admired her voluptuous body, tightly wrapped in a Travilla-inspired gold làme gown, hand-pleated to bedazzle. Her angelic voice and alluring charm effortlessly captivated her audience, including Philippe. He knew from the first night she performed there was a potential star in the making, driving her hard to improve, celebrating with equal gusto. She had Christine's voice and the body of Carlotta, an unstoppable force that would take them to the Garnier. He just had to convince

Capo and Reggi. If not for them, their intimate relationship would not need to be hidden.

The lights faded in the club as the stage lit up, revealing Viola at the front, her band behind her. They began their warm-up before the show started. Philippe again joined Reggi, two cutty sark whiskies in hand, one for his now sufficiently intoxicated companion. Mercifully, alcohol brought out Reggi's brighter side, allowing both to enjoy Viola's soothing tones and her backing band. He cast an eye across the audience, primarily enamoured men enraptured by Viola's gold dress, shining gem-like under the spotlights. She performed for them with all the skill of a woman who'd learnt to seduce to survive. That, he believed, was why she would succeed in the most challenging and most demanding industry in the world, opera.

"Good, aren't they?" Philippe said, trying to draw out positive feedback for Viola.

"The band's good. Are you sure Viola's got a good voice?"

Philippe knew Reggi was tone-deaf. He couldn't pick a folk songstress from an opera singer, probably from having fired handguns a few too many times.

"I'd never tell her, Reggi, but she could be a star," Philippe confided.

"No way! With her background? Never happen."

"No. Viola could be a star of the opera. I've worked with the best, and with the right opportunities, she could go all the way."

Reggi laughed and embraced Philippe, something he only did intoxicated. "Well, my friend, I'll never buy into your little fantasy, but lucky for you, Capo does!"

"I've heard the rumour that Capo has more than bought into the idea?"

"You heard right. Capo's bought into Teatro Verdi as a favour to a family member, on the promise that he's given a favourable audience to those who matter."

Philippe poured another whisky for Reggi, "I hear, La Scala."

"Who did you hear that from?" Reggi asked accusingly.

Philippe had heard Viola's rumour through one of the 'high-flyers' Reggi mentioned, but he'd never admit it. "From family. Who else do you think?"

Reggi sneered, letting the moment pass, something he never did sober. These intoxicated moments always emboldened Philippe. Sober, not even torture could draw from his lips what alcohol could. Even more fortunate, Reggi never remembered what he did or said drunk. In truth, most of the rumours about the family he learnt directly from Reggi.

"If Capo makes that connection, I'd quickly sign a huge deal on his behalf," Philippe said, drawing Reggi to react.

"You've been saying that for as long as I can remember. Lucky this Dr Jazz venture succeeded, or Capo would have made you pay with your blood. Don't forget it!"

Philippe laughed. "Yeah, lucky for me. But back then, you know I was set up."

"So you claim, but it was still the Marino family. Not many get away with what you did."

Philippe filled both glasses before turning to Viola and the band. He was no different from Viola. Members of the Marino had set both up. Philippe had an old friend to thank for that, and he wouldn't rest until he returned to the opera world, where he'd exact his revenge on the man who double-crossed him, Erik. That was, if as some rumours went, he hadn't perished. The thought brought a smile to his face.

"Listen to that voice, Reggi. She will sing at La Scala if Capo gives her a chance."

Reggi laughed. "Well, my limited experience with divas is they can't be trusted, but don't worry, you just may get that chance. Remember what I've told you. You get one chance to make a big play. Just one."

Philippe nodded, doubting Reggi had ever met a diva in his whole criminal life, but more importantly, Reggi revealed that Capo was making the right networks in opera circles. The Colombo head seemed to give Philippe one life-changing chance to claw his way out of his debt trap.

The opportunity arrived sooner than Philippe expected, in the space of a short few weeks. A stretch limousine ushered him through to the grand foyer of La Scala Theatre, Milan's famous opera house. He didn't look out of place dressed in a Canali suit. He stepped from the car and took Viola's gloved hand to assist her from the limousine. Viola, too, was dressed to impress in a emerald-green evening gown and ready to play her voluptuous part.

Philippe took Viola's arm and walked through the famous foyer, a neo-classical space oozing with musical history. Verdi, Puccini, Pavarotti, Callas, Caccini, to name a few, had all walked these floors of parquet, marble columns and crystal chandeliers. Tickets presented, they entered the Arturo Toscanini foyer, where Francois Levan, the Managing Director of La Scala Enterprise, was holding a private function for his guests. Francois and his wife stood at the centre of the cordoned area, mingling with their other guests as caterers served hors d'oeuvres and fine wines. Philippe and

Viola met Francois and his partner, Madmoiselle Marie Coutier, Francois's young lover since divorcing his wife.

"Welcome, Mademoiselle and Monsieur Allon! Something to drink? We have champagne or wine," said Francois, pointing to the table filled with fine wine and a selection of hors d'oeuvres.

"Please, call me Philippe, and this is Viola. You have a fine selection, Monsieur Levan. Given it is the opening night of *La Traviata*, I will enjoy the Dom Perignon," Philippe replied.

"Yes, the same for me. Merci," Viola added.

"Certainly," Francois replied, signalling for two champagnes. "If you could please excuse me for a short time, my darling, Philippe and I have some business to attend to before the opera commences."

Francois's partner smiled courteously before taking Viola's arm to introduce her to their other guests, allowing Francois to take Philippe to their private box.

The boxes were in perfect symmetry, forming a ring around the grand stage and affording the opera's best views. Surprisingly, the interiors were all different, a result of history. From the early twentieth century, building expenses were paid by the sale of boxes.

Behind the box seats, photos and paintings of the famous performers who'd performed over two centuries filled the walls. Philippe briefly studied the assembly of opera stars ostentatiously framed in gold. Caruso, Pavarotti, Domingo and Melba all stood with the directors past and present, demonstrating the global reach afforded La Scala Enterprise. A perfect partner, he thought. Seal this deal, and Philippe's financial backers would finally appreciate his considerable skills. His gaze continued to move across the different ages of opera, stopping at the photo of Carlotta Caccina, taken during her command performance of *La Traviata*. He remembered that time. Sell-out performances as she was at the height of her career. He often spoke of her abilities to Christine, knowing how it motivated Christine to practice more. Could Viola take Christine's place one day?

"Philippe," came the assured voice of Francois Levan, interrupting Philippe's thoughts.

Francois was impeccably dressed and neatly coiffured, making him look younger than his fifty years.

"Sorry, I was admiring the wonderful photos. So many stars from the past and present."

"Yes, we have a long and fruitful history. But of course, we are the home of opera. N'est pas?"

Both smiled before sipping their champagne, seemingly sizing each other up.

"Have you travelled far tonight, Philippe?"

"Not too far. I'm staying in Pisa at present."

"Oh. Have you lived there long?"

"I live between Paris and Pisa," Philippe lied.

"Ah, I hope your quarters are comfortable."

"Yes. I have many generous benefactors who take care of that."

"It makes such a difference, does it not? Pisa can be charming if you know where to live."

"Yes, my friends look after my interests."

"I miss Paris," said Francois.

Philippe sipped on his drink before openly discussing his experiences in Paris, the opposite of Pisa. The two reminisced about France, establishing a polite rapport, before turning their attention to the business at hand, negotiations for part ownership of La Scala Enterprise.

"So Monsieur, tell me of your plans for our company. The Board has reviewed the prospectus, and we are eager to find out more. In Italy, as you know, opera is more than money. It's life and death. So I was asked to find out the heart of your offer, so to speak."

"Monsieur Levan—"

"Please, Francois."

"Francois. The history of this great theatre is long and proud. The greatest operatic voices have walked this stage," said Philippe, gazing out across the theatre. "But there have been several occasions in history when the music was impacted. True?"

"Yes. In 1776 by fire. World War Two. And then a major renovation at the turn of the century."

"Finance allowed the world's greatest theatre to survive. Every box in this theatre has its financial backer. Music and business in harmony."

"That's true, Philippe, but forgive me for saying that we have benefactors and financiers express interest in our beautiful theatre every day of the year. Why is your offer any different?"

"You are seeing me tonight. Your board members must have seen something of interest?"

Francois held a poker face for a few brief seconds before smiling and levelling with Philippe. "Your organisation's networks with our labour market are strong and deep, and your ability to utilise those many labour skills would make our life more comfortable, there is little doubt. Your finances are also sufficiently deep. So we know what you bring and how. So we now wish to know why."

"We intend to expand our operations to the finest theatres in Europe. We can extend your reach beyond Milan to Paris, London, Vienna and relatively quickly."

Francois folded his arms, seemingly unconvinced. "That is quite an ambitious aim."

"Our labour and union reach, like our finances, is deep."

"This would be quite an undertaking. Who is to head this venture?"

"I am responsible for the expansion of this part of our business."

"Forgive me for being open with you, but where we know much about your organisation, the opposite is true about you. What experience do you have in the opera world?"

The moment of truth had arrived for Philippe to announce his re-emergence into the opera world with Capo's support. Those who sought him since his disappearance would hear of his return, including Christine.

"I assisted one of the great Prima donnas in the world today, Christine Dubois. My pockets are deep, as is my knowledge of the opera world."

Francois sat stony-faced as he contemplated the venture. He appeared almost relieved as the orchestra began to assemble in the pit to commence *La Traviata*.

"I shall convey this important information to the Board, Philippe. But for now, let's simply enjoy the evening," he replied, signalling a valet to invite their partners to join them.

Marie sat with Viola between Francois and Philippe. They had built an easygoing rapport and happily conversed, mainly about opera, before the lights dimmed, signalling the beginning of the performance. Philippe knew it would take more work to convince Francois of his European dream. His organisation's reach was as he'd described, but not sufficient, it seemed, to impress the Board of La Scala Enterprise. Philippe had to apply more pressure. He smiled at Viola and held her hand, softly kissing her cheek, showing a lover's excitement for the occasion but hiding his true intent as he whispered in Viola's ear.

"Your turn," he said, signalling for Viola to bring her skills to the negotiating table.

Act One opened to the atmospheric prelude as the curtains slowly rose. The diva playing Violetta was surrounded by enthusiastic friends, celebrating her recovery from illness. Viola whispered her enthusiasm for the opening scene, gaining nods of approval from Marie and reassuring Philippe that Viola's personable charm and extensive knowledge of opera was winning the day. By the end of Act One, hope was building as he listened to their ongoing enthusiastic chatter.

"Mademoiselle Gheorghiu is perfectly cast for the role of Violetta, don't you think, Viola?"

"She is undoubtedly talented, Marie. Her range is

impressive, and her expressiveness brings an added dimension to her performance that makes it sublime."

By the end of the final Act, they conversed as if old friends. Philippe and Francois both smiled appropriately as two beautiful young women occasionally enticed them into their conversation, right through to returning home as their limousines arrived.

"Thank you, Marie and Francois, for a wonderful evening. I shall hold it as a special memory," said Viola with heartfelt sincerity.

"The pleasure was ours, my darling. We must do it all again," Marie replied before looking to Francois for a consenting glance.

Philippe appreciatively farewelled his two charming hosts before assisting Viola into the limousine. Both sat back contentedly as their chauffeur drove through Milan's relatively quiet streets to their rented apartments. Viola seemingly sensed Philippe's joyful mood.

"I think Marie genuinely wants us to join them again for another opera."

Philippe smiled and squeezed her hand warmly. "You did well tonight. Francois wasn't so forthcoming, but you've tapped into the important influencer."

They arrived at Viola's apartment, both still satisfied with the night. "Would you like to come in?" Viola asked.

Philippe nodded, his mood still upbeat from the outcome. They walked to the balcony and took in Milan's expansive view before Viola brought two glasses of champagne to celebrate their victory.

"Do you think we'll pull this off?"

Philippe was studying the tree-lined boulevard below, seemingly lost in his thoughts, before finally replying. "We're close. But we must remain cautious and focused. You know as well as me, our luck could turn the wrong way without warning."

They toasted their small success, allowing the hint of victory to be enjoyed and celebrated. The icy-cold champagne and the chill of the late-night air made Viola shiver. So, both walked inside to the warmth and privacy of her cosy apartment.

Philippe held Viola close, warming her chilled arms. She looked stunning in her strapless evening gown. He caressed her shoulders and neck, unfastening the one diamond-studded hair clip and releasing Viola's silky copper-blonde hair to flow over shapely ivory-skinned shoulders. Dimmed lighting enveloped them in an erotic atmosphere. Viola responded, kissing him deeply, the taste of desire and anticipation growing.

"Stay with me, Philippe," she said, hunger in her expression.

"Philippe kissed her deeper, holding her slender neck with one hand, caressing her soft shoulder and arm with the other. He leaned in close, savouring her sweet skin, pressing his growing desire against her, teasing her of what may be, before cruelly stepping away.

"We've come this far. I won't have us fuck up when we're this close."

"What do you mean?"

"You didn't even notice. Did you?"

"What?"

"The car parked in the street."

Viola thought before responding, seemingly searching for the answer Philippe sought, before shaking her head in the negative.

"Reggi is parked outside."

Viola lowered her eyes in disappointment. She didn't need to respond. The magical evening's charm gave way to reality. Philippe turned, saying no more and let himself out, more frustrated than angry. He, too, didn't want to let go of their evenings achievement, but he firmly had his business face on by the time he reached Reggi's car and hopped in the front seat. Reggi was sipping a now cold coffee in the chill of his car, in no mood for an extended conversation.

"Capo sends his regards. He's looking forward to good

news," said Reggi, taking another sip of his coffee. All the while, he looked up to Viola's apartment, signalling his suspicions.

"She did good, Reggi."

"What the fuck does that mean? I'll go to Capo and say you did well?"

Philippe didn't offer a definitive answer, but he knew the family had reached the end of their patience for his elaborate scheme. He had reached the crossroads of a dangerous intersection. So he crossed the rubicon. "Viola did her job tonight. I expect a deal soon and amicably."

"No coercion?"

"Still possible. But as I told you, coercion would be the least favourable method. If we can keep that out of the deal, we'll make a cleaner switch into the music industry."

Reggi sniggered. "I've heard all this before, Monsieur Musique of the night. Give me a date to take to Capo."

"Two weeks. I will know for sure, then."

"Then?"

"I will seal the deal for the love of music, or I'll sign it in blood."

Reggi opened his window, sipped the last of his coffee and threw the paper cup onto the empty boulevard pavement. "Two weeks," he said before winding the window up and starting his car, ready to leave.

Philippe said no more. He'd said enough. As Reggi's black Mercedes unassumingly glided away, he looked toward Viola's apartment for a brief moment, considering returning to her willing arms. Two months had passed, both wanting each other, forging a restrained bond that frustrated and excited in equal measure. His hunger for her filled him, but the stakes had skyrocketed to another dangerous level. He needed time to consider the next fateful move — one that could return him to the world he so loved or hasten the violent death that faced all members who dared fail the family.

Two weeks had passed all too quickly. Philippe sat quietly in the corner of his nightclub, pondering life away from his Pisa club. He waited expectedly, along with the many jazz fans, mainly male, who'd become equally enamoured with Viola's performances. The club was full, except for the table Philippe occupied. The table of four, as always, was reserved for Philippe and any of his guests. He nervously checked his watch, uncertain Francois had accepted his invitation. The club lights dimmed before stage spotlights flashed on, and the MC introduced Viola and her band just as Francois arrived.

Philippe stood, warmly welcomed Francois and ordered Chateau Mouton Rothschild wine for their table. Francois gazed across the nightclub, appearing relieved to have not missed the performance.

"I'm not the only one late?" He asked, pointing to the two empty chairs at their table.

"A friend of mine may be joining us later in the evening. The other is for Viola. She will join us after the performance."

"I look forward to hearing her live."

"You received her demo tapes?"

"Yes. As you said, Viola has a wonderful range and quality to her voice. Marie insisted I follow up, so here I am."

"Then, I will not interrupt the show for you," Philippe replied, extending his arms toward the stage. His waiters ensured Francois's wine glass remained topped up, heightening his receptiveness to the performance. Viola fused jazz with some light opera, to the surprise of her fans and to Francois's delight. Libiamo ne lieti calici" charmed and invigorated Francois in equal measure as she sang diva-like with her energetic band. Philippe watched on, knowing Viola had again played her part in drawing the powerful La Scala Enterprise closer to their operations. He looked across to the bar, where Reggi leaned, his gaze constantly moving around the night club. Reggi tilted his head, questioning if he should join them. Philippe shook his head and signalled 'one' with his index finger, giving him another hour alone with his guest. Importantly, Viola had nearly finished her performance, giving her time to draw Francois further into their web.

The dimmed lights flashed back to full intensity. Viola and the band gratefully received the audience's rapturous applause before Philippe escorted the diva from the stage to his table, to a continued standing ovation. To Philippe's satisfaction, Francois, too, stood, applauding with a mixture of enthusiasm and adoration. Viola flirted with him, extending her hand, which he admiringly kissed before pulling her chair out for her.

"I hope you enjoyed our show, Francois. Many of the tunes were new."

"Very brave. I have not heard opera and jazz fusion performed so sublimely. But this is art, n'est pa?"

"We have slowly developed it, but this was our dress rehearsal, just for you, Monsieur."

"A toast to celebrate your new creation," responded Francois.

Rothschild wine was regularly brought to the table. Francois had, until now, cautiously enjoyed the wine, but Viola's appearance had loosened any reservations. Friendly conversation flowed between them, mainly about opera. Philippe joined in the chat only occasionally before excusing himself to go about his managerial duties, his first port of call, Reggi.

"Didn't I tell you? He has all but signed the contract," said Philippe, with wine-induced bravado.

Reggi downed his scotch. "All I have seen is you wasting our most expensive wines on him. The only interest he seems to have is for Viola, not signing contracts."

"That's the next step."

Reggi laughed. "You want to incriminate him? Are you serious? He's a Frenchman. He probably fucks a different woman every night. It's their national sport."

"We have already learnt there's something much more important to Francois than Viola's conquest," said Philippe confidently.

Reggi showed some interest for the first time, sliding his empty scotch glass toward the barman and studying Philippe for a moment before speaking. "Capo wants to talk to me after your meeting. Give me something that will hold his attention so I don't have to come back tonight and conclude this little farce of yours."

Philippe scoffed one of the scotches Reggi ordered, seeking courage. "Francois's ambitions extend beyond La Scala. He has a long alliance with Carlotta Caccini's husband."

"Victor, isn't it?"

"The very one. I'm sure that will elevate Capo's interest."

Reggi nodded. There was some history between the family and Victor, sufficient to buy Philippe more time to secure Francois. Reggi stood up and tapped Philippe's shoulder with his large hand as he readied to leave. That was the closest Reggi ever came to showing admiration. He was already on his mobile as he left, no doubt talking to Capo.

Philippe watched with some relief as Reggi disappeared through the exit door before turning his gaze back toward Viola. She was in deep discussion with Francois. His enamoured demeanour had changed to a more business-like expression. Viola had prepared Francois for Philippe to return to the table.

"Am I interrupting anything," Philippe asked as he approached.

"Perfect timing. I am about to start our second performance, and Francois has kindly agreed to stay to hear us," Viola replied, leaving Philippe with Francois.

"I hope Viola didn't bore you with her many views on opera?" Philippe asked.

"Quite the contrary. I admit Viola's knowledge surprised me. She truly loves opera."

"She wants to try out for the *La Traviata* production. Do you think she should?"

After their first meeting, Philippe would have given Viola little chance of being asked to perform, but she had swayed Francois with her passion and ability.

"She should try. You are aware that the *La Traviata* production will move from Milan to Paris? It will require a long-term obligation."

Philippe ordered another fine bottle of wine in preparation for Viola's next show, but also as a way of showing his commitment. "I am intimately aware of the workings of all concerned with the Garnier. I will prepare her like no other and help you in any way, should you need it."

Francois nodded to the waiter after having his wine glass filled, seemingly content with the rapport he and Philippe had. "Let Viola attend the tryouts. Should she succeed, I'll be happy to discuss our future arrangement in Milan."

Philippe raised a glass to Francois's proposition, sure he would close the deal with La Scala Enterprise. Francois didn't know that it would unleash new and dangerous players, tying them together in an unpredictable partnership that almost certainly would end in a dangerous cocktail of extortion and death.

CHAPTER ELEVEN

LA SCALA

E rik entered the Academy of Lyric Opera in a buoyant
mood. This year's intake of promising opera talent
was of high quality. The Artistic Director, Gianni Leoni,
considered them a 'unique blend of raw talent and experience', high praise. Today was when each new student
could showcase their innate talents to the guests. Erik's
success at Teatro Sociale ensured those who mattered
saw him in a favourable light. He'd invested in the
company on the proviso the Musical Director of the *La
Traviata* production would be his mentor. It afforded
Erik freedoms such as today, sitting beside Gianni in the
front row seat of La Scala as he assessed the potential
new intakes.

One singer was in the spotlight, not for her reputation or skills, but rather her age. Erik guessed she was in
her mid-twenties, unusually old to be considered. She

had either exceptional skills or the right networks to make the final selection process. All performers showed promise, currently relying on the raw talent they hoped would be refined with the Academy's guidance. A curious silence ensued as the oldest student, Viola, took her place on the stage to sing "Libiamo ne lieti calici."

Viola's inclusion intrigued Erik. How had a prodigious talent come late to opera? It was not unlike another talent he observed as head of security for the Garnier. Viola even reminded Erik of Christine as she readied herself to perform. He steeled himself for disappointment, expecting no one could match Christine's angelic voice. A hush descended as if Viola was about to be anointed Christine's heir apparent.

Her voice was indeed pure and demanded attention, but power and control were lacking. A full orchestral backing would easily overpower her understated voice. Viola's maturity afforded her a natural command of articulation, bringing a certain believability to her stage presence. She effortlessly captured the essence of Violetta, but only dedicated practice would lift the performance to diva-like greatness. Her placement in *La Traviata* would be a risky one. Rumours swirled that she had won her place in the auditions through connections, but Gianni wasn't one to be affected by gossip. As he considered this late bloomer, he knew that older intakes rarely succeeded.

Viola half bowed to the small group, who applauded unenthusiastically before the art director invited Erik to say a few words to the new students. He welcomed the chance to warn overconfident young talent of the unrelenting competitiveness they would face.

"Welcome, everyone, to one of the most important days of your life. You have all no doubt battled an infinite number of hurdles to be here today." Erik paused to emphasise the moment. "This is the last hurdle. Should you succeed, remember the challenges never cease. If you are fortunate, you may be the one who soars to the greatest of heights, but you will need to work diligently, hone your unique skills and honour the great composers who imagined this world. The season of *La Traviata* commences soon. I advise you to spend time researching and understanding its composer, Guiseppe Verdi. By seasons end, I hope those whom we select will better appreciate Verdi. Be prepared to push yourselves to the limit to honour his creation. Good luck. I shall watch your development as performers with great interest."

All applauded enthusiastically, then Gianni thanked Erik before delivering his final message.

"That brings to a close today's audition. Tomorrow, we

choose who moves to the rehearsals proper. We shall begin with Act One of *La Traviata*. Use what is left of the day to practice. I will expect you all to know each song's lyrics so that tomorrow we can concentrate on the nuances that make it so special. Good luck!"

Ashen-faced students filed out of the auditorium, relieved but aware of the demands they would face tomorrow. Erik studied them as they walked away, some determined, others seemingly fearful and uncertain. Erik shot Gianni a knowing smile as he approached.

"The challenges of youth," Gianni said.

"Not all are young." Erik countered.

"Yes, Viola. We haven't had a mature student for many years. It's always an interesting dynamic. We will see," he replied, rubbing his chin, uncertainty in his expression.

"There's a rumour she was favourably considered."

"Really? I've not heard that. Any favours have not and will not come from me," Gianni replied, closing his notebook indignantly. He was a proud man, good at his craft, and any insinuation of favour got a reaction. "Where has this favour come from?"

"It's only rumour, but she has a friendship with Philippe. Some say more."

"That, I have heard. We will meet Philippe tomorrow."

"Yes. Philippe's group brings much-needed support, it

seems. Hopefully, your new student is equally supportive, musically speaking."

"All companies come with strengths and weaknesses.
Even yours. True?"

Erik had worked hard to convince them of his genuine desire to make a difference. Money certainly helped,
influencing many on the board, except Gianni. He
balked at the thought of a director on the board wasting the musical director's time, pushing Erik harder than
anyone. Erik had earned Gianni's support, as too would
Viola, should she be selected.

"Ultimately, she'll survive or fall on her talent. I do feel
there is something unique about her, Gianni."

"Yes. I felt the same way. Her tone reminds me of
someone I can't place. But a rough diamond, no?"

Erik smiled in agreement, thinking of the precious
time he spent helping Christine become a diva. "This is
why you love what you do, is it not?"

"Yes. If I find one new diva among these students, it
will be worth all the struggle. Unfortunately, many
will leave tomorrow, and many more will leave within
the first six months as they realise the rigours of their
challenge."

Erik had learnt not to waste too much of Gianni's
time with small talk. "Then, I shall leave you to consider

who will join the *Traviata* production. I have to assist the directors on some operational issues."

"The industrial disputes seem to be getting worse every month."

"Well, from what I hear, our new director will bring much-needed respite from the union's demands."

"Let us hope. Do you think opening night can be a success?" Gianni asked as Erik was about to leave.

"A triumph! Not even a nationwide strike would stop them from coming." Erik displayed confidence, but in truth, a strike would be damaging. The introduction of a new director would be timely. A year of hard work had partly lifted the burden of Erik's troubled past, making him believe music would be an integral part of his new life. Were the sins of his past fading?

The board meeting's glum mood matched the morning's traffic gridlock, courtesy of the nationwide rolling strikes that had endured all year, disrupting La Scala services from catering to ticket collection. Erik sat beside Francois, who appeared to be in a reflective mood. The industrial disputes took their toll on all, but especially Francois, who carried the primary responsibility.

"It's a miracle I made it here on time," Erik offered, not needing to explain the reasons.

"Our new board member just contacted me. He's caught in traffic, also."

Erik chuckled. "Ironic. I hear Philippe may be the one who can fix this problem, Francois?"

"I'm not sure his reach extends to the transport union, but I'm confident he can help us in the restructure of our services and administration."

"That would be timely."

"Opening night is close. I hear good reports?" Francois asked, looking for any good news.

Erik accommodated. "I think it will be memorable for all the right reasons. The performers are ready and eager to showcase their considerable talents, and Gianni is inspiring the new interns."

Francois looked at a message that arrived on his phone. "Ah, Philippe has arrived," he said, excusing himself to welcome the new member.

Erik sat back and listened to the chatter around the boardroom table, not feeling the need to join in. His mind turned to the opening night, which was approaching fast. Concerning problems lingered that he didn't wish to share with Francois. Erik was accepted on the board to solve them, but the industrial disputes had meant late deliveries of sets and wardrobes, creating chaos behind the scenes and affecting the confidence of all.

"Excuse me, ladies and gentlemen," said Francois's secretary, tapping a glass with a spoon to draw attention. "Francois and our new member of the board are about to join us. As a show of courtesy, could we all stand as they enter?"

Erik waited eagerly to learn more about the new member, quietly hoping he was as knowledgeable, skilful and enthusiastic about the industry as he'd heard. Francois walked in first, standing at the table's head, before introducing the new member, Philippe D'Arenberg. All applauded. Erik, too, but less enthusiastically.

Philippe D'Arenberg was the man he'd sent to Rome two years earlier. The man he believed long dead was very much alive, and he greeted the welcoming board members with the assurance of a professional. Erik knew this side of him well, but he also knew the hopeless gambling addict. It was Philippe's gambling addiction that prompted Erik to send him to Italy in the first place. Make his competition, Philippe, disappear. And yet, here he stood. Philippe's reappearance drew out repressed memories of terrible years he thought he could leave behind.

"Any more questions? Erik, you've been surprisingly quiet," Francois asked, drawing him from his introspection.

Erik cleared his throat, buying time to collect his thoughts before he asked him a question in his best Italian accent. "I admit to being surprised, Monsieur D'Arenberg. You were a substantial supporter of French opera for many years, and then you disappeared."

Philippe hesitated, seemingly intrigued by his question. Had he recognised Erik? "I decided to spend time away from my home to pursue new interests here in Italy. Given my notoriety, I worked under another surname. This meeting seemed the perfect occasion to announce my return. Do I detect a slight French accent in your voice, Signour...?"

"This is Signour Erik Rossi," Francois replied on Erik's behalf.

"I worked in Paris in my youth as a struggling musician before returning to Italy to work in my father's business, so I'm fluent in Italian and French."

"Then we share a passion for music. My love for opera crosses all geographic boundaries, and my dedication to opera is a thirst I shall never quench. Perhaps we can discuss that passion at another less formal occasion?" Philippe enquired.

Philippe held a questioning gaze as if he'd recognised him. Erik allowed the moment to pass. He held his tongue for the remainder of the meeting, which by all accounts was a success in the eyes of the board directors. All warmly shook Philippe's hand as they departed.

Erik was the last to leave, preferring to listen to Philippe's interaction with his new colleagues and collect his thoughts.

"A most informative presentation, Monsieur D'Arenberg," Erik said, warmly shaking his hand.

"Please, call me Philippe. I must admit that I feel I have met you before. You remind me of someone, but I can't place it."

Erik deflected Philippe's reaction. "It must be my time in France. That makes us brothers of a sort, don't you think?"

"Of course, that must be it."

"And as any good Frenchman would do, I invite you to the final full rehearsal tomorrow night. I usually watch it alone in the stalls, taking notes for our musical director. You can join me if you wish. I can introduce you to the cast afterwards, should you have the time?"

Philippe nodded, firmly shaking Erik's hand. "I welcome the opportunity."

Erik left the boardroom with mixed feelings. Philippe seemingly didn't recognise him, but an evening together would test his anonymity. It was also a chance to find out more about the missing years in Philippe's life. While he knew Philippe's plans for La Scala, he was less sure of the role his deadly family backers had.

Erik sat high above the La Scala stage as Gianni boisterously engaged all cast and crew for their final preparations. For the first time, all the cast were in full dress because Philippe had come good on his promises. Gianni glanced Erik's way as the fully assembled cast posed for publicity photos. Erik acknowledged him, pleased with the improved industrial situation. Whatever Philippe's intentions, he was grateful for the positive impact he'd had on *La Traviata's* production. The casts' demeanour was as buoyant as the costumes they adorned, lifting Erik's mood.

"Come sit down, Philippe."

"Have I missed anything?"

"No. We are finishing photos before the rehearsals. As you can see, they're in full dress," nodding to Philippe in appreciation.

"I don't expect any more industrial problems, but let me know if you have any," he confidently replied, as if he expected none.

Photography complete, the orchestra opened the rehearsal with the atmospheric prelude. The curtains swept open to the cast, positioned in the grand hall of

Violetta's home, amongst her party guests celebrating her recovery from illness. Angela Gheorghiu shone beside some of La Scala's future stars as she set the scene for her fateful love.

"She is every bit as good as her reputation," said Philippe in admiration.

Erik would have grown to like Philippe under any other circumstance, but he knew too many of his secrets, namely expensive gambling habits that destroyed all those who cared for him. Christine and Raoul had learned that lesson. How significant were his debts now? His success with the unions was the Colombo family's doing, casting him ever deeper into their debt. Was this his last chance to escape their web?

"She has been compared to Carlotta Caccini by some, but I feel her tone and range is not unlike Christine Dubois," Erik replied, looking for a reaction and getting one before Philippe's mobile ring tone interrupted.

He checked the caller before speaking. "Excuse me, I must take this," he said before courteously sitting at the back of the stall.

Erik nodded obligingly before standing up and peering toward the stage to give Philippe the impression of privacy while straining to hear Philippe's every word. The call sounded urgent, based on his reaction and the subservient tone of his voice. It had to be his benefactor.

"I'm at La Scala. Final rehearsals are in full swing. Yes, tell him the problem's rectified. I expect a faultless opening night. I have the tickets."

Erik heard only snippets but enough to make him think Philippe had risen in the ranks of Colombo. It reminded him of an earlier time when he, too, needed money and was prepared to borrow from families he should not. However, when you live a life one step removed from a death wish, why not? That spiteful abandon led Erik to make promises hard to fulfil. If not for his military skills, he may not have survived the perils of owing the mob money.

"They're for you, Reggi....insights....opera....okay?"

Philippe kept referring to Reggi. Was this his go-to man? How high was he in the chain of command? Erik would make enquiries ; though, doing so risked exposure to his enemies, especially if Reggi had access to the top. Whatever Reggi's standing, Erik needed Philippe as an ally, not an enemy.

"Sure, sure, okay. Let me know," said Philippe before his call ended abruptly.

Erik called out to Gianni, creating an impression he hadn't been listening in. "The lighting should be more subdued for this scene, Gianni." Gianni complied, getting the lights lowered. Then Erik sat down beside Philippe and watched the rehearsals. "I think this will be a very successful opening night. Mademoiselle Gheorghiu is singing sublimely."

"Yes, you're right. She's similar to Christine Dubois, particularly in her expressions."

"I only saw her perform once. At the Garnier in *Macbeth*."

"Yes, a magnificent performance in the greatest of opera houses," said Philippe, his gaze distant, seemingly visualising that night.

Erik saw an opening. "I hear French opera is suffering the same fate as La Scala. Perhaps your network tentacles spread further than Italy?"

Philippe grinned with delight. "The Garnier does suffer some industrial dispute, but word has it their problems are more of a financial nature," he confided.

It didn't surprise Erik that Philippe remained interested in the Garnier's workings, so he pressed him to find out more. "I doubt French aristocracy would allow such a jewel to fall for too long."

"You're right. It's more a question of whether management would ever know. Word has it that those responsible for running it may be less than open and accountable," Philippe replied.

Philippe's tentacles spread long and deep. He

confirmed what Erik already knew. Victor had again resumed control of the Garnier opera house, the man Erik had dethroned two years earlier. Carlotta's breakdown had allowed Victor undeserving influence, again.

Erik let Philippe's judgment pass, directing his attention to the rehearsal."La Scala had its financial difficulties, but we are in a better situation now."

"In no small part due to you, Erik."

"The bleeding has stopped, for now. With one other sufficiently enthusiastic director, I believe we will fully heal the patient," Erik offered openly.

Philippe nodded his head knowingly. "That is my intention. It would help to know what an acceptable level would be?"

Erik had his chance. Philippe wanted to know if they would be friends or foes. Erik looked him square in the eye. "I believe a director with twenty per cent holding would be an ideal offer for the long term survival of La Scala," he said, holding his hand out as a gesture of trust.

Philippe shook Erik's hand. "Twenty per cent stake, it is."

They had informally set their partnership in motion in a fitting place, the stalls of an opera house. If he followed through on Erik's suggestion, they would soon be allies, holding a substantial stake in its future. Then

Erik's enemy would be close to him, the best place for an adversary.

Rehearsals continued smoothly, building the rapport between them and loosening the cautious barriers of a developing friendship.

"If *La Traviata* is a success in Milan, perhaps next year may be Paris?" Philippe suggested.

"From what you've told me, they will need a strong team of directors."

"It's almost certain, Erik."

Philippe must have maintained his alliance with Victor even while incognito in Italy. They had to be close friends, meaning Carlotta was vulnerable to their manipulations. Erik had to act, so he played to Philippe's suggestions.

"This could be the beginning of a long and fruitful friendship. Although I read some bad business happened there. Murders and whatnot."

Philippe's expression turned serious. "That was all the work of a thoroughly despicable character who thankfully no longer is there."

"I read about him. The head of security and a band of other unsavoury characters doing his bidding."

"Yes. Your namesake. The most despicable man I ever met."

"I lost touch with the newspaper reports. Did they catch him?"

"Unfortunately, no. I think he perished in the Seine."

"Then, the way is open."

Philippe nodded. Erik had told him what he wanted to hear. Philippe's return to opera appeared to be the single strategy to free himself from debt. Ultimately, the Garnier figured in his calculations. Unknown to him, Erik wanted precisely the same. He had to act swiftly and manoeuvre himself into the Garnier before Philippe and warn Carlotta. To make it work, Erik also had to help Carlotta regain her memory to deal with Victor before it was too late. Unlike Philippe, he was running low on finances. The only means of matching Philippe was through reestablishing contact with his mafia connections. The risk was revealing he had not died, as was commonly reported, a gamble he was now prepared to take.

CHAPTER TWELVE

RETURN TO GARNIER

arlotta sat in the front row of the Garnier, observing Claude, the assistant artistic director, as he welcomed the performers on stage. It was the second week of winter rehearsals for the spring release of *La Traviata*. Wrapped in a woollen blanket and sipping on warm coffee, Carlotta looked anything but the shining star who once ruled the Garnier opera world. Claude expressively clapped his hands to motivate performers and keep his hands warm. As always, she sat alone in the darkened theatre, bar one other. Carlotta cast a sideways glance up to Box Five, where the shadowy outline of Madame Giraud sat, seemingly previewing the new performers. Her presence pervaded the Garnier like the supposed opera ghost, saying little but always observing. A shiver ran across the back of Carlotta's neck at the thought of her. Carlotta cast the idea aside, putting her full attention on the stage. All were present for rehearsals except one, Christine.

"Musicians, let us start with 'Dell' invito trascorsa e gia l'ora.' Cast, assemble in your places. Gina, you will sing as Violetta until Christine arrives."

Carlotta smiled at Gina's willingness. Gina needed no prompting, for Christine's double hadn't been announced, and she was the favourite to be selected. Gina had a pleasant enough voice, but Carlotta worried about her limited range. At these times, she regretted retiring from performing. Carlotta had not practised since her fateful final performance in *Macbeth* years earlier, but she knew her range was greater even without training. She'd had many quiet conversations with Claude along those lines, but they continued to scan the opera world for another double as there was still time. Halfway through the performance, Christine scurried onto the stage, halting the rehearsal.

"Welcome, Christine. We are so glad you could make it today," Claude said, looking anything but happy. He twisted his conductor baton firmly with his hands.

Christine didn't reply, merely nodding to Gina before taking her place. She turned to Claude, but not before glancing out to the stalls directly at Carlotta and raising her eyes indignantly, expressing her displeasure at her attendance.

"Maestro, again, please," said Claude.

Carlotta admired Christine's youthful beauty as she sang, but today she rehearsed with little passion. Her performance was understated, sufficiently worrying Carlotta enough for her to join the rehearsals. She, more than anyone, could read the mood of a diva, understanding the emotional pressure that came with being the best. By the time rehearsals reached the third act, the cast's singing overpowered Christine's inadequate tones. Carlotta had seen enough, walking toward the stage, her patience at end.

Claude knew what Carlotta required. "Everyone, take a break for twenty minutes, please."

As they filed out, Carlotta signalled for Christine to sit with her. Christine joined her, putting two seats between them. Her expression was the cold type normally reserved for unwanted media.

"I don't like to interrupt rehearsals, but I felt it was important. I think I can help you."

Christine's raised eyebrows revealed her scepticism. "Why are you here, again? Do you want my part?"

"No! I've retired from singing, but in case you weren't aware, my company owns the production, Christine."

"Your husband is the manager. Can't you leave the

people hired to carry out their duties alone? Including me," said Christine, turning away from Carlotta and leaving only a cold silence between them.

"What did I do to you?"

"You don't know?"

"I have a good idea, but I want to hear it from you."

Christine faced her, arms folded. "I don't know what your game is, Carlotta, but this innocent facade doesn't fool me. You never offered help to any performers while you ruled opera. That's your true nature."

"Everyone makes mistakes."

Christine laughed ironically. "Ten years of doing all you could to hold me back. Even threatening me. That's a little more than a mistake, don't you think?"

"You're right. I behaved outrageously, and I wish I could have my time over. Give me a chance. I'll never undermine you again. I promise."

Christine unfolded her arms. "I will think about it, but don't expect an answer any time soon."

"I understand and will wait for as long as you need."

Christine slumped back in her chair, seemingly relieved. "That's all I'm asking of everyone. Time." Silence ensued, both gazing at the stage as performers returned. Christine stood to join them but looked Carlotta's way almost as an afterthought. "This isn't just about our history. You know that, don't you?"

"Yes. I heard about Philippe."

"I spent years searching for him without a word. I accepted he was dead, only to learn he'd been alive all this time." Christine stopped to control her wavering voice. "Now, the man I loved won't even talk or write to me, as if....as if I meant nothing to him. Why, Carlotta? Tell me why."

"Only Philippe can answer for his actions. One day he may return to the Garnier, and on that day, he will have to tell you why."

"Will he? That one day could be a year from now. What should I do in the meantime?"

"Do what you were born to do. Perform like no other. You are the greatest diva in Europe. Bring happiness to others and allow your heart time to heal."

Christine looked away, hiding tears that welled in her eyes. She turned and walked away from the stage to the back of the stalls. Carlotta thought to call out to her, but what else could she say to console her? Time was the only process that would heal her, but time was not on Christine's side. *La Traviata* was just months away, requiring difficult decisions. Should they scour Europe for a new diva?

That decision could wait a while longer. Carlotta had

learned that lesson, having placed her faith in a new friend who had disappointed. Unlike Philippe, her friend, Erik, had at least contacted her after a long absence. She'd accepted his invitation to meet in Montmarte, but she would be more cautious this time. She did know that the Milan production of *La Traviata* had been a success, so meeting Erik was justified, business-wise. Carlotta's memory had improved from becoming involved in the *La Traviata* production. For some reason, she still felt Erik could play an integral part in her continued recovery. Exactly how alluded her, but she couldn't help feel as if she'd met Erik before Como, and she had to find out when and where. Perhaps that could unlock the mysteries of her past life.

She'd seen enough for today and walked up the aisle to the exit doors. The chill of the darkened theatre weighed down on her, making her look directly up to Box Five as she passed. Madame Giraud no longer sat at the front of the box, but she could see a silhouette of activity at the back of the stall.

A shadowy outline of two people talking before both looked her way.

CHAPTER THIRTEEN

REUNIONS

It had been a decade since Erik walked through the gothic doors of the Basilica of the Sacre-coeur, the landmark church overlooking Paris from the summit of Montmarte. Ambling through its quiet pews, he made time for prayer, wishing Rose happiness in her next life. She deserved more in her short life, but he'd failed her. Erik looked up to the morning-lit gothic windows, admiring the coloured hues shining through stained glass. It reminded him of the unique light that adorned his home beneath the Garnier, where he plotted revenge for Rose. A tide of anger built in him, threatening to overrule his new purpose. In that dark mood, Carlotta was his enemy. He stood up from prayer, fists clenched, screaming out across the empty chamber. "Help me understand!" He looked up to the highest windows. A dim silhouette danced across the light before circumnavigating the church like a flock of crows. Erik followed the shapes, but they disappeared as if a phantom controlled the Basilica's lighting. The event startled him enough to leave. Erik walked to the viewing area, not turning back, fighting old notions that invaded his mind, phantoms he could not forget.

Erik admired the panoramic view, taking deep breaths of Montmarte's crisp spring air. The sights and sounds of the ascending funiculaire came to his attention. He could see Carlotta sitting by a window. In a short time, she joined him at the viewing point. It had been a year, enough time to notice the change in her. She walked confidently toward him, smiling briefly in recognition. She'd lost the paleness of her poor health, making him smile involuntarily. He opened his arms, offering a hint of affection. Carlotta nodded politely, showing a well-deserved wariness toward Erik, who'd broken the promise he made in Como.

Erik deflected the slight, pointing to the view. "We're in luck. It's a perfect day to roam Montmarte."

"There have been many blue skies this last year," Carlotta replied, admiring the view and avoiding his gaze.

"Has it been a year?" Erik replied, drawing a stern glance from Carlotta.

"A good friend would know how long it's been."

Erik opened his arms apologetically. "I'm sorry. I should have contacted you. You deserve better."

She nodded in agreement. "I feel like a walk. I always enjoy the street art exhibition. Shall we?"

Erik nodded and pointed for her to lead. Sunday was market day. Montmartre's narrow streets filled with a kaleidoscope of traders in everything from food to art. They weaved through the bustling crowd, sampling fresh bread and cheese, occasionally buying.

"You will have to carry that back to Como," Carlotta said.

"No. I'm staying at Le Chat Noir hotel for a few days. We will have lunch there, if you'd care to join me?"

Carlotta smiled, not answering, so Erik embellished his invitation. "I have a charming balcony with a view of the Eiffel Tower. It would seem a pity to dine alone."

"Will this be an annual event?" Carlotta replied, looking more interested in the food stalls.

"I am sorry, Carlotta. It won't be a year when I gain the position as artistic director of *La Traviata* for the Garnier production."

"Ambitious. It will be a competitive process. What makes you sure you'll be selected?"

"I have the financial support you are looking for."

"Then become the financial manager."

"You know the *La Traviata* productions in Como and Milan were both overwhelming successes. I was heavily involved in both, making me more qualified than anyone in Europe."

Carlotta merely raised her eyebrows at Erik's claim. They strolled through the streets of Montmarte before descending the stairs of the Rue Foyatier to the base of Montmartre hill. Carlotta remained aloof but finally accepted Erik's invitation to dine on his apartment balcony. Chilled wine had been readied on the terrace table, which overlooked panoramic views of Paris. The sound of bustling streets vibrated up to the hotel's top floor, heightening the vibrant feel of Montmarte.

"It makes me want to go to the real Le Chat Noir," Carlotta said, taking a seat and relaxing.

"We could go there, but unfortunately, all that remains is a plaque."

"How it must have felt to attend the very first cabaret in Paris, perhaps the world?" Carlotta imagined.

"Exhilarating. That's how I want the audience to feel about La Traviata." He opened a chilled white wine and filled both glasses

"Why are you pitching to me, Erik. You know my ex-husband will choose the team."

"Do I?"

She studied Erik for a time, touching the rim of her wine glass. "There is still so much I don't remember. For now, it suits me that Victor runs the Garnier operation. I can set up the meeting. The rest will be up to you."

Erik nodded in appreciation. "Let me prepare the charcuterie, and then we can talk about anything but business. It's been a year, and I want to know more about you."

Carlotta raised her eyebrows, showing her suspicion remained. He filled her glass then went to the kitchen to prepare their lunch. He needed Carlotta's support, and she knew it. Victor would welcome any financial offer put on his desk, and Erik's proposal would not disappoint. Money matters were relatively easy, but Carlotta would decide his fate regarding his input into musical directing.

Erik arrived early for his meeting with Victor and used the time to stroll through Paris's most famous drawing room, beneath Baudry's interpretation of French music history. The famous ceiling painting was on show, free from the glitz of countless chandeliers in light. He preferred the Grand Foyer in the twilight, as the Garnier in natural light allowed him to speak to those who once strode its famous corridors before performing. Even the grand marble staircase took on a different hue in the semi-darkness, giving way to Apollo's triumph as he gazed down on those who ventured up to its heavenly stage. The stillness engaged his senses, allowing a calm meditation of what was and what might be.

The calm soon broke. Victor descended the Grand Staircase as if it was his own private dwelling. Erik looked on smiling, not at the sight of him but because he recognised that feeling. The opera house had its energy, filling occupants with a sense of unique grandeur. He bowed his head slightly, playing along with Victor's false sense of superiority. Erik would reclaim power soon enough. Erik even endured his guided tour of the famous corridors, feigning attentiveness. Victor proudly presented the myriad of stories he'd rotely learned, maintaining his civility and masking his lack of respect. Victor's tour ended at a vantage point Erik knew well — Box Five.

"This has been home to two phantoms who terrified this opera house a century apart."

"I'm aware of the famous Phantom of 1902, but I know only snippets of this latter-day phantom," Erik lied.

"Well, the latter-day phantom's reign was far shorter than the original's, but both owned Box Five."

Erik perused the Box that Victor offered him as part of the contract to be the Producer of *La Traviata*. "Well, it's time the occupier of the infamous Box Five focused on music, not mayhem. What happened to the last Phantom?"

Victor looked out to the stage, seemingly searching for any ghostly presence in the empty theatre.

"He wasn't a phantom, as many have since embellished. He was the head of security, a manipulative and dangerous man."

"How dangerous?"

"Very. I suspect Erik was the murderer of a ballerina who was to perform in *Macbeth*. The police never solved the case, but I believe he was more than capable of committing such acts."

"So, they didn't catch him?"

"No. The police closed in after the abduction of our leading light of opera, Christine Dubois. He was in the process of taking her from the Garnier when they discovered him. The police shot him as he tried to escape, but somehow he managed to allude them and disappear. They believe he was fatally wounded and probably died somewhere in Paris."

"Then we can breathe easily?" Erik said, pressing Victor's arm reassuringly.

"Yes, the Garnier is a happier place now. I never feared the monster, but I felt for poor Christine Dubois. She remains one of the finest singers in Europe, but I believe she has never really recovered from that incident."

"Then we should work together to revive her majesty, should you accept me as your new producer, of course."

Victor took an envelope from the inside pocket of his jacket and passed it to Erik. "I have already considered your application and accepted, Monsieur. You'll find my offer more than generous. What do you say?"

Erik didn't open it. He would have taken this position for no pay. Instead, he shook Victor's hand in feigned appreciation. "Your reputation for managing opera is second to none, Victor. I want to work with you and your impressive team. So I accept the position of Producer of *La Traviata*."

"As you are aware, there is a second proposal for financial backers to join the Board. That proposal is also in the envelope. Take your time to study it, and should you have interest, I'll arrange a meeting between you and my accountant."

"I shall give that serious consideration, Victor. I'm happy to meet your business accountant while I'm in Paris. I return to Milan in two days, so a meeting any time tomorrow would suit me."

"Consider it organised! Where would you like to meet him?"

"Ideally, right here in Box Five, given it's my new meeting place."

"Would the evening suit? My ex-wife, Carlotta, will be viewing rehearsals then. You could meet her as well."

"I would be happy to meet Carlotta. As you know, she graced our Como Opera awards dinner last year. It would be an honour to get her thoughts about the production."

"She could introduce you to the team. I know you can't start for a month, but it would be a nice way to break the news to them."

Erik raised the contract and glanced at it. "I have not yet signed, Monsieur."

Victor grasped his hand and shook it again. "I trust the handshake of an honest man, Monsieur. You are officially the artistic producer of *La Traviata*. Our house is now yours!"

He slapped Erik's shoulder, and Erik reciprocated. Erik truly wanted to work with the team Victor had assembled, even if it meant pretending to be his friend.

"I must head to another meeting. Feel free to walk through our beautiful opera house," Victor said before leaving.

"Thank you. I will. I want to breathe in the atmosphere."

Victor nodded and left, leaving Erik alone in Box Five. His mind turned to earlier years when he freely roamed the Garnier as head of security, nearly fulfilling his dream.

He studied the neatly framed photos that adorned the back room. Most were of Carlotta when she ruled the opera world. *La Traviata, Turandot, Macbeth*, all of Verdi's classic creations, carefully assembled for Erik, Box Five's new owner. He ran his hand along the wall just under the line of photos, occasionally tapping it until he reached the corner, where the tapping noise had the slightest change in tone only a musical ear could detect. The familiar hollow sound made him smile. The secret compartment behind the wall was still intact. Unbeknown to Victor, Erik's purchase of Box Five included a hidden network of corridors and rooms he once ruled. He walked from the back room to the front stall, well pleased with his work in Paris. Both Carlotta and Victor supported him.

Erik studied the stage, now fully enclosed by its famous red velvet curtain. Where he had once ruled the shadowy caverns of the opera house, he now sought its brightest light — centre stage.

The thought calmed Erik before movement around the curtain distracted his thoughts. Someone was walking behind the security curtain protecting the famous painted curtain used for performances. He or she moved slowly toward its centre, likely barefoot, for there was no sound. Erik held his gaze toward the stage, waiting for the mysterious intruder to reveal his or her identity. He believed it a stagehand, but the mystery enthralled him as he imagined the many ghosts claimed to have haunted the theatre. The curtain slowly opened, revealing only a shadowy outline of the famous painted curtain. Something or someone parted the curtain, making a ghostly flutter like a magicians trick.

"Who's there?" Erik exclaimed without reply. He was staring at an empty stage, but he sensed eyes were studying him. "Reveal yourself!"

"Pardon, Monsieur?" A muffled voice replied from behind, making Erik turn around.

A woman approached. One he knew well from a past life — Madame Giraud. She looked at him with concern, as if Erik had seen a ghost. Perhaps he had.

"I'm sorry to have startled you, Monsieur. I heard your voice and thought I should investigate. Are you lost?"

Erik felt disoriented from what had occurred and took the time to collect his thoughts. "No. Quite the opposite. I'm the new artistic director of the *La Traviata* production, and this is my new office. And you are?"

"Madame Giraud, Monsieur. I am the concierge of the opera house. Welcome."

Erik nodded in a restrained manner, careful not to show he knew her. "What brings you to Box Five, Madame Giraud?"

"I come here often, Monsieur. Box Five has special memories for me. It's the most famous box in the world. You know of it?"

"I have read of the rumours."

Madame Giraud nodded, then turned to the photo frames, adjusting one. "I like it always to look perfect. I would very much like to continue doing that for you, Monsieur, if that does not offend?"

Erik watched her attend to the photos as if they were her children, children she'd watched for decades. Where Victor and Carlotta represented the opera house's brain and heart, Madame Giraud was its soul. Winning her support would be essential if he was to flourish in Garnier's corridors.

"You would always be welcome in Box Five, Madame. I do not yet know you well, but I am aware that you have been part of this magnificent theatre for a long time. It would be an honour if you shared some of its secrets with me."

Madame Giraud stopped adjusting the frames and joined him at the balcony of Box Five. "Merci, Monsieur...."

"Monsieur Rossi."

"Ahh. I had heard the name floated around the crew. So it is official."

"Just one hour earlier. I will commence in a few weeks."

Madame Giraud proudly looked out across the theatre until something she saw changed her good mood. "Someone has been playing with the protective curtain again." She turned to him. "Is that what startled you?"

"Yes. I thought there was someone there."

"Perhaps. I should warn you to prepare for strange occurrences in our famous opera house, Monsieur Rossi."

"The famous phantom?"

"Do you believe in such tales, Monsieur?"

Erik had more than belief, but he was not about to reveal the truth to Madame Giraud, at least not yet. "I have an open mind."

"That is a good thing, for as the owner of Box Five, I believe mysterious events will test you. But I'm sure you are too busy to hear tales from an elderly woman. Again, please forgive me for interrupting you. I look forward to meeting again on your return."

Madame Giraud politely nodded and left. Erik had now seen all he needed to secure his tenure at the Garnier, which was a substantial financial stake. Carlotta and Victor were now his business partners. Would he also inherit a more ethereal partner? He looked a last time toward the stage. The security curtain was closed as if his most crucial benefactor also approved of the proceedings. He would find out soon enough on his return.

CHAPTER FOURTEEN

PHILIPPE'S RETURN

Philippe signalled to his chauffeur to amble the remaining stretch of Chateau de Primard's long driveway, making his brother, Raoul, wait that little longer for their reunion. He looked out to the familiar Jacques Witz designed garden. The many hedges, trees and vast lawns were all freshly sculptured. Even the farm component was in pristine condition with the assortment of animals lined along the barrier seemingly greeting their former owner's return.

Servants met Philippe on his arrival, assisting his chauffeur with luggage and car arrangements. Philippe greeted his younger brother formally, too. Their many phone conversations before this first reunion in years ranged from terse indifference to harrowing disappointment, but at least they were talking.

Philippe watched his chauffeur disappear to the

service area behind the home before looking back across the expansive 44-acre family property.

"It's never looked better. Is the interior as impressive?"

"Come, let me show you around. There have been a few changes," Raoul said, leading Philippe through the four-storey property with an air of pride.

Raoul had modernised their family home. Even Guainville had changed as more Parisians took up residency in the small village. The tour ended at the ground-floor sitting room, where refreshments awaited them. Philippe finished his tea and cast a final glance at the new architecture before removing and placing his jacket on the corner of the coffee table, much to his brother's displeasure.

Pleasantries put to one side, Philippe's manner became severe. "You did as I requested?" He asked, almost as an aside.

"Christine knows nothing of your visit, but I will make her aware next time I see her," Raoul retaliated, picking up Philippe's jacket and calling to a servant to take care of it.

"And when do you intend to see her?" Philippe enquired.

"Tomorrow. One of us cares for Christine's feelings."

"I need a few days. Not a lot to ask of a brother?" Philippe replied, unmoved.

Raoul pushed his empty espresso cup in Philippe's direction to emphasise his feelings. "She is my friend, and I'll bloody well see her when I want to. You come here after years of absence with your demands and not so much as a word of explanation."

"I will explain everything if you give me some time."

Raoul poured a tea for himself, shaking his head and half smiling at the brevity of Philippe's request. He'd left years ago, leaving Raoul to face his considerable gambling debts, not contacting him once.

"It took years of hard work to recover our estate. I won't risk that again, and I won't help you until you convince me you're cured of your gambling addiction," Raoul demanded, his gaze unwavering.

Philippe took out a letter and slid it across the coffee table, revealing a signed contract from Garnier Opera. He sat back in his seat, seemingly self-satisfied with his accomplishment, waiting for Raoul's reaction.

Raoul absorbed the details before offering a single word,"Congratulations," a simple but ironic utterance, demanding an explanation.

Philippe sat up straight, recognising the challenge. "I also worked hard every day of those years I was away. Furthermore, I built a business respected by my financial backers, a dream we shared, Raoul. I have made it real."

Raoul sipped his tea, seemingly seeking composure. Philippe's success had surprised him, but his suspicions remained. "Who are your backers?"

Philippe threw his arms in the air, exasperated. "I have come here to offer you the chance to have part owner-ship in the Garnier Opera company, and you tear it down. Join me, brother, and together we will have major-ity ownership within the year."

Raoul knew he'd have little chance of finding Philippe's backers, not immediately anyway. "What do you want of me?"

"Work with me. First, work with Victor's accountant, so we know exactly how the company is performing. You've always been the financial expert in our family. You were helping father from an early age. It's natural for you, whereas you know I prefer to be the entrepreneur."

Raoul's lips parted slightly. The first hint of a smile formed. He wanted to believe his brother had reformed. They had shared a dream to own the Garnier ever since their father failed in his attempt. "We both know Victor. He always keeps some secrets."

"That's why I made him agree to open the books to us. I can set up a meeting with his accountant for you. Spend the week going through all their finances. If it looks suspicious, I'll follow your advice, Raoul. Help me, brother," Philippe implored.

Raoul took a deep breath and nodded his head slightly, doubts eased for the moment. "I will give you a week, but you will agree with my terms."

"Yes," Philippe acknowledged in wholehearted agreement.

"If I do that, you will see Christine and explain yourself. She has lived with a broken heart too long, Philippe. Promise me you will do that."

"I promise to call her tomorrow and see her this week."

"I consider Christine a close friend now. If you slight her, you slight me, so speak honestly with her."

"I will. Now, will you be honest with me? Is she a close friend or perhaps more?"

"We're not lovers if that's what you're suggesting. I don't know why, but Christine has held out with the hope of you returning. Her love for you remains should you want her affection."

Both sat quietly for a time. The thought of Christine had touched a chord for each, but for very different reasons. Raoul wanted more than their friendship, but that could never be while Philippe stood in the way. Resolution would help Raoul move forward with his own life. Either way, he knew Christine's loyal affection would continue.

Whereas Philippe shared many memorable moments with Christine as young lovers, but time had changed him. Philippe had endured years of hardship under an unforgiving mafia family that demanded absolute loyalty, beyond anything he could ever offer Christine. He would do anything for that freedom, including deception.

Philippe walked into L'astrance, one of Paris's finest restaurants. Little had changed since they last dined there, three years earlier. It remained a three Michelin star destination with a reputation as one of the world's finest. Chef Barbot had toiled hard to reach his position, just as Philippe had struggled. Time and events had changed him. His dream to own the Garnier remained as strong as ever, but circumstances had changed his justifications. Back then, Christine was the centre of his life, a gem in the operatic crown offering opportunity. She possessed only raw talent back then, whereas now she was the toast of Paris. He should have helped Christine, but another did, Erik, ironically the very man who oversaw his demise. Philippe paid heavily for his addiction, leaving himself vulnerable to a cruel adversary. The thought that Christine had befriended Erik overpowered any affection that remained. Just as they had blindsided him, so would he.

"Anything from the menu, monsieur?"

"A bottle of your finest Fleur Petrus merlot. Mademoiselle Christine Dubois will be joining me shortly. Is it still to her liking?" Philippe asked, knowing it remained Christine's favourite wine but more intent on gaining favourable service befitting a famous diva. He studied the menu before an incoming call on his phone interrupted. It was Viola.

"How did you go?"

"I was accepted!" Viola proudly announced.

"Wonderful! What did I tell you."

"I'm sitting in a hotel room, hungry and ready to celebrate."

"I have some business to take care of first."

"You promised to show me Paris by night."

"I will, but it'll have to be after dinner. Order some food from the hotel's restaurant, and I'll meet you after for drinks."

A long silence followed before Viola made her disappointment clear. "This is the biggest night of my life. Don't be too late, or I'll find someone else."

"If I don't do the business in Paris, you won't have an opera company to join," he snapped. He was about to rage further, but he caught sight of Christine entering the restaurant. "Got to go," his last words before hanging up.

Philippe sat on the restaurant's second floor with a bird's eye view of the diners below. Christine's appearance drew admiring glances from the diners. She thanked her chauffeur for escorting her to the maitre d', who graciously welcomed her before slowly guiding her past their patrons for maximum exposure. Christine walked with a manner of someone accustomed to attention, occasionally stopping and talking to acquaintances of the maitre d'. Christine knew how to perform on and off the stage, generously accommodating her fans and admirers and lighting up the subdued mood, effortlessly drawing all eyes her way.

Philippe stood to welcome her, kissing her extended hand and slightly nodding as befitting a diva, then waited for Christine to be seated before sitting down himself. Christine's mood was like the hourglass double-breasted wool-blend jacket she wore, slightly formal but 'tres chic'. The waiter quickly followed up with the wine Philippe had ordered.

Christine eyed the bottle as if it were a white flag. "You remembered," she noted.

Philippe feigned admiration while trying to read her expression, but where once he could feel her soul through those loving blue eyes, there was now only distance. "How quickly life passes," he offered, raising his glass and waiting for an extended period before Christine acknowledged.

They toasted, initially to silence. Christine tilted her head, waiting for Philippe to describe what they were celebrating. "To your success, Christine."

"It should have been our success," she retorted.

"You never needed me. Your talent was so sublime, you were always going to succeed."

"So you decided not to support me. Is that it?"

"I would have dragged you down with me if I'd stayed. I had to leave and face my addictions alone. There was no other way."

"How admirable. Don't you think if you cared, I deserved some explanation before you left to face your problems?"

Christine was restless, seemingly deciding whether to remain or leave. "I'm sorry, Christine," Philippe said, brushing her hand, willing her to stay. "I didn't trust myself. I had spent a great deal of the inheritance and would have squandered it all if Raoul hadn't intervened. I'd have spent your money too if you tried to support me."

Christine looked out across the restaurant and waved her hand to a waiter, signalling she would stay to hear more. "You could have made at least one phone call."

"I'd have tried to convince you to help me. No, I had

to do it on my own. I'd resolved not to return until I permanently stopped gambling."

"Raoul and I risked our lives trying to find you."

"That's why I have returned now. When I found out about your experience, I worked twice as hard to return to Paris. I paid my debts with shrewd investments so that I could again pursue my dreams. Manage the Garnier Opera company and help you."

Christine's expressive eyes glazed slightly, showing a hint of sentiment. "These people you worked with are killers, Philippe."

"A gamblers desperation knows no bounds. I fell into the deepest crevice and gambled all I had left. My life."

Christine's demeanour softened for the briefest of moments before she collected her emotions to address the waiter, who'd arrived to take the orders. "I recommend the seafood 'Legine au miso'. The taste is a unique experience," she said, diva-like, exchanging real emotion for pretence.

The meal continued in the same vein, courteous formality until they drank enough wine. "Another bottle, monsieur?" The attentive waiter asked.

Philippe tilted his head in Christine's direction, waiting for her to agree. "Just chilled water," she responded, allowing the waiter to fill their glasses. "I'm meeting with the musical director after this to discuss my double. I will have to leave soon."

"Of course. Are you pleased with the cast selected?" Philippe asked.

"We lost several talented singers this season. So there will be extra pressure on the new intakes to develop quickly. I hear you know one of them?" Christine asked, fishing for a reaction.

"Viola worked in my nightclub as the lead jazz singer, but she has always wanted to perform opera," he replied, deadpan.

"Jazz is hardly a suitable training ground for *La Traviata*."

"I'm sure the musical director will make a good decision, with your advice, of course."

"Of course," she repeated sarcastically, signalling to the waiter to call her chauffeur as she readied to leave. "Thank you for dinner, and explaining yourself. Your decisions still mystify me, but I'm glad you survived your ordeal against the odds. Raoul tells me that he is helping you with the business finances?"

"He's looking at the books for me, in case Victor is up to his old tricks."

"Victor will never change. You are wise to use Raoul. He has always been a loyal brother to you, despite your behaviour."

"I know. I want to repay Raoul for his support, and now I have the chance, Christine. I want to do the same for you."

"Helping Raoul is enough for now. So, why the lavish dinner at our favourite restaurant? What do you want from me?" Christine asked, ready to leave.

Philippe took Christine's hand. "I've only ever wanted you to be the brightest star in Europe, just as I want the Garnier Opera company to be the best in the world."

Christine's cheeks flushed, showing her feelings for him lingered. Slowly, she removed her hand from his and left.

Philippe watched her descend the stairs with the maitre d's assistance and get into the waiting chauffer's limousine before he made a call. "I'm about to leave. I can pick you up from the hotel foyer in thirty minutes."

"The evening is ours?" Viola asked.

"As I promised. An evening in Paris for the rising star of the Garnier."

"Hardly a rising star, but I do want to celebrate joining the cast," Viola replied humbly.

"More than just a cast member. Your musical director has selected you as Christine's double. So enjoy this night, as there is a lot of work ahead."

"How could that be? I'm not ready, Philippe."

"You're ready if I say so. See you in thirty minutes."

Philippe ended the call and paid for the meals before slipping into a waiting taxi, feeling satisfied with his work. Raoul was helping him. He believed Christine's feelings left her vulnerable and Victor fully supported his demand for Viola to be Christine's double. He'd fully entrenched himself into the Garnier's machinations, comfortable he could quell any resistance through a single request to his Italian backers. He'd waited a long time for the moment, and all he wanted to do was celebrate into the night with Viola. In time, this would be their victory.

CHAPTER FIFTEEN

DIVA'S DILEMMA

The first of five remaining rehearsals before the opening night started smoothly, pleasing Gianni, the musical director and the audience of just two, Erik and Carlotta. All scenes flawless until the appearance of Violetta in her opening scene. Christine performed Violetta's celebratory song without conviction, looking more like the sickly Violetta before her tragic death in the final scene. Christine didn't even try to hide her indifference, and five minutes into her solo, 'el tagrio', Gianni made his dissatisfaction clear to all.

"Where is your head, Christine?" Gianni asked, tapping the podium in annoyance.

Christine looked to the floor, murmuring to herself and drawing quiet chatter from the cast. She had become the main talking point over the past week, with rumours she may not perform. Gianni's patience had slowly dissolved as opening night approached.

"Would you like to take a time out, Christine?"

She looked past Gianni, out to Carlotta, seemingly seeking her counsel. Their friendship had developed over time, surprising many, given their turbulent history. However, Philippe's return had brought many changes to Garnier opera. There had been numerous staff and cast changes, unsettling many, particularly Christine, who struggled with his new manner. While he supported Christine, he also encouraged Viola, a relatively unknown singer, beyond her capabilities, fostering a competitive and sometimes combative culture. It didn't help that she hadn't seen Raoul since Philippe's arrival. So she increasingly turned to Carlotta, who nodded her way before standing and walking to the back of the theatre.

"Yes. I have developed a cold. I shall rest today," Christine announced, walking from the stage, following Carlotta to the back of the theatre.

"Viola, take Christine's part. From the top, please."

Christine walked hurriedly from the theatre, not wishing to hear her stand-in, Viola. There was little rapport between them, a situation Philippe appeared to encourage, and everyone knew it. Worse, Viola revelled in her opportunity, seemingly enjoying undermining her.

Christine slammed the exit doors behind her, shaking

her head. "I can't work under these conditions," she said to the waiting Carlotta, who took her arm and headed to the nearby Cafe de la Paix.

They were seated outside at a prominent table, which both gave them the best view of the Garnier and allowed locals to see them, the opera stars who frequented the establishment. Both sipped on their espresso, taking in the sweeping presence of the famous building. Christine studied the building, but her mind seemed anywhere but on the Garnier.

"We are lucky to work in such a famous building," Carlotta said, tapping the saucer with her cup and drawing Christine's attention. "I've been told I had difficult moments in my career, too. I wish I could remember. Even the worst of them."

"I know I'm lucky to be where I am. But this. Philippe." Christine shook her head in frustration.

"Give him time. I know he's pushing everyone, just as he is pushing himself. He is so hungry to succeed."

"Too hungry." Christine slid the espresso cup away from her, spilling the remaining contents on the table.

A concerned waiter quickly cleaned up the mess. "Was the coffee not to your liking, Madmoiselle Dubois?"

Christine ignored the waiter, drawing Carlotta to respond out of courtesy. "It won't help to take your frustrations out on others. You'd be better to use your energy on singing. That's your gift."

"And ignore Philippe? I wasted years of my life searching for him. I cared, yet he seems indifferent to my feelings. We had lunch together, and I felt his detachment, as if it were purely business. He professes affection, yet he seems more concerned about Viola. Then he pushes Gianni to make her my double. She has no experience, and yet he places her ahead of a handful of girls more deserving. I want no part of it. If there was a placement somewhere else, I'd take it."

"I haven't been so lucky with men either," Carlotta offered sympathetically.

"You seem to be happy with Erik."

"It didn't start so smoothly. Time changes feelings and attitudes. It could happen to you and Philippe, too." Carlotta sipped the last of her espresso, "I promised Erik I'd watch today's rehearsal. Why don't you come back with me?"

Christine declined Carlotta's extended hand. "I can't, but I promise to be at rehearsals early tomorrow."

Carlotta bent down and hugged Christine with a sincerity that reflected their growing friendship before returning to the Garnier and taking her place in the front stalls beside Erik. Philippe was on stage with Victor in tow, making his feelings known and brandishing a smile of delight for Viola before exiting the stage.

"Did I miss anything?"

Erik lifted his eyebrows. "The usual," he replied. Both had witnessed Philippe's incessant micro-management across all company levels, from the finances to the performers. "His favourite performer is about to commence 'El tagrio'. So your timing is impeccable."

Gianni tapped his podium, attempting to salvage normality after the irritating interruption. The orchestra commenced, and the spotlight brought Viola into focus. "This will be interesting," Erik said, seemingly expecting the worst.

Viola commenced cautiously, but she rose to the occasion, confidently vocalising Verdi's lyrics. "She's done her homework," Carlotta murmured. Viola's performance began to lift the confidence of those around her, including the musical director, who brandished his baton with a flourish.

Carlotta leant into Erik, allowing Viola's fresh tone to draw a personal reaction, tears. She enjoyed the feeling, for it drew some precious memories from her current blank canvas. Carlotta performed in the very place that Viola did now, but it felt an eternity removed. Back then, Christine stood backstage as her double. The

silhouette of a man stood in that same place, reminding her of another man. His name was Erik, but not the
Erik who sat with her now. He once cast a terrible gaze
toward Christine, and she strained to remember why.
She moved closer to the Erik she now knew, fearing the
other and what he meant. They had done something
together. First, she remembered they'd been lovers, but
there was something more sinister, a recollection that
evaded her.

Erik caressed her arm, showing he too reacted to
Viola's performance. Carlotta sighed, appreciating the
momentary warmth. She ceased her struggle to recollect
until an ethereal light formed above the stage, shining a
soft hue across the cast and orchestra. No one on stage
seemed to notice the object, so she turned to Erik.

"Do you see it?" Carlotta asked, turning her gaze in
its direction.

Erik shook his head. "The light above the stage,"
Carlotta said.

Erik still appeared mystified. "Sometimes the lighting
can play tricks on the mind," he reassured.

Carlotta wanted to believe Erik. She searched for a
logical reason, turning her gaze to the lighting equipment high above them. It streamed a straight line to
the cast, whereas the separate obelisk's light emanated

from another source. It was then Carlotta first noticed Madame Giraud. She sat at the front of Box Five, staring directly at her, a knowing look, telling Carlotta she too saw the object. Madame Giraud leaned her head in the direction of the strange light, as did Carlotta. The light flashed for a few seconds, revealing the silhouetted man who stood backstage. Philippe watched on, oblivious to those around him. He felt sufficiently anonymous to reveal his true feelings towards Viola, unabashed adoration. A deadly secret had been revealed and only to Carlotta and Madame Giraud. As quickly as the light emerged, it also vanished, leaving Carlotta mystified but determined to speak to the mysterious tenant of Box Five.

CHAPTER SIXTEEN

BROTHERS IN ARMS

Erik studied the framed images of Carlotta's triumphs, Paris Garnier; London Royal Opera House; Staatsoper Vienna and Bolshoi Moscow, to name a few. A world star of opera and Erik's lover, cut short by their shared evilness, now both allowed to start afresh. Erik felt some self-satisfaction with how quickly he'd advanced, owning a sizeable portion of Garnier Opera. He touched one of the images, wishing their bond grew with equal stealth, drawing a smile. His private reflections were interrupted.

"She will need your help, and more, for what is to come," said Madame Giraud, walking into the light of Box Five.

Erik turned around, warmly greeting her. "I will do all I can to help her. That's why I'm here. Carlotta would like to meet you."

"The Opera Ghost revealed a deadly secret to her," she

replied, running her frail hands over the same image Erik had just touched. "Challenging riddles," she said, turning directly to Erik with an unnerving gaze belying her small, ageing frame.

Erik reacted subconsciously, rocking back on his heels away from her intense expression. *What did she know?* Erik wondered. Most who worked at the Garnier maintained a respectful distance from Madame Giraud. Rumours had it she and the Opera Ghost shared a lifelong connection that at times ended in untimely disappearances. Erik himself had experienced enough to sense an ethereal presence radiated through this opera house like the grand chandelier illuminating the theatre.

"I will do what I can," Erik offered, maintaining a stolid expression.

"What affects her will affect you. You're about to learn that."

"I'm heading to Victor's office. Are you referring to him?"

"You're dealing with more than Victor's influence, but you already know that."

Erik nodded slightly. He expected Philippe to be in attendance, as the two had been inseparable since Philippe's arrival at the Garnier. "I'll take that into account. Thank you." Erik turned to leave then stopped to ask a favour of Madame Giraud. "Carlotta will be joining me for the rehearsal. Could you meet us in Box Five afterwards?"

"Of course, I view every rehearsal," she replied, looking out to the Garnier theatre as if someone hid in the empty theatre listening to their conversation.

Erik followed the direction of her gaze to empty leather seats and silence. A cold breeze wafted up to Box Five, as if an unearthly presence approved of their arrangement. "Until this evening," he added, before nodding courteously and leaving.

Erik walked into Victor's office at their arranged time, but Victor was already engaged in a group discussion. Three of the four, Erik knew. Philippe sat at the head of the long table, his brother Raoul to his left and Victor beside Raoul. A fourth man sat to Philippe's right, talking on his phone. Erik was offered the remaining empty chair at the far end of the long table.

No one invited him to move closer, so Erik settled some distance from the group. He was happy for Victor to take the lead, but Philippe spoke first, reaffirming his rapid ascendancy, the meeting shaping as Philippe's victory speech.

"Thank you for joining us, Erik. I don't believe you have met my brother, Raoul."

Erik nodded courteously, "I haven't, but I've heard many good things about you."

Raoul responded, walking to Erik and warmly shaking his hand. "Enchante, Erik. I, too, have heard favourable comments. You are helping Christine during a difficult period." He offered a knowing smile before Philippe interrupted.

"Yes, we can save the chit chat for another time, given the deadlines we are facing," Philippe asserted, shifting Raoul's chair back to illustrate his impatience. "We have just finalised new arrangements for the Garnier Opera Company, and I want you to be aware of the changes, Erik." Philippe turned Victor's way, inviting his confirmation.

Victor sunk reluctantly low in his chair, clearing his throat before dutifully announcing the new resolution. "I have agreed to a rearrangement of the company shares. I will be transferring around half of my shares to Philippe so that he will hold a majority 51 per cent stake."

A stony silence followed. Victor could not or would not lift his gaze. The others studied Erik. He remained coy, offering no more than a congratulatory nod in Philippe's direction, leaving Philippe to do the talking.

"I don't want you to look at this as a hostile takeover, Erik. I greatly value what you bring to this organisation."

He glanced toward the man unknown to Erik, who'd concluded his phone call. "Pass the proposal to Erik."

Erik studied the contract. Sure enough, it listed Philippe as the majority owner at 51 per cent, leaving him and Victor as minority partners. He looked at all three pages, noting Carlotta hadn't signed or initialled any part of the contract. "I'm sure you and Carlotta are pleased with the outcome," Erik cautiously offered. There was time enough for retaliation if needed.

Victor cast an unconvincing smile before Philippe cut off any chance for him to reply. "We anticipate all parties to sign the final contract by week's end," he declared, looking firstly to Raoul then the unknown man.

Erik studied Philippe's assistant, believing he'd met him but unsure of when and where. He was small in stature with a youthful face that belied his thinning hairline. He wore an expensive suit that wouldn't look out of place in a legal firm. His quiet demeanour was one of caution rather than introversion, making Erik believe him to be a mafia legal connection.

"Have we met?" Erik asked, more as a backhanded aside to Philippe than any wish to know him.

"This is Ritchie Esposito. He will be taking over for Victor's lawyer," Philippe offered on Ritchie's behalf.

Ritchie extended a formal handshake, a courteous

gesture. He showed no hint of wishing to talk, so Erik returned the contract to him. "This all looks in order, so I look forward to remaining a contributor to your team, Philippe," Erik said, walking to him and shaking his hand. "I wish I could stay and discuss your plans further, but the rehearsals begin shortly. Are you joining us tonight?"

"Not tonight, my friend. I want to finalise the contract by the end of the week, so more work ahead for us tonight. Please, go ahead and watch the rehearsal. Is Carlotta joining you?" Philippe asked, glancing Victor's way.

The reference to Carlotta was a deliberate slight, but Erik humoured Philippe. "Yes. She has taken a keen interest in Christine. Do you want me to pass on any messages?"

"No. I'll see her soon enough," Philippe replied dismissively, turning to the business with his team.

Erik didn't press Philippe's deliberate indifference, although he felt increasing rage toward his adversary. At another time, he would have responded to his intimidation. Philippe's bravado was born from his connections rather than any real strength. Erik could crush Philippe's confidence, and he'd do so soon enough, but first, he had to find out how much Carlotta knew. It seemed Madame Giraud's prophecies were quickly coming to fruition.

By the time Erik arrived, rehearsals had already commenced. Carlotta was on stage talking to Christine. Both waved to Erik as he sat in the front stall, as did many of the cast. Where Erik's stocks in the company's finances had declined, his popularity with the cast was strong. He'd attended every rehearsal since joining and contributed positive feedback evenly distributed to all the performers. Both he and Carlotta were genuine assistants to the musical director, Gianni.

By the time Gianni tapped the podium to commence Act One, Carlotta had joined Erik in the front row. She squeezed his hand, and he reciprocated. They had learned to tone down their affections for each other in public. Rumours swirled about their obvious chemistry, so they did their best to contain them, particularly given the delicate stage of Board negotiations.

Erik watched the lead diva as she positioned herself centre stage. "Christine's ready?"

"As ready as can be expected."

Erik shook his head. "Why does she bother worrying about Philippe? He doesn't care for her."

Carlotta removed her hand from Erik's. "You don't know that."

"I met Raoul. It's clear he cares more for Christine than Philippe ever will."

"That will be for Christine to determine. Won't it?"

"Yes, you're right," Erik offered, quickly changing the subject. "The meeting with Philippe was interesting. He has more clarity when it comes to business dealings than romance. Are you aware of the takeover?"

Carlotta breathed deeply, ignoring Erik's questioning gaze, seemingly focused on the performance. Erik knew that expression, so he settled back in his chair and watched the opening song of Act One in silence. By its end, Carlotta responded. "All I care for is the performance. I want no part of the business side anymore."

"You want Philippe to head the Garnier? The cast detests him. If it weren't for Christine, they'd openly complain."

"Is Victor any better?" Carlotta retaliated.

"I'm not suggesting Victor. You should control the Garnier."

"If I could, I would have already taken control but I'm not ready. I may never be ready. Is that the life you wish for me?"

"I would support you, Carlotta. More than Victor ever did."

Carlotta turned to Erik for the first time. "How would you know how much Victor has supported me?"

Erik wanted to tell her exactly how much he knew

about Victor and Philippe, but the truth would only drive her further from him. "You're right. I overstep the mark. At least speak to others before you sign their contract. You can start with Madame Giraud. She will meet us in Box Five after the rehearsals."

"Us? Why does everything have to be us? Perhaps you want to be in charge of the Garnier?"

Erik held his hands up in defence. Any argument with Carlotta would be pointless, and in truth, she was right. Erik was no different from Philippe. Ultimately, he did want to hold power. A year earlier, he and Carlotta would hurt anyone who got in their way, including Christine. But Carlotta had changed. He knew more than most about Carlotta's dark past, but telling her could irretrievably drive her from him.

"You're right again. I want to see our maestro about some of the musical arrangements, anyway. You spend some time with Madame Giraud. She has known you for a long time. Perhaps she holds the key to helping you remember."

They watched the remainder of rehearsals in silence, enjoying the growing confidence of the performers. Even Christine was beginning to smile more as the thought of a successful opening night approached. Carlotta, too, smiled, before kissing Erik's lips for the first time in public. "Thank you. We can talk about all of this tomorrow," she whispered before leaving for Box Five.

Erik watched her walk away. What would she know after her meeting with Madame Giraud? Nothing, everything? He walked an emotional tightrope with Carlotta, surrounded by vipers who would stop at nothing to get their revenge. He peered up to Box Five, where Madame Giraud sat, looking down at him. Her strange gaze disconcerted most in the cast. Could she see through people who moved too close to her psychic orbit, as the rumours suggested? He would find out soon enough.

Carlotta sat beside Madame Giraud in the front seats of Box Five. They peered at the empty stage, the only sign of activity coming from the noise of stagehands moving equipment into storage until the next rehearsal.

"It was our best rehearsal yet," Carlotta offered nervously.

Madame Giraud smiled warmly, sensing Carlotta's uneasiness. "You have changed. Do you remember anything of our conversations in the past?"

Carlotta studied the stage as if searching for lost memories hidden in its famous French curtains. "Small images come and go. I remember the view from behind the curtains and seeing you here in Box Five, but no conversations. Did we speak often?"

"No. You maintained a professional distance, mostly. Understandable, given your fame."

"More infamous than famous from what I read and hear."

"Well, divas must strike the pose of a wildflower rather than a shrinking violet," Madame Giraud confessed, smiling broadly and drawing laughter from Carlotta, putting her at ease.

"It's a heavy burden. It's why I worry about our new diva," Carlotta said, her eyes uncommonly innocent, seeking counsel.

"Ahh, Christine. Our new shining light. Your fears for her are well-founded, and I think you know that many are concerned for her," Madame Giraud said, staring to the stage. "These famous boards are a unique platform for the worlds most gifted to display their genius. I have seen many over the decades, all of them talented, full of life, but also flawed. The world is entertained by what unfolds between these famous curtains. Some look deeper than they should. If you do the same, be prepared for surprises."

Carlotta brushed her hair back from her cheeks, seemingly wanting to see Madame Giraud more clearly. "You saw it too, didn't you?"

"I've seen many things on that stage. What did you

see, Carlotta?"

"The light—"

Madame Giraud interrupted, pressing her. "Answer truly, or you will learn nothing. What did you see?"

"The mysterious light shone on Philippe. He loves her."

"Loves who?"

"The new performer. The rumours are true. He loves Viola. That's what I saw. I thought my imagination was inventing it. Erik hadn't seen anything, but then when I looked your way, I felt you'd seen the same thing."

Madame Giraud nodded her head instead of speaking. Her eyes were wide, seemingly inviting Carlotta into her mysterious world.

Carlotta pressed her. "What is that light? Is it the Opera Ghost everyone talks about?"

Madame Giraud chuckled at the thought. "I have spent a lifetime wondering about that. You may need to experience more than a single flash of light before drawing any conclusions."

"Everyone believes you are the Opera Ghost's ally. You must know that."

"People fall too quickly into beliefs instead of believing their own eyes. If there's an Opera Ghost, he preys on rumour and gossip."

"I wish only to remember again. It's as if my mind

refuses to cooperate with my will. I read and hear terrible things about my behaviour. Are they true?"

"I'm not sure. I can say if there's an Opera Ghost, you truly gained his attention. Your fall from grace as Europe's finest diva was a dark period for our opera company. Deaths, deception, revenge all pervaded that time. I have learnt that dark times evoke a force that can become a wrathful master. You felt it more keenly than most."

"Will I remember again?" Carlotta implored.

"Memory will always return, but only when the time is right. You're repaying a debt by helping Christine. That will surely go a long way to recalibrating your emotional disturbance."

"She's in distress. I don't know whether to tell her of my experience with Philippe, for she stubbornly holds on to her love for him."

"Forces in the past have been deadly, but they always seemed to protect the music of love. Stay faithful to that, Carlotta," said Madame Giraud. She was about to say more, but something caught her attention.

She reached out to the seats behind them as if feeling for the strange force she spoke about before, swiftly retracting her hand. "I must go now. We will speak again, but for now, cast your gaze to the stage and try to remember your last performance." Madame Giraud brushed Carlotta's hair as if clearing her troubled mind before leaving her alone in Box Five.

Carlotta looked down to the stage, studying the area where she saw the light float above Viola, then tried to remember back to the time she reigned the opera world. A flash in her mind jolted her, giving rise to a single powerful memory. She stood in precisely the same space, performing Violetta in *La Traviata*. It was where she collapsed on stage. That same light had ended her performance and career. Was it the Opera Ghost?

Then a second, more disturbing image returned, making her feel feint once again. Another man stood in Philippe's place who had the same expression for Christine that Philippe had for Viola. It was Erik Destler, the man she had desired and perhaps loved. He had deceived her in front of the world, embarrassing her in front of her loving fans. His evil eyes terrified her, not because of what he did but of who he was. She recognised his eyes and realised they belonged to someone she thought she trusted. Carlotta fell back into her chair, physically shaking from anger and despair. The life blood had drained from her face, leaving her as pale as the opera ghost who'd haunted the Garnier. If she could summon the phantom from the depths, she'd do so now and unleash his deadly form of justice.

The old Carlotta had been reborn.

CHAPTER SEVENTEEN

MYSTERIES

Carlotta left Box Five, making it appear empty to the naked eye. Behind her, shimmering light rays intertwined with the sole security light, its vibrations discernible only to those with rare sensitivity.

Flynn and I communicated at wavelengths imperceptible to human ears.

"Christine is surrounded by a nest of vipers. I must warn her!" I exclaimed. My force lit Box Five for an instant.

"They cannot hear you," Flynn said.

"Madame Giraud senses us. Both saw our light force."

"They only see what they want to see. Human biases will distort anything you try to communicate. You could set off a chain of events that is the opposite of your intentions. Do not try to play God in their world."

"Why give me God-like powers then?"

"Diva hired you to play for her final performance. Learn of her life, then write her a fitting epitaph."

"How can I decipher her life if I don't understand myself? Am I human, AI, or merely a puppet machine?"

"You'll only find your core by taking this journey. Follow your powers of reasoning, but remember you can only function on this plain for a limited period safely."

"And when the medication wears off?"

"The medication was merely a placebo. Your core source is like all AI's. It can be transferred to a different plain but for limited periods. You will gradually tire until your core weakens into what your body interprets as slumber, signalling the technology that delivered you here to return you to your Earth-bound body."

"So if I decide to walk away from our agreement?"

Flynn's light force intensified in reaction to my threat. "Do what you think's right, but I will erase all memories of your time with the Diva. You'll return to your previous life as if nothing had happened. Is that what you want?"

"Give me something, Flynn. It could be the difference between having or not having the right music for Diva. If she is so important to you, do that."

"You have been programmed to undertake what you are doing. No more, no less. Knowing more of your origins would only confuse you. Even if I showed you your origins, you wouldn't understand it. I may as well show an ant how the human world operates. Help the Diva. You know that feels right."

I shrugged my shoulders in resignation. "Where will you take me next?"

"My task is almost done here. You can function properly in this world. Where you should go is up to you. I have one remaining matter you need to be aware of."

Our two forces swirled across the Garnier theatre, piercing curtains, walls, concrete, boulder and finally water, until we hovered in the dark recesses of the Garnier underground above an old piano positioned near its shore. Musty musical scores lay scattered around the piano, deteriorating chairs, tables and assorted furniture. Deep inside the cavern was a dimly lit space containing just a bed and a desk. It too looked long abandoned, and the strange-coloured light gave the room an eerie tone. We stopped just outside the room.

"This is where I leave you."

"Why here?"

"Do you recognise the bed, Benny?"

"No. Should I?"

"You saw it less than a day ago."

"The dying man's bed?"

Flynn nodded. "The very one."

"How could Erik have found a hundred-year-old bed?"

"He didn't. It's a mystery, as are many things in this cavernous expanse."

"Perhaps it's a replica?"

"No. It's the original. We can't explain it, like the final mystery I should tell you."

I followed Flynn as he retreated toward the lake, the dimly lit space now little more than a speck of pale light in the bleak darkness.

"The light from the room is part of that mystery. If you look closely, you'll see there are no electricals in or around that room. The power source, like the bed, can't be explained."

"A naturally occurring phosphorous chemical in the surrounding rock formation?"

"None have been detected. The power source is unknown. It is an unexplained phenomena that has occurred in the past. You are likely to experience these phenomena."

"Some unknown entity is haunting the Garnier?"

"It's a mystery that has impacted those who visit and perform at the Garnier. Help Diva tell this ethereal tale with your music. The story will be remembered for a long time."

Those were Flynn's final words before he vanished, leaving me alone in the Phantom's lair.

CHAPTER EIGHTEEN

MEMORY REBOOT

A frosty climate descended over the Garnier opera company, testing alliances old and new and generating rumours daily. The most significant talking point had become Carlotta's sudden withdrawal from rehearsals, Erik becoming the lone figure in the theatre as the cast prepared for the fast approaching opening night. Many believed she had feuded with Erik and refused to return to the theatre until his departure. Still, the conjecture ended when she officially called a board meeting directly after rehearsal.

Erik took his place at the board table, unsure of what to expect. Ever since Carlotta's meeting with Madame Giraud, their friendship had waned. Surprisingly, Carlotta sat at the head of the table with Philippe to one side and her lawyer on the other. The only person missing was Victor, an ominous sign.

Carlotta's lawyer called the meeting to order before handing the chairmanship to Carlotta. Her hair was tied back, revealing large gold earrings complementing her navy Chanel suit. She scanned all attendees, casting a particularly fleeting glance toward Erik before commencing her presentation. Had the Carlotta of old returned? Erik wondered.

"Thank you for your attendance at such short notice. As you can see, I have made some changes to the management structure, starting with Victor, who has resigned his tenure after accepting a payout for his services."

Philippe interrupted Carlotta, not hiding his displeasure. "Who will be managing operations now?"

"My lawyer will be running operations while we decide who is the most appropriate replacement for Victor," Carlotta retorted, her steely gaze showing there'd be little room for negotiation.

Philippe persisted. "He signed a binding contract I expect you to honour. Otherwise, I'll settle it in court."

Carlotta was seemingly unaffected by Philippe's threat. She reached out to her lawyer, who placed Victor's contract on her open palm. "I'm the major shareholder of the Garnier Opera Company. I don't see my signature anywhere on this poorly crafted document. Do you?" she asked, defiantly sliding it across the table to Philippe.

"So, you're saying the word of your husband counts for little?"

"Any thoughts I have about my ex-husband, Victor, shall remain between us. I expect any members of the board to be frank and honest in their dealings with me. If they can't, I suggest they move on."

Carlotta remained expressionless as she stared down Philippe, then, for the first time, gazed at Erik. "Do I have the support of my board members?"

A tense standoff ensued before Philippe broke the silence, sliding the contract toward Carlotta's lawyer and abruptly leaving in silence.

"Does anyone else wish to engage in theatrics?" Carlotta turned her gaze to Raoul, questioning his brotherly loyalty to Philippe, but he remained seated.

"Very well. Given we're all agreed that my lawyer should run operations," she paused briefly for any hint of dissent, "his position is a short-term appointment. I will choose our next operations manager before opening night. Aside from any potential outsiders, Erik and Raoul are the most qualified. If you are interested, please state your case in formal documents my lawyer has prepared for you." He handed the documents to Raoul and Erik. "Any questions?"

"I apologise for my brother's actions, Carlotta. Perhaps

I'm not a suitable choice?"

"We've known each other a long time, Raoul. I can't question your loyalty to the Garnier. Your financial expertise is ideal for the position," Carlotta replied, turning her gaze from Raoul to Erik. "In contrast, we have recently met," she said through pursed lips, and glossed eyes, the only hint of her disappointment.

Erik's secret had been exposed to her, in turn making her remember what they once were, and her coldness revealing what she once was. "If you have doubts about my dedication, I will change those concerns through action," Erik replied.

His promise drew a feint wry smile before she looked away to Raoul. "Thank you both. Let's turn to the position of artistic producer. I don't wish to make any changes at this point. Erik has given considerable support to our artistic director, and he recommended you remain in the position. Do we all support that Erik remains?" All nodded in agreement. "Then I will call this meeting to a close if there are no further questions?"

"Could I have a brief word in private?" Erik asked.

Carlotta showed the first hint of emotion, gripping the contract as she seemingly struggled to reply. "Only a moment. I have another meeting," she replied tersely.

Erik showed no emotion, simply nodding appreciatively.

The boardroom emptied, leaving Erik to face Carlotta's wrath. "When did you remember?" he asked, ending any attempt at hiding the truth.

"You shouldn't have organised the meeting with Madame Giraud."

"She knows?"

"Madame Giraud didn't tell me. I believe the Opera Ghost may have."

"I wanted to tell you," Erik replied, his eyes lowered regretfully.

"But you didn't, Erik. You preferred to masquerade as a genuine friend as if I'm some playmate to manipulate. I trusted you! If you weren't so loyal to the performers, I'd have terminated your employment along with my conniving husband."

"I'm sorry. I'll do everything I can to make it up to you."

"I have only remembered some of our past. I'm not sure I want to know any more. The shame of what we did would be unbearable."

"We both have dark pasts, but let me help your future. I'm not sure you realise the peril you face. Victor opened the doors to more than just Philippe."

"Yes, you too. Victor's already paid the price."

"Philippe's connections are far worse than anything Victor could do."

"Don't expect me to lap up your stories anymore. Do your job, Erik. Help my artistic director, encourage the cast, support Christine and leave me alone. Am I clear?" Carlotta ended the conversation and left Erik without a further word, closing the door firmly.

Erik clenched a fist and slammed it on the mahogany board table, angry at the situation he had put Carlotta in. He should have revealed his true identity to her, for she had trusted him. Now, he'd lost her confidence just when she most needed him. He had to warn Carlotta of the potential dangers, just as he too had to better understand the threats. To learn more meant revealing his true identity to his enemies, a deadly game he'd played before.

Erik took his phone and made a fateful call. "Come to the Garnier. We need to talk."

"Where?" Bernard asked.

"The underground. We need to reopen our fortress before we learn who exactly our enemies are," Erik replied.

"Understood. You want me to make some enquiries."

"Yes. Find out who the backers are and meet me in the lair tomorrow."

Erik hung up, saying as little as possible. He couldn't be sure how many knew of his true identity. At the very least, Carlotta and Madame Giraud were aware, but that would certainly grow. Erik left the boardroom and disappeared into the dark corners of the Garnier before slipping between secret doors into the underworld he once ruled, his private kingdom he vowed never to return to. Within minutes Erik wound his way through the darkness to the one source of light that never faded, the Opera Ghost's lair. There he would plan how best to protect Carlotta. He just hoped the Opera Ghost, if he existed, would be his ally as he brought vengeance on the influential Italian families that sought control of the home of opera.

Bernard moved through the dark cavern, guided by torchlight that announced his imminent arrival at the lair where Erik waited. He scanned the ancient chamber, lighting the dim enclosure and surveying all corners, taking in his connection to their infamous underworld. The underground had been their base for a year as they planned to rest control of the Garnier.

"Can it be rewired?" Bernard asked, rubbing his arm where he'd struck a rocky outcrop on his way through the dark maze.

"The damage is too severe. We'll have to operate on lanterns and torch fires."

"I'll get on to it," Bernard said, sitting and accepting a hot brew Erik poured from a flask.

They savoured the steaming tonic in the cold, breathing in the coffee aroma and earthy scent of the damp boulders and the lake. They made their plans with soldier-like precision, ready to enact them with haste.

Both finished their coffee, then Erik spoke. "You made contact?"

"Yes, but it was not easy. The bagman set it up, but I suspect he acted alone."

Bernard's observation alarmed Erik. Their connection with the second-most powerful Italian mafia was needed to take on Philippe's more powerful backers. "Mateo has gone to ground?"

"He wouldn't say. There's a rumour he was pinched by federal agents. Most of the soldiers I knew aren't on the street. It feels like some spring cleaning."

"How many G's for his update?"

"I gave him ten G. He wants fifty G for our next meeting."

Erik's eyes narrowed. "A lot!"

"Agreed. Seems to me he has no backing. Smelled of fear, the cement shoe kind of apprehension ."

"Tell me it was worth it," said Erik.

"Philippe is a pawn trying to become an associate. His bagman is a wise guy named Reggi with close connections to Capo. He's a long-term, loyal soldier with a reputation as an expert on shakedowns. Take on Philippe, and we certainly face Reggi and his soldiers."

"Did he talk about the Garnier?"

"Not a peep, which spells trouble for Carlotta."

"Did you tell him I need to speak to the family?"

"I pushed the thought, which surprised him. He was sure somebody smacked you. I tried to set up a follow-up meeting with Mateo, but he looked anything but eager."

"Does he know Philippe's lawyer?"

"Reggi organised him, but he's Capo's associate. Long-serving and well connected in legal circles. He brings heavy financial and legal knowledge, so they aren't going to play games. My guess is the family will quickly spread their tentacles right around Carlotta and her lawyer."

Erik twirled his Legionnaires ring, seemingly contemplating his next move. "When do you see the Bagman again?"

"He was elusive about timing. The streets are dealing with shakedowns, but he did want to know more about you. That will buy us follow-up meetings."

Erik had heard enough to know they had little time to act. "Play that card and organise a follow-up. Offer more information about my plans. That will spark their interest. I'm just not sure if it will be of the supportive kind. Meanwhile, we have to rebuild our fortress before they come for us. Buy me time to convince Carlotta of the threat she faces. Can you do that?"

"Sure. Do you want me to talk to our soldiers?"

"Yes. Our two best for the job. We have to make the lair impenetrable."

Bernard nodded before leaving in his usual determined fashion. He was a legionnaire to the core. No assignment was too big for Erik's loyal deputy. Erik had the same attitude, but this time his position was weakened by his feelings for Carlotta. If he could not convince her of the peril she faced, he left himself exposed to a ruthless family that didn't take kindly to losing. He looked to the unearthly pale light that constantly filled the chamber, and for the first time, he whispered for help from a ghostly presence he hoped existed.

Erik returned to the theatre, clear on what he should do next. He had to win back Carlotta's trust, then convince her of the dangers she faced. The cast had assembled for rehearsals, but the mood was sombre. Christine stood in front of the stage, talking with Raoul while Gianni studied his musical score, patiently waiting for Christine to join the rest of the cast. Erik approached, fearful Christine's dark mood had worsened. He expected the worst. Raoul welcomed him, relief in his face, seemingly that another could help lighten Christine's situation.

"I'm looking forward to this performance. The cast has come a long way," Erik said, lightly stroking Christine's arm in encouragement.

"Is she joining you?" Christine asked, her expression troubled.

Erik was unsure of Christine's enquiry and turned to Raoul for clarification. "Christine had a lunch engagement with Carlotta, and she didn't show up."

"I wouldn't worry. Carlotta has a busy schedule since taking over from Victor," Erik replied, trying to reassure her.

"She is not answering calls. It's unlike her. So I tried her lawyer, and he's not answering either."

Erik remained calm. "Let me look into it, but for now, you should begin rehearsals. It will help take your mind off Carlotta."

Raoul supported Christine and walked with her to the stage, leaving Erik to follow through on his promise. He called Carlotta, then her lawyer, without reply. Their behaviour was unusual and troubling. Had Philippe's backers moved quicker than he had anticipated? If they had, Carlotta faced extreme peril. After numerous unsuccessful calls, Erik decided to go directly to the potential cause, Philippe.

CHAPTER NINETEEN

HOSTILE TAKEOVER

Erik knew where to find Philippe. Every morning he sat on the terrace of Garnier's most iconic cafe, engaging its 'Joie de Vivre', discussing anything but French philosophy or news. He sat with his lawyer, the busy street their cover. Both had wry expressions as Erik approached, as if signalling victory. Philippe moved a spare chair to his side, inviting Erik to join them and signalling a waiter.

"Another coffee, s'il vous plait."

No sooner had Erik nodded in appreciation, Philippe's lawyer, Ritchie Esposito, abruptly left, not acknowledging Erik or Philippe. "You have to excuse him. He can be single-minded." Philippe offered, inviting Erik to take his chair at the table.

Erik used the slight to draw out Philippe's knowledge of Carlotta's whereabouts. "How did he take Carlotta's new decree?"

"He broods at the best of times, but his mood has darkened."

"I was going to give my formal application to Carlotta for the Artistic Producer's position, but I can't find her."

"Really? I'm surprised. I thought she'd be showing off her newfound power."

Erik studied Philippe for any sign of irony, but his expression was inscrutable. "She's expressing what is rightfully hers."

"Then she should have kept a lid on her deceptive husband. I wasted a lot of time and money drawing up those contracts. Now I'll waste more money in the courts while I sue his ass."

"That's another reason I want to see her. Her last meeting was low on information. Why don't you join me?"

Philippe scoffed before leaning toward Erik, seemingly confiding in him. "You would do well to negotiate your way out of your company share holdings. Things are about to get ugly here."

Erik nodded appreciatively, maintaining his facade of friendship. "Negotiate with her or you?"

Philippe leant back in the chair, pleased with himself. "My lawyer may seem a moody loner, but he has many connections. Work with us, and I'll see to it that you are handsomely rewarded. You can even stay on as the Artistic Producer."

"Generous," Erik lied, drinking his coffee as if he were seriously considering Philippe's offer, "but you understand that I need to see what Carlotta is prepared to offer as well." He finished his coffee and stood, ready to leave.

"You do that, my friend, but don't sit on the fence too long. As I said, things will get messy, and I don't want you caught on the wrong side."

"Thanks, Philippe," Erik replied in as a conciliatory tone as he could muster, but when he turned and left, he had only one thought. Carlotta was likely in the hands of ruthless operators, and Philippe wasn't even aware of it. He was no more than a charismatic pawn.

He walked into the Garnier, his mobile in hand, talking to Bernard. "I suspect they abducted Carlotta. See the Bagman as soon as possible and find Carlotta's location."

"We run the risk of exposing you," Bernard replied.

"They have already infiltrated swiftly and silently, as should we. Move forward cautiously."

Bernard agreed before signing off. *He was right,* Erik thought. Rescuing Carlotta would be dangerous and certainly expose his identity, but ultimately he needed powerful supporters capable of fighting back against Philippe's ruthless backers. He returned to the shadows of the Garnier's lair to be alone in his thoughts. His enemies may have promptly moved to control the Garnier opera company, but he was sure they had not infiltrated his underground caverns. He looked out across the lake, taking strange comfort in its familiar waters, remembering lives lost in the past and potentially the future. His discomfort grew in the dark underground as he allowed evil thoughts of revenge to reemerge. The permanent light cast from the lair reflected across the lake, directing his thoughts to the opera ghost's influence. Just then, the light grew in intensity as if reacting to Erik's thoughts. He looked below the waters, anticipating an ethereal visitor to rise from its depths, but none appeared. Erik was alone, but he could not let go of the thought in his head.

Someone was watching his every move.

Bernard drove through the location where he was meeting the Bagman, an obscure run-down factory on the outskirts of Rome, one of a dozen eroding depots long past their use-by date for business, except trade of the illegal kind. He pulled up outside the last factory and exited his car, studying all corners for signs of soldiers the Bagman had planted as protection. The location told Bernard a lot. The information he had offered earlier had likely not progressed much further up the family chain. He was about to find out just how far. A black vehicle cruised into the narrow road linking the chain of factories.

The driver slowed, seemingly hesitating, making Bernard remain close to the security of his car. Fifty metres short, the driver pulled his car over and exited. He looked familiar to Bernard, perhaps a foe from the past. He considered driving away until the man opened his coat, signalling he didn't carry a gun. Bernard glanced at his pistol resting on the front seat before closing the door and walking toward the man. He, too, opened his jacket, revealing he had no gun but not revealing a concealed switchblade, his insurance if it turned sour.

Bernard approached cautiously. "Where's the Bagman?" Bernard asked, looking for any concealed pistol. He was a stocky man with large, heavily scarred hands that matched his battle-drawn face. It was inevitable he carried a hand knife, too. They were both warriors of war, and soldiers never entered situations unarmed.

"You won't have to see him again. I'll give you all the information you want. You'll just have to fight for it. I considered having you executed, but I'm not an uncaring man," Reggi countered, in no mood for conciliation.

Bernard faced two choices, flee or fight. Either way, their cover had been exposed by the Bagman. He had no choice. He took his switchblade in hand, flicking the sharp silver knife in full view. "And I'm in an obliging mood," Bernard retorted, flashing his knife and inviting the fray.

Reggi drew his knife and attacked without fear or caution, swinging his blade with a force and ferocity Bernard just evaded, but Reggi didn't miss with a low roundhouse kick to Bernard's knee that felled him. Stunned by the speed, Bernard took another kick, a grazing blow to the side of his face. Struggling with double vision, he rolled away from Reggi, buying time to stand and return to the battle.

He circled his deadly foe, the taste of blood in his mouth, and his sight impaired from a rapidly closing eye. Now lacking the clearness of vision to attack with confidence, Bernard knew the battle would be won in close, needing the loss of more blood. Reggi moved counter-clockwise, exposing Bernard's diminishing sight. He struck his assailant with speed again, breaking Bernard's defences. Reggi struck a second kick into his foe's wrist, dislodging Bernard's weapon. Then, Reggi blocked Bernard from retrieving his knife, leaving him unarmed. Reggi's blade had blood on it from a gash that had opened up across Bernard's waist, its red flow seeping across his white shirt.

Bernard awaited the inevitable attack and possibly death, all the while hatching his final defence. He could yet win, but there would be a heavy price. Bernard moved forward toward Reggi, vision in just one eye now, easy prey for a skilled killer. He had only one chance, and he took it, throwing a feigned punch with his right hand, inviting an easy retaliation to his left. Reggi took the bait, plunging his knife toward his face. Bernard only just held the killer's decisive thrust at bay, using all his strength to halt the advancing sharp blade. His foe slowly moved his dagger ever higher toward the kill zone. Wide, wild eyes met in their dance of death, only Bernard's strength saving him from a quick demise.

A stalemate of wills ensued as both men pushed sinews to their sweat-filled limit, seemingly locked in a statuesque tribute to the macabre. Bernard focused his mind into a single thought to survive Reggi's final attack, even though his position was hopeless. He could measure his declining powers as the sharpness of the dagger slowly cut into his cheek. Blood began to seep into his good eye, blurring his vision. He could only lash out with a final attempt at a lethal punch to Reggi's abdomen. He heard Reggi's pained groan, but it wasn't enough. He felt the force of a large fist crash into the side of his head before losing consciousness.

CHAPTER TWENTY

INVESTIGATION RE-OPENED

Erik walked into the final day of rehearsals, showing no sign of the anxiety he felt. A day had passed,
and no one had heard from Carlotta. Equally ominous,
he couldn't contact Bernard. The calmness of rehearsals belied the building tensions that grew in Carlotta's
absence. He sat with Raoul, who'd taken it upon himself
to be there for Christine now that Carlotta wasn't. Erik
was intrigued by Raoul's loyalty to friends, an endearing
quality his brother, Philippe, lacked.

A day on and Victor had returned by Philippe's side,
demonstrating their version of solidarity to the Garnier
Opera Company, a dedication few believed,. They chat-
ted with cast and crew. Christine's dwindling confidence
was evident. She requested Viola perform in the opening
hour while she sat with Raoul and Erik. Gianni obliged

without argument, having learnt debate would only exacerbate her mood.

Surprisingly, Philippe and Victor moved to join them in the front row before Philippe received a call. Whoever the caller was surprised him as he and Victor hastily exited the theatre, drawing relieved chatter from the cast and crew.

"Have you heard anything?" Christine asked.

Tired eyes indicated she'd had little rest, prompting Raoul to gently stroke her arm. Both hoped Erik could offer a resolution. "Nothing, but I'll tell you if I hear anything," Erik replied.

"Thank you. At least someone cares," Christine replied, glancing at Raoul, indicating her displeasure with his brother.

"When Carlotta returns, I will fully support the team she puts in place," Raoul said before turning to Erik. "She should give you more prominence," he proposed, determination in his tone.

Erik nodded. "I have my best people looking, so we should soon find her. But, for now, I'm sure Carlotta would only want you to be ready for opening night."

"She's the reason I'm still here," Christine replied.

They all turned to the stage as rehearsals began with Viola performing the lead. Where Christine had suffered under Philippe's rule, Viola had prospered. She hadn't the range or power of Christine, but she had worked hard to develop into solid support. Viola performed Act One with confidence, prompting Christine to rejoin the cast for Act Two, she, too, performing perfectly.

Erik joined Gianni in congratulating everyone, lifting the spirits of all. For a short time, the fears surrounding Carlotta's disappearance were put aside as the cast and crew planned for a celebratory drink. However, the buoyant atmosphere was cut short. Philippe and Victor returned to the Garnier, along with a man well known to many cast members, Inspector Moreau.

Philippe took Christine and Erik to one side but still within earshot of most. "The inspector wishes to interview you both at police headquarters."

"Is it to do with Carlotta? Have they found her?" Christine asked in anticipation.

"I'm not at liberty to say anything. You will need to ask the Inspector directly," he said, pointing to where Moreau patiently waited near the exit doors.

Philippe then left Erik and Christine to hasten the assembled cast from the stage. "Thank you, one and all, please go to the dressing rooms now," he said, clapping his hands to emphasise his directive. Meanwhile, Christine and Erik were left to join the Inspector, whose intense gaze indicated their meeting would not be cordial.

Inspector Moreau ushered them to the small interview room consisting of a table and three chairs. Erik and Christine sat together facing Moreau, a single one-way viewing window behind him, where officers no doubt observed and recorded the proceedings.

Christine didn't wait for the Inspector to speak. "Is this about Carlotta? Is she okay?"

Moreau looked surprised by Christine's question. "Shouldn't she be?" he responded, leaving Christine to speak her mind.

"We haven't seen her since yesterday. Everyone is worried about her. I thought...."

Christine broke off mid-sentence, aware Moreau hadn't brought them to discuss Carlotta. Moreau jotted a few words on his notepad before putting it in his shirt pocket. He remained calm and unmoved, seemingly relishing the uncomfortable silent pause. Erik mirrored Moreau's reaction, knowing the inspector would prefer he and Christine talked about their concerns.

Moreau had aged since they last met. His loose white shirt protruded from an old favourite jacket, showing he'd gained considerable weight in the last few years.

"I did call Carlotta, but Philippe answered, who is the

operations manager while she is away. On business, he informed me, which Carlotta's husband verified."

"Thank you. Philippe hadn't told the cast," Christine replied, looking to Erik for support.

"That's true. Carlotta speaks with the cast every day, so when she failed to turn up, and so close to opening night." Erik slightly shook his head, indicating his concerns. "Well, you understand, the cast would talk."

"It would be premature to follow through on your concerns, but let me know if you don't hear from her by the week's end."

Christine shuffled in her chair, demonstrating her agitation.

"I'm sure she had other business, Inspector. But I will ring you if we do not hear from her by Friday," said Erik.

"Thank you, Monsieur....." Moreau nodded, inviting Erik to introduce himself.

"Rossi, " Erik replied.

Moreau raised his eyebrows as if he believed otherwise. Another uneasy silent pause ensued. Moreau seemed to relish Christine's growing agitation, removing his notepad to write in it a second time. Moreau was like a caterpillar among two butterflies, enabling remonstration, encouraging revelations.

Finally, with none forthcoming, Moreau returned his

notepad to his shirt and spoke. "I have called you both in because we have decided to reopen an old case. The disappearance of a ballerina. You remember?" Moreau asked, looking directly at Christine but glancing at Erik for a response.

"How could I forget? Our ballerina was popular with the cast. We were all shocked by the incident. Have you found her?" said Christine.

"I'm afraid not. It remains a mystery, but one of the suspects of that case has turned up."

Moreau placed two photos on the table in front of Christine. "Do you remember this man?"

"Yes. Bernard was part of the crew that worked with our head of security."

"Correct. Bernard disappeared, along with the head of security, Erik Destler."

Christine nodded. "Rumour was, Erik died."

"It remains a rumour. Both had disappeared, until now." Moreau sat in silence for a time before addressing Erik. "I apologise, Erik. We are talking about the Garnier's dark history of which you know little." Then he moved the photos closer to Erik. "Do you know this man?"

Erik briefly looked at the picture. "I most certainly do. I have hired him on several occasions as a security officer. He works freelance and is very good at his job."

"Is he currently under your employment?"

Moreau was fishing, immediately warning Erik that Bernard's absence had taken a deadly turn. "I'd discussed potential security work at the Garnier, but it was in a preliminary stage."

Moreau took the photos back and stacked them beside the second bundle of images that remained face down. He glanced at them before looking directly at Erik, inviting him to ask about them, but Erik stayed silent.

"Were you aware that Bernard kept some pretty unsavoury alliances with associates the opera industry would not welcome?"

Erik held a blank expression, even though inwardly his mind raced. *How much did the Inspector know?* "I never really considered that, Inspector. He seemed good at his job, which is what I paid him to do. Has he done something wrong?"

Moreau sat back in his chair, taking time to respond. "Quite the opposite," he replied, waiting for Erik to react to his perplexing reply, but Erik remained expressionless, bar a slight raising of an eyebrow signalling bewilderment.

Moreau took a deep breath, seemingly conceding to Erik's reaction. He picked up the second stack of photos and laid them in front of Erik one at a time to emphasise

Bernard's fate. A half dozen photos graphically illustrated Bernard's violent physical injuries. Erik displayed suitable shock at the violence laid in front of him, as did Christine, who looked away.

Erik signalled for Moreau to remove the images from the table. "Was he in an accident, Inspector?" Erik lied. The signs of a struggle which he ultimately lost were evident to him. What he didn't know was whether their enemy had extracted the truth from Bernard. If they did, Erik was exposed and vulnerable to the most powerful family in Italy.

"He certainly was involved in a dangerous activity, but he didn't end up like this by accident," Moreau replied.

"What do you mean?"

"This is the work of an Italian cartel. They have taken an interest in your business associate for some reason."

"He's hardly an associate. I contracted him on a couple of occasions while I was working in Italy."

"You never worked with him in Paris?"

"No. The work was in Milan and Como. I understand your need to see me, but I fail to understand why you would draw our premier diva into these investigations. Opening night is less than a week away, and she is stressed enough without this," Erik replied, fishing for more information from Inspector Moreau.

"Unfortunately, we have reason to believe that these cases overlap," Moreau replied, deliberately miserly.

"I feel responsible for Christine. Are you planning to keep us both much longer?"

"No. These are preliminary investigations, so we shouldn't be much longer."

"Is there anything I should tell our board on my return?"

"I already briefed Victor and Philippe, but you can update Carlotta. I hear you are friends?"

Erik ignored Moreau's insinuation. "I will when she returns. Is there anything specific you want me to tell her?"

"Tell her we have reopened the ballerina case. She is familiar with it. I will interview many cast in the coming days, including her, at a convenient time."

Christine impatiently looked at her watch, intervening in the conversation, "I need to return to the theatre soon, Inspector. If there is anything else you want from me, could you ask me now?"

Moreau gathered the photos, still unhurried by Christine's plea. "Just one last question. We didn't take these photos. They were sent to us by an unknown source. There was a letter, and it referred to the Garnier, so it seems someone is trying to tell us something. I was hoping one of you could enlighten us?"

"What did this letter say, inspector?" Erik asked.

"I'm not at liberty to say."

Erik sat back in his chair and shrugged his shoulders, and Christine shook her head. Moreau stood, "then that will be all for now," he said, abruptly ending the meeting. "My detective will drive you back. Thank you for your cooperation," he said with a tinge of cynicism in his tone.

Erik and Christine sat in silence as they were driven back to the Garnier. Once out of the car, Christine opened up about the strange and deadly occurrences when the Phantom ruled the Garnier. "Perhaps Erik has returned," she said, glancing at Erik, "I mean Erik Destler."

"I have only read the rumours. So they say Destler was the Phantom of the Opera?"

Christine had a faraway look in her eyes as she thought about that time. "Everyone had their rumour about the Phantom. Then, after the ballerina disappeared, those rumours multiplied. Very few would walk alone in the theatre after that."

"That would seem a normal reaction. You all must have been terrified."

"Nearly everyone. I remember Madame Giraud was the only one in the theatre alone. She would often be sighted in Box Five by the early morning crew. Some thought she was the opera ghost, issuing ethereal commands to the earthly Phantom, Erik Destler."

"The stories go that you became close to Destler. Did you sense he had ethereal powers?" Erik asked.

"His musical skill was sublime, but was he connected somehow to another plane of existence?" Christine paused and looked at the paintings lining the grand foyer, seemingly yearning to find the truth in the famous artist's work. "I believe he was a tortured genius capable of anything from pure art to unspeakable violence. I experienced both under his spell."

"Do you think he has returned?"

Christine turned from the artwork to face Erik. She looked deeply into his eyes, momentarily holding her breath. "When it is deadly quiet, like now, I feel his presence, in the halls, in your voice." Christine's voice faltered as if, at that moment, she realised Erik had returned, but then the moment was lost as Madam Giraud entered the grand foyer, her manner more urgent than usual.

"Philippe sent me to find you after the detective informed him you'd returned. He has called a meeting on stage. All the cast and crew are there."

"Is it about Carlotta?" Christine asked in anticipation.

"I do not know, but I feel the changes he has been steadfastly working towards are about to be revealed."

Christine looked to Erik, waiting for him to accompany her. "You go, Christine. I just want a few words with Madame Giraud. I won't be long."

Erik and Madame Giraud faced each other, their expressions of resignation revealing both knew more than most about recent events. "Powerful forces are at play," said Madame Giraud.

"What do you know of Carlotta's whereabouts? If you tell me, perhaps I can help her," Erik implored.

"Events will quickly unfold. It has always been this way. You would do well to retain a nimble mind and a true heart."

Erik nodded, "I should join Christine," he said, about to leave, but Madame Giraud held his arm.

"View Philippe from Box Five. It will reassure Christine," Madame Giraud proposed, and Erik willingly consented.

Proceedings had already commenced as Victor invited Philippe to the artistic director's lectern. Both were business-like in their manner, not bothering with idle conversation. Erik had a bird's eye view of everyone. Christine stood with Raoul at the back of the group, whereas Viola stood at the very front beside the artistic director, Gianni looked particularly downcast as if aware of what was about to unfold.

"I will be brief and to the point this evening. You have a challenging week of rehearsals ahead, and we need continuity. Unfortunately, an investigation from the past has to be faced as well, so expect Inspector Moreau to be visiting us all week. He has agreed to carry out interviews from one of our offices, so you will not be required to go to police headquarters, as Christine and Erik have just done."

Philippe's momentary pause was met with murmurings among the cast before he tapped the lectern, drawing their attention back to him. "On the Inspector's advice, we will be making some changes. However, before I announce them, I want everyone to be clear that they are only short-term changes until Inspector Moreau advises otherwise."

The earlier murmurings turned to loud, unbridled chatter, making Philippe turn to Gianni for assistance. "Quiet, please. We need to hear the directives from our local police!"

"Inspector Moreau anticipates multiple interviews with Christine and Erik while the investigation unfolds. I can also announce that the investigation has broadened. There is the reopened investigation into a missing ballerina and a concurrent investigation into the disappearance of Carlotta. As such, we have decided that

Christine and Erik step down from all duties until the investigation ends. I shall undertake Erik's duties, and Viola will take the position of the lead singer during that period."

All eyes turned toward Christine, who clung to Raoul's arm, visibly shaken by the announcement. Many of the cast moved closer to console her, whereas only Gianni congratulated Viola.

Philippe and Victor left the stunned cast and crew without further word. Philippe briefly acknowledged Viola before looking up to Box Five, signalling Erik to meet with him in his office.

Erik stood ready to confront Philippe, about to exit Box Five but not before Madame Giraud spoke. "Past conflicts have returned. So act cautiously and do not rush to choose friend or foe."

Erik studied Madame Giraud, seemingly deciphering her warning, "I choose you as a friend. Help me find Carlotta," he implored.

Madame Giraud looked at one of the framed photos of Carlotta prominently hanging in Box Five. "The walls of the Garnier have ears. We must use them well."

Erik briefly nodded, then he was gone as swiftly as a phantom, ready to begin the inevitable war.

Erik walked into Victor's office, where neither he nor

Philippe waited. Instead, Esposito sat at the desk, signalling for Erik to join him. A single contract and a pen lay on the desk, which Esposito pointed to before speaking. "Philippe asked me to attend to this matter. I have prepared a contract offer for your share of the Garnier," he said, sliding the contract towards Erik.

Erik didn't look at it. "I'm happy to have my legal people look at it."

Esposito held a stern look as he leant forward on the desk. "Our people are concerned about how the investigations will affect the organisation. Take a look. It's a handsome offer."

"Well, that's just it. My leaving in the middle of an investigation will look suspicious. Give me a week, so I can address the investigation and respond through my legal people," responded Erik with steely eyes. He gazed directly at Esposito, determined not to look at the contract.

"I can't guarantee the contract will hold, given the fluid situation we face. However, I suspect that the longer the investigation goes, the more tenuous your situation."

Erik sat forward on the desk and eye balled Esposito. "Are you threatening me?"

"No. But let's just say that your lack of cooperation will put your friends in a difficult situation."

Esposito had as good as confirmed that Carlotta, along with Bernard, were likely held hostage. The question was how much did they know about him. He guessed precious little for now, but it would only be a matter of time before they uncovered his new identity.

"It's true. I have developed a friendship with Carlotta since joining the Garnier. Where is she?"

Esposito laughed at Erik's naive request. "Either you're playing a dangerous game, or you don't know with who you're dealing. My people don't take kindly to indecision. In their world, life is cheap. I'm not here to barter. Either sign it or never see your friend again," Esposito threatened.

Erik picked up the contract and stood up, ready to leave. "I will respond by the week's end. If your people can't wait that long, I will presume you have no intention to negotiate sincerely," he said, turning and walking away from Esposito, not looking back.

Erik moved swiftly through the corridors, vanishing from the Garnier via hidden passageways down to his lair. He was sure Espisito's threats were no more than a bluff. More importantly, he'd bought enough time to finish what he and Bernard had begun, installing wiretaps throughout the Garnier, his best chance to find where they were holding Carlotta and Bernard. He also had to find out who was running Philippe's takeover. Madame Giraud's warning was accurate, for, at this moment, he was fighting an invisible foe.

CHAPTER TWENTY-ONE

BERNARD

Bernard gained consciousness again. How many times was it now? His rib cage throbbed from the last interrogation. His unnamed interrogator, Bear, the nickname Bernard gave his attacker, inflicted punishment via enormous fists powered by a stocky bull-like frame. Bernard's ordeal was made all the more savage by being bound tight and strapped firm in a straight jacket. Bear's ravaged prize-fighter face revealed few emotions but the desire for victory at any cost.

Ironically, the straight jacket offered Bernard his best opportunity for escape. Bear took liberties, believing his victim's situation was hopeless. A recurring cycle of hourly beatings and equally regular breaks where he was left alone had continued. Despite his battered frame, Bernard fought through the pain to loosen his straight jacket. Deep breaths expanding his chest muscles slightly stretched the thick canvas. Then he exhaled only after advancing his fingers, gripping precious loose cloth, ever closer to that vital space for his arms to escape.

Morning daylight arrived, signalling Bear's return. His mood was bitter at the best of times, but his expression was particularly severe. Bear said little, preferring to use his eyes as intimidation, wild animal-like eyes that only ever threatened. He breathed in the stale smell of vomit and blood permeating his dungeon of death, exhaling with the satisfaction felt in ones true home. He circled Bernard for a time. As his breath grew faster, he walked directly to Bernard, wrapping his enormous hands the whole way around Bernard's neck and lifting him effortlessly until their eyes met, just inches apart.

"Where is he?"

Bernard could hardly breathe, let alone speak, but he mustered all his strength to whisper, "Who?"

Bear inhaled, expanding his massive frame. His face turned red ; his vice-like grip tightened. He kicked the chair hard into the wall and ran forward, holding his prey in one hand. He rammed Bernard's head hard, cracking both wall and skull. Satisfied with his assault, he let go, pacing in front of him, glancing down at his victim while rolling his neck and shoulders, preparing to unleash fury.

"Playtime is over. You have one last chance to live. Think it over while I eat," he threatened, pulling out a single knuckleduster from his jacket and fitting it on his massive right hand. He faked a punch to Bernard's head. "Tell me or die," he warned, leaving no doubt Bernard would die in their next confrontation.

He slammed the door and locked it, leaving Bernard precious little time to affect his escape. Repeating the process, deep breath, flex chest, inhale, grip the canvas, repeat. A dozen runs gave sufficient leeway to manoeuvre his arms over his head. Challenging at the best of times, Bernard groaned at the pain it caused to his fractured ribs. Ignoring the pain, he snaked his arms further from his chest, straining to raise the top arm higher, falling just short of release. *Legionnaire! Make pain your saviour!* He grunted to himself, dislocating his right shoulder to force the first arm then the second to the front of his body, exposing the buckles of the sleeves. Bernard gnawed at the sleeve buckles while his freed hands worked beneath the canvas, unhooking the neck and body buckles. Finally, he stepped on the ends of the sleeves and pulled upward violently — and release.

Bear would return any minute, so he adjusted the straight jacket to make it appear he was still secured. His best attack against this monster was the element of surprise. Before sitting, he risked looking out from the one small window in the room. There was a small cottage where he momentarily saw Bear and at least one other. It wouldn't be enough to overpower Bear. He'd have to do it quietly.

Bernard sat back against the wall, wrapping the loose sleeves of the straight jacket behind him, and waited. His assailant soon returned, satisfaction in his expression, ready to kill on a full stomach. He didn't rush this time, seemingly wanting to draw out Bernard's agony. He paced from side to side, admiring his knuckle duster and occasionally glancing Bernard's way, gloating with power. Bernard imagined this brute's life, one of constant combat, feeling only fleeting joy until the next conflict, raw savagery in his eyes. Bernard would not die peacefully.

With a final stretch of his bull neck, Bear approached his prey, grasping Bernard's neck with one hand and clenching his other metal-gloved hand, ready to tear flesh. Bernard's one chance, the element of surprise, arrived. He bashed Bear's arm hard, freeing him from Bear's chokehold, then instantly pulled the canvas jacket down around his head, gripping him with all the energy left in his battered body. He rammed Bear's head hard into the cement floor, using his own skull as a second battering ram, crashing heavily against Bear's face.

The force would have killed any other man, but not Bear. Bernard tightened the canvas jacket, suffocating his foe of breath and sight. Bear struck out with increasingly desperate blows to escape Bernard's death grip. The brutal dance ebbed between two trained killers, a macabre medley of frantic movement and sweat, climaxing with the final breath. Bernard fell beside Bear's collapsed body, holding his fractured ribs, pushing through the pain and standing.

The room began to spin as he staggered to remain upright. To his shock, Bear moved, making him retreat. "Fucking die," he said, more to himself, as Bear removed the jacket from his head and stood. Blood streamed from his fractured skull and nose, one eye puffed and closed.

Bernard faced a cornered, deadly beast, knowing he only needed to land one desperate blow to finish him, so he circled cautiously, waiting for an opening. Bear knew his situation was deteriorating, so he launched one full-frontal assault, a last desperate attempt to grasp his foe. Bernard sidestepped, crashing his fist into the back of Bear's skull. Bear fell heavily into the wall, not moving from where he lay, slowly choking in his own blood. He managed a final disbelieving groan before slumping to his end.

Bernard collapsed against the opposite wall, the pain welling through his body, knowing he had to get up but unable. He sat in the silence, watching Bear's blood slowly flow to the base of his shoes. Finally, he mustered the energy to fight through the pain a second time, preparing to face his other captors, an unknown quantity in the adjoining cabin. The maths was simple. Win and escape or lose and die.

CHAPTER TWENTY-TWO

WIRETAPS

E rik secured all the secret passageways connecting his underground lair to the theatre above. No
one, including Inspector Moreau, would find their way
through his maze to the one last remaining connecting
tunnel. Erik's last safe stronghold was in place.

Dust and fragments of the destroyed tunnels filled the
hideaway, reaching even his beloved grand piano. With
care, he sat and cleaned the keyboard cover before opening it, revealing pristine ivory and black keys. Reassured
that his music had survived the controlled explosives,
Erik closed the keyboard cover and walked out to the
lake to make a call. All the while, he listened through
earphones to the many wiretaps he'd secretly installed.
If anyone knew of Carlotta's whereabouts, he'd know
next. Then, an incoming call rang out, echoing across the
cavernous underground of his lair. He didn't recognise

the number, but he instantly knew the voice.

"Is this the council for registrations?" Bernard asked.

"Sorry, you have the wrong number," Erik replied, hanging up and returning his call on an untraceable phone. "You're safe?"

"As safe as I can be. I'm still in Italy."

"Inspector Moreau was good enough to show me some of your travel photos. Do you need treatment?"

"I'll need treatment, but it'll have to wait. I found out the hard way that Philippe's supporters have thick wallets."

"Capo?"

"The very one. It seems Capo has taken a personal interest in the Garnier. We may need a team of helpers for this one."

"That depends. Is Capo aware of my identity?"

"Not from me. My interrogator tried, but I took care of him and his soldiers. They won't be worrying us anymore, but Capo's sure to send his enforcer, a guy called Reggi, for revenge. He has my phone, so he'll investigate all the contacts on it."

"Do we have to warn any other contacts?"

"Only one. Doc, but he's on a long list of contacts. It should take him a while to work through it."

"Fix it now. Get Doc out of Italy and set him up abroad.

Secure his new place, then let him work on your injuries while you're there."

"A week should be enough. Anything to do on your side?"

"Send me everything you can find on Capo and his lieutenants, particularly this Reggi character. I want to be ready for him, so I have to locate Carlotta before he turns up."

"Move carefully. Reggi made one mistake, losing me, but he won't make a second. They'll be ready for you. Is Carlotta worth the risk?"

"She's the current major stakeholder of the Garnier Opera Company, and I want it to stay that way. Call me when you've settled Doc," Erik said before hanging up.

The window for Carlotta's rescue was closing. Capo wasn't one to draw authorities his way. Carlotta would disappear, becoming another statistic on the national missing person list. If Erik was to permanently rid the Garnier of Philippe and his associates, his message had to be deadly and decisive. Even a man with Capo's power knew when to steer clear.

Erik walked from his lair to the underground lake. What he'd told Bernard was true. Carlotta needed to lead the opera company, but Erik wanted more than that. He came to the Garnier a year earlier to strike back at the horrors of a violent past and, most notably, to avenge the loss of the true love he'd lost, Rose.

A familiar chill crossed the lake, drawing his gaze to its centre. He thought he saw a ripple form on the surface, just where the young ballerina had disappeared into its depths a year earlier.

"Are you coming for me again? Are you not happy with me?" Erik cried. He strode into the water toward the ripple. "Take me if you dare, for I'll pursue you across a hundred lifetimes if you let another die. I won't rest until I drag you to an eternal inferno if you don't protect those who bring music to the world."

Images of Rose formed in his mind. A singing virtuoso taken in her prime by monsters who cared little for the world of music. Now, another diva faced an uncertain fate against mercenaries who cared only for money and power. Erik dove into the deep centre of the lake, desperately stroking to the bottom. He searched for his victim, who perished in its depths, trying to undo the violent madness of his past. *Take me now*, he thought, willing the Opera Ghost to end their ethereal battle of wills, but all he could hear was the sound of two divas singing a duet of reconciliation above him. He pushed up toward the surface, where he saw images of the divas. He thought they serenaded him, but they were singing to another not from this world. Were they soothing the Opera Ghost?

Erik broke to the surface, gasping for air. He looked for the divas, but the image had disappeared. He staggered to his lair, stripped and lay shivering under blankets, more from the terror he felt than the cold. Had the Opera Ghost won? The thought alarmed him so much that only sleep could erase the idea from his mind.

The pitch of Erik's phone woke him. "Erik. Can you join us?" said Christine.

"When, where?" Erik replied, still disoriented from sleep, not even sure of the time.

"We've been trying to contact you. Where have you been?"

"I've been organising a few things."

"Raoul and I are going to see Philippe this evening. The cast is upset with what has been happening. We want you to join us."

Erik checked the time. It was late afternoon. "Where are you meeting him?"

"At Philippe's place, in three hours. Can you come? We need you."

Erik saw advantage in joining them, as it was a chance for him to lay more wiretaps. "Name the time, and I'll be there."

"Raoul will pick me up near the Garnier entry. Can you meet me there at 8.00 pm?"

"Fine, but don't get your hopes high. I met Philippe, and all he wants from me is to sell my ownership share."

"Well, Raoul doesn't support his brother on this. So we owe it to our cast to convince him not to let you go," Christine implored.

"I'll see you at 8.00," Erik replied gratefully before ending the call, keen to review his wiretaps for any more information.

Several wiretaps confirmed Philippe's link to Capo, but also Philippe's dissatisfaction with Carlotta's abduction. Importantly, he'd learned her hiding place was close to home, figuratively and perhaps literally. Erik peered out to the lake and smiled. Maybe his pleas to the Garnier's ghost hadn't fallen on deaf ears. He was close to finding Carlotta, and when he did, he'd make sure he left a clear message to those who wished her harm. A battle of wills had commenced that would reverberate throughout the famous opera house's walls, far beyond their lives.

Raoul led Christine and Erik through the foyer of Philippe's residence, a central apartment that shared an internal garden, a collective quiet space free from the noise of Rue d'Amsterdam. The major thoroughfare was a popular rental area, given its reasonable price and proximity to metro lines. Erik guessed Philippe's neighbours were associates of Capo. The whole place was under extensive surveillance and security, from the electronic cast-iron gates into the common area to the fortified internal entries to all the apartments, including extensive internal and external surveillance cameras. Once past the secured entry, they endured further waiting time in the long hallway before Philippe allowed them through to another room.

His lounge room looked onto the internal courtyard. The window side was filled with a modern leather lounge setting, and the other side was set up with an office where Philippe sat behind a modern white desk with three chairs opposite. He dispensed with formalities, not standing, merely signalling for them to take a seat. Rudimentary refreshments, coffee and cups were placed on the corner of the desk, but not offered, so Raoul commenced the conversation.

"Thanks for seeing us, Philippe. As I said on the phone, there's a lot of ill feelings among the cast over your latest decisions."

Philippe silently nodded, seemingly unaffected by Raoul's assertions. Erik listened on, sure their conversation was taped.

Raoul looked to Christine for support, but she sat stony faced with her arms folded, so he continued. "This may be hard for you to hear, but nearly everyone is upset with the changes you have brought. I don't wish to embarrass Christine, but everyone believes she should be the lead, investigation or not. She is the finest opera singer in Europe, whereas your replacement is very inexperienced. Similarly, they want Erik to remain on the board. He brings valuable experience, and all the performers have appreciated his assistance during rehearsals, particularly our artistic director."

Philippe heard his brother out, seemingly in no hurry to respond. But his eyes darted accusingly across the three participants, revealing impatience. Once Raoul had finished, Philippe droned out a well-rehearsed take on the company's financial peril as his defence.

"You know better than I that we cannot afford headlines of impropriety. But if Moreau's investigation drags on, we will be at the centre of a media storm that could irreparably damage the Garnier's reputation. We have to see out the season without that. Surely that is not a lot to ask, Christine, if you care about Paris opera?"

"I'm prepared to do that if you hold on to Erik," Christine challenged, much to Raoul's consternation.

"The decision of board members is a delicate one that

I'm not at liberty to discuss," Philippe replied, his uneasiness with the matter obvious.

Erik took advantage of the awkward pause. "I haven't come here to negotiate my position. So it might be an opportune moment for me to step out and use your restroom. If you want to discuss board matters, use this moment," Erik said, standing and receiving directions from an appreciative Philippe.

Erik walked back into the hallway and down to the back of Philippe's apartment, deliberately opening the wrong doors along the way and faking confusion for the cameras. All entries were locked bar the restroom. Security was extreme, convincing Erik that Philippe shared the apartment complex with his financial backers. The restroom door locked behind him, and Erik hastily went about his real agenda, planting a high-range listening device in a camouflaged space. If Philippe's apartments were Capo's French headquarters, he would soon find out.

The task completed, he returned to the meeting. The two brothers had seemingly reached a silent impasse. Whatever they discussed in his absence had visibly upset Christine. Any hope of successful negotiation had appeared to end. Philippe drove this home by laying out the contract he wanted Erik to sign.

Erik didn't pick it up. "I already have a contract, and

as I said to your lawyer, I will make my decision by the week's end."

"This is a substantial contract. My backers will not remain so generous if they believe you're stalling."

"Tell your backers that I'm moving back to Italy and that the delay is only to allow my lawyers to study the details properly."

"A wise move, my friend. This investigation can only harm your reputation. In time, when all this clears, I'll be the first to invite you back."

Erik knew that to be a lie, but he played along with Philippe's charade. Christine's demeanour showed she also knew. Philippe would shred friendships, even loves, to get what he wanted. That was how desperate people behaved.

"Please, some coffee?" Philippe offered, the look of victory in his manner.

Erik declined, using the moment to leave. "If you don't mind, I have another meeting not far from here. Many arrangements to be made for my return home."

Philippe escorted Erik to the exit, using the moment to press him. "I shall tell my backers Friday morning. No more extensions. Is that understood?"

"I will personally deliver the papers to you," Erik said, the intensity in his gaze drawing a nervous chuckle from Philippe before he returned to the safety of his fortified apartment. Erik studied the courtyard for a few minutes, pretending he was checking his phone for directions. In reality, he was tuning his listening device and filming the six apartments bordering the internal courtyard, preparing the actual response he would unleash on Philippe later that evening.

Erik strolled down Rue d'Amsterdam, looking like any other late night revellers, dressed all in black from his dress jeans, skivvy and jacket, to his small backpack. He disappeared from view into a small alley bordering Philippe's quarters, ascending a pre-selected apartment to the rooftop then down into the darkest corner of the fortified courtyard, where he removed his jacket and backpack. The backpack was actually a bulletproof vest with purpose-built side pockets that carried his tools of the trade, a saw, files, knives and assorted implements to pick any manner of locks. He refitted the vest to the front of his body, then headed for the front gate.

He quickly matched the appropriate pick with the gates lock and left it with his jacket. His escape route prepared, Erik turned his attention to the surveillance camera pointing to Philippe's and neighbouring apartments. He aimed an electronic device at it, rotating the surveillance camera 180 degrees so it pointed toward the opposite apartments, and waited. If someone viewed the camera's monitor, they would investigate. A full minute passed without response, thus commencing the incursion of the apartment he believed Carlotta was held hostage in.

Erik adjusted his black skivvy to a full face mask and fastened night vision goggles in place, staying in the fog of darkness. He quickly picked the front door lock and moved directly to the electric switch box, killing all the lights. The hostage-takers had locked all interconnecting hallway doors, so he waited in the pitch black, ready to strike. Philippe's goons would soon investigate. The first of them stumbled into the room, hands stretched out as he maneuvered his way toward the fuse box. He was easy prey for Erik, who landed a single sharp blow to the side of his head, felling him on impact into his waiting arms. Erik left him in full view beneath the fuse box.

Erik softly stepped to the opposite side and stooped behind the open door, preparing for another accomplice to investigate. The next soon did, calling out to his partner, the silence drawing him into the pitch black room.

"Tony?" No response, so he activated a torchlight. "Tony, are you okay?"

Erik heard the sound of his cautious footsteps and the click of his pistol as he readied it to fire. His torchlight illuminated the opposite wall as he moved through the threshold of no return. Erik could quickly kill him, but he had to disarm him with minimum sound, particularly gunfire. Erik unleashed a decisive blow, successfully knocking the pistol from his hand, but allowing the assailant time to respond with a swift martial arts kick to Erik's left leg that felled him. Erik's assailant grounded his torch in Erik's direction, facing him, ready for combat.

Erik regained his balance just in time to face his knife-wielding assailant, just avoiding his every thrust of the knife. Equally matched fighters, Erik used the element of surprise as his weapon, parrying several times before exposing his abdomen to an attack. His assailant took the bait, ramming the knife solidly into his exposed torso, failing to penetrate the security vest. Erik used the opening to drive his fist into his exposed neck, instantly crushing his larynx, and followed with a second blow that broke his neck.

Two soldiers decommissioned. If Erik faced a third, he'd be waiting in the next room. Erik picked up the dead man's torch, a phone, and pocketed it before moving into the second room, which was empty. Any more guards could only be behind the one last secured door facing him. If Carlotta was in the apartment, she'd be there.

He forced the lock with the swift skill of an artisan and cautiously opened it, sweeping the room with his night goggles. The space was empty, bar a single bed in the corner where Carlotta lay, asleep, likely drugged.

Erik swept the rest of the apartment in darkness before lighting the apartment, and setting about reviving Carlotta. Erik repeated the combination of cold water towel and coffee for a half hour before Carlotta recognised him and uttered her first words.

"Where am I?"

"Somewhere you don't want to be. When you can stand, I'm taking you home," Erik said, towelling Carlotta's forehead. "Drink a little more," he said, helping her drink the hot black coffee.

Carlotta started to take in her surroundings, sparking some memory recall. "Some men took me here, against my will," she said, holding Erik's arm, fear in her expression.

"Yes. I've taken care of those men. You're safe for now, but we have to leave here soon. Do you think you can walk with me? I have a car not far from here."

"Yes. Help me up. I want to go home."

Carlotta stood up, immediately swaying, so she leaned into Erik as he took her to the front door and sat her on a chair. He again killed the lights, leaving the apartment in darkness, before helping Carlotta out to the courtyard to the main exit. "Stand against the gate and take in deep breaths. It will help revive you," he said, quickly returning to the apartment and securing it from any prying neighbours. Capo's people would discover and erase any evidence of what happened.

In a short time, Erik took Carlotta to safety, not to her home, but to his lair, where she could recover from the ordeal under his watchful surveillance. Her slumber was erratic as nightmares woke her sporadically. Erik sat close by, casting a watchful eye her way and offering support when she woke.

One dream made her abruptly sit up, drawing Erik to comfort her. "Why did you lie to me? I trusted you."

"There are dangerous people who want me to pay for what I have done to them. I couldn't risk exposing you to them."

"The people who abducted me?" Carlotta replied pointedly.

"I believe so. They want to scare you with threats so that you hand over ownership of the Garnier company. Did they hurt you?"

"Outside of the abduction, no. I mostly slept. Have you informed the police?"

Erik breathed deeply before taking Carlotta's hand

and shaking his head. "I don't believe they can help. They're more likely to make it worse."

Carlotta lay back on her pillow, withdrawing her hand from his. "Make it worse for you or me?"

"For both of us. You are dealing with a ruthless family that will stop at nothing to take control of Garnier opera."

Carlotta sighed before giving way to her fatigue. Erik could keep her safe here, but she wouldn't willingly stay in Erik's fortress too long. He had to clear the way for her to run the Garnier. Perhaps his resignation was the only answer. The phone rang, taking him from his deliberations. It was Bernard.

"The game seems to be up. Doc has disappeared."

"Any signs of foul play?"

"No, but Capo left a message for Erik Destler to meet his man at the viewing level of the Arc de Triomphe at sunset. Come alone, then call the number I just sent you and wait."

"Where are you, Bernard?"

"Boarding a train to Paris."

"How's your condition?"

"Not great but I'll recover. Do you want me to bring in reinforcements?"

"No. Come to our base. There's medication here and I

have some important property for you to protect until I return."

Erik slammed his phone to the ground. His identity revealed, he had little room to manoeuvre. Capo was pulling resources into this project that Erik couldn't match. Why had he taken such an interest? Philippe was anything but a reassuring operator. It had to be more than that. Whatever the reason, he agreed to the meeting. At least the public location was a signal that there would be no bloodshed. Still, he would do a thorough survey anyway, beginning with dressing appropriately, choosing a bulky jacket with a bulletproof vest underneath, pistol and knife.

He was ready to leave within the hour, his last action to leave a note for Bernard. He sat beside Carlotta, who hadn't stirred, as he wrote his message. Usually, he'd retaliate to Capo's message with all-out war, but his feelings got in the way. So instead, he had to negotiate with the devil. He folded the note and left it on the bedside table, then took a last glance at Carlotta. As she slept peacefully, he found himself wishing he could keep her here, always safe from the coming war.

CHAPTER TWENTY-THREE

ARC DE TRIOMPHE

E rik arrived at the famous Arch with time to spare and had a chance to check for irregularities. The rectangular platform afforded the best views of Paris as the three arrondissements collided into one of the busiest roundabouts in Paris. As a result, a steady torrent of tourists filled the Arch, matching the constant stream of cars navigating their way through the streets below.

Erik's only potential threat would be a sniper, but firing a weapon into a crowd would be risky even for the mafia. Satisfied with safety, Erik called the number as the sun set over one of Paris's best views. His contact arrived, a stocky man exuding the confidence expected of Capo's enforcer.

"Monsieur Destler, I presume?" He said, a slight smirk revealing his satisfaction with knowing Erik's previous identity.

Erik nodded, "You have me at a disadvantage, Monsieur....?"

"Reggi. No need for formalities here, Erik," he said, nodding toward an unoccupied viewing section and walking over to it. There was room enough for a half dozen tourists, but Reggi spread both hands out across the railing, taking up most of the space. Reggi eyed Erik from the corner of his eye, seemingly sizing him up. He unbuttoned his long black overcoat, revealing part of an inside pouch that likely carried a pistol.

Erik ignored Reggi's arrogant stance, mirroring an equally aggressive posture and a tone of impatience as he responded. "Does Capo have a message for me or not? You're his messenger boy, aren't you?"

Reggi managed a forced smile, straining not to react to Erik's slight. Instead, he adjusted his coat and turned to face him, grasping the rail with his massive hand. Scars adorned both hands, touting his life of violence. "Capo wanted me to meet you here. It's one of his favourite spots when he's in Paris. You know why?"

"It's just about every tourist's favourite location," Erik replied with a disinterested tone.

Reggi clenched the rail harder, his only visible reaction to Erik's sarcasm. "It offers the clearest view of Paris. Capo likes clarity in everything he does. That's why he's where he is."

"Then perhaps he can explain why he abducted an opera star. That action seems to lack any clarity."

"An ex-star of opera, but importantly a romantic interest of the rat he needed to draw from the sewer," Reggi retaliated.

"Well, from one rat to another, can you relay the message your king of sewers has for me?"

"You did a good job of hiding, Destler, so he had to bring you out. He never wanted her. He just knew it was the quickest way to reach you."

"Well, his little exercise cost him a few soldiers, didn't it?"

"Capo won't forget that. End your little musical project, or you'll start losing more than your soldiers."

Erik sighed and turned to look out at the fading daylight view as Paris's night lights came to life. "My colleagues offer hope in people's lives. Tell Capo I won't give up on them."

"Then leave the Garnier. Let Carlotta work with Philippe. If you stay, it won't go well for her or her friends," Reggi threatened.

"Carlotta is the majority owner of the Garnier. So if I leave, it has to stay that way."

Reggi smiled. "Capo is a reasonable man. He only

wants you out. Carlotta 51%, Philippe 49%. In appreciation for her not reporting her recent incident. You make
her aware of that, seeing as you took the trouble of rescuing her. I take it she's in your hands?"

Erik ignored Reggi's question. "Christine is to be
reinstalled."

Reggi shook his head, "Capo doesn't want any more
heat. She has to stay out until the police finish their
investigations. You have to stay out permanently, or
news may filter to Inspector Moreau that Erik Destler
is alive and well."

"Who knows about this?" Erik asked.

"For now, Capo and I, as long as you leave and never
return to the Garnier."

"Christine will be reinstalled to the lead as soon as the
investigation ends?"

"That will be Carlotta's call," Reggi replied, about to
say more, but a phone call interrupted them. "Yes. I'm
here with him. Sure," Reggi replied, handing the phone
to Erik.

"That was a good disappearing act you pulled,
Monsieur Destler. So befitting of the so-called Phantom
of the Opera," Capo said, chuckling at his own words.

"Well, that's the thing, Capo. Phantoms don't die
easily."

"You've heard my offer. Take it, and we'll never have to find out if that's true. Because if you don't, I'll make you the phantom of Paris prison, but not before some of your colleagues suffer. It would be a shame if your beautiful divas permanently lost their voices."

"Keep them out of it, or I'll make it my life's work killing you and your goon."

"Charming till the end, Erik. Do we have an agreement?"

"Yes. You'll not see me again. I've tired of the place," Erik lied.

"That's the spirit. Then our time together is unfortunately at an end."

"Why this spirited interest in opera ? I understand your thirst for power, but opera? It's hardly a money-making exercise."

"My interests, first and foremost, are family. You're not the only one with an interest in music."

"You're telling me you have a hidden interest for music?" Erik asked, chuckling at the thought.

"Not me, my family. A sister-in-law to be precise, who happened to have a daughter with a promising career in ballet, a sweet innocent girl who loved music and dance, just as you now claim you have discovered."

"The ballerina who disappeared?"

"Don't pretend innocence. You insult my intelligence.

You or one of your soldiers killed her and now you have to pay. My request is simple. Leave your Garnier dream forever. Never return. Live what's left of your miserable life hiding and running. Do that and I won't carry my vengeance out on those close to you."

Erik had heard all he needed. He handed the phone back to Reggi, realising the enormity of his past actions. "Tell him I'll settle the contracts this week, before opening night," Erik capitulated.

"Then we don't want to see you anywhere near the Garnier on opening night, or we will hand Inspector Moreau all the details necessary to arrest you. Understood?"

"Very clear," Erik replied, leaving without further word and descending the narrow spiral stairs down to the entry of the Arch. He had until the weekend to organise his next strategy, starting with convincing Carlotta not to go to the police, a tall order, given the lack of trust she now had in him.

Erik called Bernard, "Everything fine at home?"

"She's still resting. How did the meeting go?" Bernard asked.

"A lot of empty promises on both sides. I've agreed to their terms, so we need to make them think we left the Garnier. I secured all the secret channels between the lair and the theatre. Double check my work."

"Understood."

Erik hung up and headed to the Metro and directly to the Garnier to help Bernard prepare for the coming war.

Capo was a ruthless leader who would hold the Garnier in a vice-like grip, given a chance. Erik would need an ally, and he knew just the person to see.

CHAPTER TWENTY-FOUR

SURPRISE VISIT

I returned from the past, not in the Diva's home, but slumped in the middle of the Garnier. My last memory was a threatening conversation between Erik and Reggi at the Arch De Triomphe. I could still have been in the previous century, if not for the telltale signs, crew decked in 22nd-century clothing. My mind raced, continually reviewing the ordeals that had happened in Diva's early life and feeling helpless to do anything about it. Then a familiar voice broke my introspection.

"You look like you're carrying the weight of the world's troubles on your shoulders, Benny," said Flynn, sitting a row back.

"The mafia has gained control of the Garnier. I fear that the Diva faced terrible ordeals. There must be some way I can help her."

"Her past can't be changed," Flynn said, shaking his

head with frustration. "But you're learning more of her life. She's here in Paris, preparing for her final performance. She will want to rehearse with you soon. Talk to her of your new insights then."

"I haven't written anything new since our last meeting."

"You can address that soon enough," Flynn said, seemingly unconcerned. "It's a nice view here, don't you think?"

"Most seats have a spectacular view. I prefer Box Five."

Flynn smiled at the irony. "The professionals say this is the clearest view in the theatre with the purest acoustics."

Flynn didn't often engage in small talk, so I used the opportunity to get some answers. "I think you know way more about the Garnier than you let on. Isn't it about time you told me more?"

"Such as?"

"The point of all this."

"It's simpler than you believe. Diva's wealthy enough to buy whatever she wishes on this Earth and the Sensorium. That brings certain privileges."

"She could just as easily have told me her story."

"Do you think so? I think the best stories ever told evolved from the myriad of human experiences, from suffering to ecstasy. You have a chance to be part of that storytelling."

"I'm a musician. I entertain. Apart from that, all I want is to help Diva and show her I care."

Flynn smiled warmly at me for the first time, lightly touching my shoulder in a show of appreciation. "Then you are offering her what she hoped for. Support Diva in her final quest."

Flynn came and sat beside me, and we both watched the crew assembling props to their designated positions.

"That's Ziggy Stardust," I said as a crew member stacked some props in the corner.

"The Diva has organised an exhibition in the main foyer to run before her final tribute concert. She's planning a memorable send-off. Look, she's arrived." Flynn said, returning the Diva's wave as she strode onto the stage, inspecting the assortment of props. "She wants you to join her, Benny. Go now," said Flynn.

I walked toward the stage, admiring her calm assuredness as she directed the crew on how she wished the props be displayed. Her confidence gave her a youthful appearance. Between her enthusiasm and the supportive post-human technology, she could live another hundred years. I approached her, determined to achieve just that.

"Ah, come to me, my love," she said, her eyes lit up by my presence. She opened her arms, inviting me close, kissing my lips and embracing me. "I'm so sorry for my stern words when we last met, darling."

"It's okay. I'm beginning to understand why," I replied, holding my gaze to hers.

She studied me as if reading my mind, "I believe you are." She took my hand. "Come, let me show you what I've organised for our night of nights."

We walked out of the theatre to the grand staircase, where a hub of digital artists were creating art for the planned exhibition.

"You'll need AR vision," she said.

I removed AR sensors from my jacket pocket and put them on, making the artists' creations spring to life. A kaleidoscope of art and music filled either side of the staircase, most familiar to me, from opera stars to famous music celebrities of the past century.

The exhibition preparation continued on into the main hall, a surreal blend of digital and classic art filling Garnier's historic grand hall. The Diva turned to me. "Once the artists finish their work, an artistic director will position them around the staircase, grand hall and side rooms. We will have over a hundred exhibits overall."

I admired the artists, many famous, busily stroking their digital brushes. "An expensive exhibition."

Diva looked on like a proud mother. "We will auction all of them in the evening. I have pre-purchased the

NFT's and will donate the profits to a worthy cause. By the end of the night, I expect the values to have soared, so I locked in long-term percentage clauses for every resale."

"A wise investment. There are many great artists."

"They will become infamous, given what I have in mind. The works will become classics."

"Seems strange you don't want to be around to see it?"

"Darling! Such concern," the Diva said, gently kissing me. "What have you been uncovering with your research?"

"It seems your love was cursed. No one deserves the deceit you faced."

The Diva's buoyant mood mellowed from my words. "You must capture that in your lyrics. Sugarcoat nothing for my adoring audience. It will be important on the night."

"You could have died at the hands of those monsters."

"But I'm here, dear Benny, preparing to sing your song to the world of opera. Make them remember it. Finish your research." She was about to say more, but a text message interrupted her, its contents lighting up her face with joy. "I want you to see Flynn. Tell him that your research is near completion. He will know what I mean."

She hugged me and turned to leave, but I called to her. "You know about me, don't you? You've always known?"

Diva turned back and kissed me full on the lips. "I

adore you, darling, and admire your talents. That's all I've ever seen. Talk to Flynn," she said, avoiding the question, then leaving.

I returned to Flynn, still sitting where I left him. I immediately questioned him. "She's always known what I am, hasn't she?"

"That's why she selected you. No one else would be so loyal."

"So the whole lover thing is no more than a facade. A reward for services rendered."

Flynn looked at me sternly. "You are working with a world-renowned artist who lives by her emotions. She doesn't play with people. You became her lover because she felt something for you. Isn't that enough? Isn't that more than you could ever have hoped for?"

"But she knows that I can't love her the way she wants and deserves."

"Don't be too sure of that. You've seen what Christine has experienced. Love has not exactly been kind."

"She was surrounded by more danger than she realised. Yet, she survived it all," I said, relieved at the thought.

Flynn's eyes narrowed. "At what cost?" He asked, waiting for a reply.

"Some of those she loved betrayed her, but others were supportive."

Flynn stood and looked up to Box Five. "You need to finish your music for the Diva, Benny. Tell me what you see up there."

"Box Five?" I answered, unsure of what he meant.

"That is the window on Diva's life. Go back and write her song," he implored, his gaze profound as if his mind had taken control of me. "Look again."

I turned to Box Five, and the vacant seats now had two occupants. With a single thought, my energy source floated up to Box Five. I was back in the past. Madame Giraud sat in the front row, and another sat further back in the shadows. I looked down to the now full theatre, calm and waiting in expectation for the opening night of *La Traviata*. Madame Giraud looked on with antici- pation, whereas I couldn't see the second person's face, a male dressed in black. A black mask covered his face, but I guessed it to be Erik. They were looking at the front row seats, where in the middle sat three VIP guests, Carlotta, Christine and Raoul.

As the overture to *La Traviata* played, Viola took her place centre stage, confirming Philippe and his gangland benefactors had taken full control of the Garnier.

CHAPTER TWENTY-FIVE

OPENING NIGHT

Twenty hours before Viola's opening night debut, two cloaked figures stole their way into the Garnier. Their aim, secure the finest and deadliest views of the evening's performance of *La Traviata*. The nimblest of the pair and a skilled climber painstakingly navigated Reggi across dangerous platforms and ladders to the giddy elevation forty-five metres above the stage. Their first destination was the main gantry, a metal grid that ran vertical wires for raising and lowering scenery, the work area of the specialist crew charged with bringing the stage alive with colour and atmosphere. Reggi's guide gave him a much-needed rest from the challenging climb before pointing to a higher camouflaged platform. There, Reggi would patiently lie in wait, his lethal weapon by his side, ready to perform his unique, deadly overture to Verdi's musical.

Twenty hours later, Raoul escorted two famous divas to their reserved front-row seats. Christine and Carlotta waved to the appreciative house. Christine dressed in a pearl gown, and Carlotta in sapphire, both shone as bright as the stage. Carlotta waved to the royal box, where Philippe sat beside his special guest, Inspector Moreau. Christine notably ignored them, waving to her many fans in the auditorium. The applause continued until the spotlight faded, and the sound of the orchestra took its place, tuning instruments.

"You should have acknowledged them," Carlotta said, still reeling from her abduction, fearful of more threats.

"I wouldn't give him the satisfaction," Christine replied sharply, drawing a supportive caress from Raoul.

"How have negotiations fared?" Raoul asked.

"Early discussions have been positive," Carlotta replied, looking to the empty seats beside Philippe, reserved for Victor. "I will not discuss majority ownership until Christine is back in her rightful position. I hope that you support me, given others have chosen not to."

"I was sorry to hear Erik left the company. I assure you that I will undo what my brother has done, no matter the cost."

The familiar sounds of the orchestra's warm-up subsided as the artistic director and conductor for the evening, Gianni, walked to the podium of the orchestra pit to applause. Hushed expectation took over. A tap of his lectern followed by passionate commencement of his baton initiated the haunting beginning of *La Traviata*, Act One's overture.

Philippe sat proudly in the Royal Box, satisfied he'd persuaded the Inspector and his wife to join him, further building his trust. Philippe was the VIP guest to all in attendance, but he knew otherwise, casting an appreciative glance to his important attendee. Settled in the shadowy back stalls of the auditorium, Capo watched his unfolding achievement, orchestrating his plans from the safety of anonymity, only his wife beside him and his most trusted soldiers scattered strategically around the theatre. Philippe basked in the limelight, having pulled off the coup of a lifetime, knowing he had the most influential Italian mafia leader in support. What he didn't predict would haunt him forever.

The performance progressed to Act Three, and even though Erik sat a metre to Madame Giraud's left, no contact was made, fearful Philippe's people observed them. Instead, Erik intermittently peered through binoculars at the stage and across the theatre. All had gone smoothly until the closing stages of Act Three.

Madame Giraud spoke for the first time. "There is a disturbance above the theatre gantry."

Erik moved from the anonymity of the shadows to take a clearer view. What he saw confirmed his fears. Carlotta was in danger. Without hesitation, he slipped the hidden lock to the adjacent secret passage that ran above the viewing boxes and was a shortcut to the climb that reached the gantry. He opened the door, revealing his secret to Madame Giraud. She studied him, seemingly unsurprised, sharing a knowing gaze before Erik spoke.

"I have to stop them."

"I know. Philippe's backers won't stop until they have control," she replied, nodding in agreement.

"How do you know these secrets?"

"I have told you before, these famous walls have ears. They hold all the secrets of the past, present and future."

Whatever doubts Erik had about Madame Giraud had faded just as his stern expression gave way to one of hope.

"Whatever happens, remember that the Phantom's fighting spirit will live on through the music. Go now. There's little time," she said, revealing the slightest of smiles before Erik vanished into his secret world.

The sounds of appreciative applause floated high

above the theatre, echoing around Erik's chamber of metal and vertical wires. Ironically, the last time Erik scaled these passages two years earlier, he wanted to kill Carlotta. Now his thoughts were only to protect her.

He deftly leapt across metal platforms to a position well behind the gantry, where operators skillfully managed the many scenes of *La Traviata*. Then he saw his target. Reggi was in a sniper position, his rifle aimed and ready to shoot. The thunderous applause camouflaged Erik's approach across metal scaffolding, allowing him the element of surprise.

Violetta's final dramatic death scene was in play below. The calm theatre halted Erik metres short. Reggi's finger was on the trigger, ready for the kill shot. He, too, would be waiting for the applause to take over, muffling the sound of rifle fire. Erik would attack him at that precise moment.

The final death scene played out to an enraptured audience. Even Christine appreciated the quality of Viola's performance as she sang the last lines. "A strange joy has brought me to life," she sang under a star-filled stage, her final view of life before her stage death. Raoul squeezed Christine's hand, showing he, too, admired Viola's performance. They exchanged glances, a tender momentary gaze.

"I think it was destiny," she said.

Raoul squinted his eyes in a questioning manner. "What destiny?"

"To experience opening night beside you. I love you, Raoul," she whispered.

Raoul's eyes lit with joy as he replied, but applause drowned out his response as the crowd admiringly acknowledged Violetta's dramatic performance. People began to stand and cheer, including Carlotta and Christine, looking like two angelic pillars on either side of their melancholy host, who unexpectedly remained seated.

The stars made for a surreal backdrop as Erik prepared his assault. Reggi lay statue-still in the kill position, poised to pull the trigger when the applause commenced. The timing was critical. Too early, and Reggi would turn his weapon on Erik. Too late, and his target would surely perish. He held a high calibre Barrett M82 semi-automatic capable of destroying enemies behind concrete cover, power unnecessary for his prey. A direct hit with its recommended ammunition would leave a bloody mess over anyone within five metres. Erik feared he carried more subtle ballistics, 'heart attack' darts, a lethal charge that disintegrates upon entering the target — an undetectable kill.

He crawled to his best attack position without being heard, tensing his robust frame, prepared for his one chance to halt the silent violence Reggi readied to unleash on his unwitting target. In the seconds between the star-filled interlude and the burst of commotion, he thought again of his true love. Erik couldn't protect her. He had to save Carlotta or die trying.

Thunderous applause filled the theatre, drowning out the dramatic scene unfolding on a hidden platform high above the stage. Erik leapt at Reggi panther-like, driving his right boot full force into Reggi's ribs. He couldn't be sure if Reggi got a shot away before the assault, but he was certain there wouldn't be a second. Reggi rolled away from Erik, giving him the time to draw a flick knife. Erik stood and faced his wounded prey, one hand protecting cracked ribs, the other pointing his blade in front of him, ready to thrust into the fray.

Erik didn't rush, knowing Reggi had broken ribs. Reggi had the desperate gaze of a wounded animal cornered, a singular thought, survival. The faceoff, a surreal battle, unfolded to the sound of adoring applause below. The irony made Reggi smile. He brushed blood trickling from his mouth, as if to camouflage his imminent defeat.

Reggi looked at the blood and said something to Erik before he attacked, his angry utterances drowned out by the noise. Reggi moved swiftly, belying his stocky frame, surprising Erik with three swift thrusts of his blade, all just missing, until the fourth slashed Erik's forearm, drawing blood. But Reggi's initial victory came at a cost. Erik drove a fist square into his damaged ribs. The searing pain made Reggi drop his weapon and stagger backwards, unable to protect his ravaged torso. Erik advanced toward his disabled foe, showing no mercy, viciously punching and kicking until and after Reggi's demise. What he left behind on the platform was a blood-riddled message to Capo that would permanently drive him and his family from Erik's home of music.

Reggi lay slumped, his final expression one of shock over his downfall. Erik stooped over his opponent and looked him square in the eyes. "This is for Bernard," he declared, ramming a violent punch square into his face.

Applause thundered from below, drawing an ironic smile from the victor. Erik stood over his vanquished opponent, a wild glare, as if Reggi symbolised all the killers he'd faced in his lifetime. "And for Rose," he said, suddenly remembering why he had killed again. He looked down to the front row. Carlotta and Christine stood with everyone, oblivious to the crime scene above them. Erik wanted to stand with Carlotta in celebration, but he knew he never could. In that one violent moment, Erik had become a pariah, an outcast feted never to belong to the world of opera. He turned away, knowing that he could not be with Carlotta again. Just as the curtain closed on the successful opening night of *La Traviata,* so too the curtain on Erik's dreams.

Raoul sat and gazed at the two divas joyfully applauding along with the house of opera lovers. Their friendship had blossomed during these trying times. Raoul, too, had felt his bond grow with both of them. He even dared to believe love could follow. About to stand and join Christine, a wasp-like sting on his neck halted him from doing so. He touched the pain with his hand. There was a tiny smear of blood on his middle finger, making him instinctively look around him for the flying intruder. The generous applause lingered, turning his joy to annoyance, as if every clap thundered against his skull, surging louder by the second until he had to leave the auditorium.

Raoul motioned to Christine he was heading outside, instantly concerning her before he signalled he'd soon return. Raoul touched his throbbing neck, looking for a sign of more blood, but the trickle had dried. He reached the exit doors, welcoming the silence, and headed for the quietest corner he could find, away from the glare. He slumped into a shaded chair, the throbbing from his neck moving down his arm. He lay back in the seat, breathing deeply and trying to contain a rapid heartbeat. Pain swelled in his chest, immobilising him and ultimately shutting him down into unconsciousness.

CHAPTER TWENTY-SIX

CLOSING NIGHT REHEARSALS

We walked into the Garnier, our composition ready to perform after some heartfelt days of auditions. I'd captured the savagery of the previous century's incidents, although I still wondered if Diva's enthusiasm for our final song was born from her not wanting to relive those events. Since then, I practiced alone, honing the piece, wondering if Diva did the same. I'd find out on the night, just a day away.

We arrived early so the Diva could inspect the spectacular Grand Foyer art exhibition, featuring some of the 22nd century's icons of digital art: Van Gough Alive, Yayoi Kusama's Infinity Mirrors Room, Banksy's culture wars, Lia Chavez's meditation nightclub and Global Art's algorithmic foreground, the top collections.

Satisfied, we went straight to centre stage, where a Steinway piano and standup microphone were set up for our final rehearsal. Background props for *La Traviata* filled the sparsely decorated stage floor as crew prepared *La Traviata* scenery for the following weeks opening of the opera season.

Diva called out to the crew working in lighting. "Can we have the lighting on now?

"We can have it ready in fifteen minutes," came a reply from the back of the hall.

Diva nodded and walked over to one of the props, a table and chairs, and sat down. "Refreshments Peri!" she asked, which Peri quickly organised. Diva sipped on her lemon and water, occasionally engaging in scales, preparing for a rehearsal.

I sat at the piano, waiting for lighting. "Would you like me to play?"

"Soon enough. We have the stage for the next few hours," Diva replied, looking out to the theatre, her gaze directed toward Box Five. "Sometimes, I swear I see her."

"Madame Giraud?"

She didn't reply, lost in her reflections, making me think of those events. "I'm sorry for what happened to you."

Diva remained silent for some time, as if she didn't

hear me. "Love carries a considerable toll. Would you pay such a price?"

I shook my head slightly, unable to honestly answer. "What became of everyone after the opening night?"

The Diva drew a deep breath, seemingly struggling to revisit that time in her life. "Events unfolded quickly, and it all started with Madame Giraud."

"How soon did you learn about....." I didn't finish, fearing I'd push her too far before our final rehearsal.

Diva flashed an angry glance at me. "If you don't know that, you're not ready for tomorrow's performance." She brushed past me to the microphone, immediately practising scales, signalling we rehearse. The two hours continued professionally, ultimately delivering a perfect-pitch song.

"I'm ready, but you are not. See Flynn and tell him what I said. I'll see you tomorrow," she announced, walking away briskly, showing her displeasure.

"What time is our business appointment," I retaliated, making the Diva stop and turn.

"Are you upset, Benny?" she asked, an irony in her tone.

"You know that can't be, but at least I'm trying."

Her annoyance melted away as she affectionately placed one hand on my neck. "I know, darling," she whispered, kissing my lips. "Do what I ask. Because, then, when you know more, you'll be ready for what I will ask of you."

I gazed at her inquisitively. "What do you want? I feel like it won't include me."

"You must do this for me, Benny. I ask a lot of you, but it's what you seek. Trust me and see Flynn. He will prepare you."

I nodded, resigned to my fate. "I've searched for an elusive diamond and failed at every turn, no matter how hard I try. I have nothing else left but to trust you."

She kissed me passionately. "Until tomorrow, my love," she whispered, then left.

So I returned to Flynn in the Grand Hall where he was standing in front of one of the digital exhibitions. "Your rehearsal went well?"

"Not well enough. I'm still not ready. I have to return to the opening night."

Flynn nodded. "Soon enough, but first, there's something else I want you to see," he said, turning toward the exhibition. "Set augmented sight," he said, and we walked into the digital adaption of Kusama's famous 'Chandelier of Grief', a stunning dark three-dimensional space lit only by a single crystal chandelier but illuminated and infinitely replicated in every direction. The original 5-hectare area of a real chandelier and mirrors were recreated within the confined space of the Grand Hall, making for an ethereal world above and beneath the infinite platform on which we stood.

"I wanted you to see this before your final journey back." Wherever we walked felt to be the centre of the chandelier universe. I stopped and turned a full 360 degrees to take in the infinite realm. "You asked me what the Sensorium looked like," Flynn said, signalling to the vastness.

"If the Sensorium designed me, why would I be denied passage through it?"

"At first sight, this creation is spectacular, but in time, you'd lose purpose in a sea of images that made little sense to you. The Sensorium would dazzle then overwhelm you. You're programmed to live on Earth."

I was about to ask more when a small light in the distance caught my eye. "Do you see that?"

"Yes. Let's walk to it together."

A short walk revealed the Garnier Grand Hall's magical light, seemingly floating in the digital creation.

"It's a recreation of the Grand Hall inside the art?"

Flynn shook his head. "No, it's the actual hall."

We walked into the Garnier just as the theatre exit doors swung open. Satisfied Parisians streamed from the theatre hall, some heading outside for waiting cabs, many queueing for bistro food, open for a few more hours. Some revellers opted for the quieter corners to enjoy a celebratory wine and talk about the night's spectacular performance. One solitary figure sat sleeping in a chair, seemingly having overindulged in the fine wine on offer. I cast a momentary glance before realising that it was Raoul. I turned to question Flynn, but I was alone, returned to a past century of opera, the night named in opera folklore as the infamous opening night.

CHAPTER TWENTY-SEVEN

RAMIFICATIONS

The mood was upbeat in Philippe's box as the appreciative crowd began to file out of the theatre, lively chatter signalling the show's success. Philippe exchanged congratulatory nods with Capo, their private acknowledgement for the evening's triumph. Their company would be the talk of Paris and Philippe was one step away from taking full control of the Garnier. Erik had left the company and Carlotta had been convinced to cooperate, leaving the signing of new contracts a mere formality. His confidence soared as he turned to Inspector Moreau and his wife to accept their congratulations.

"You must be proud tonight," Moreau said.

"I couldn't have wished for more. Come and join me for the cast celebrations," Philippe said, guiding Moreau and his wife back stage where the cast and crew gathered. Philippe introduced them to a number of the cast before leaving them to mingle with the crowd, so he could join the group with Viola and raise a glass to her performance. He hadn't felt more proud in his life than that moment, that was until he saw Madame Giraud hand Inspector Moreau a letter that he opened. Upon reading its contents, Moreau's mood turned decidedly sombre. He immediately phoned someone before signalling Philippe to come to him.

He folded the note and placed it back in the envelope. "Madame Giraud just handed me a letter. It was hand written and signed by the Opera Ghost."

Philippe laughed at the suggestion, but Moreau's serious mood deepened. "This ethereal guest has made some disturbing accusations that may incriminate you, monsieur."

"Inspector, you aren't seriously going to listen to the meanderings of an ageing woman who has heard and told one too many stories about her imagined phantom?"

"I take all accusations seriously, monsieur. That's my job."

Moreau turned and summoned one of his officers who approached. "Have you protected the potential crime scene?"

"There's a cordon of officers in place, awaiting your instructions, Inspector."

"Has Monsieur D'Arenberg been located?"

"Yes. He is in the Grand Hall. We have cordoned the area. He's—"

Moreau interrupted him. "Thank you, officer. That will be all. I will join you shortly," he replied, turning to Philippe.

"I have to attend to a potential crime scene here in your opera house. I will post officers around this room to make sure no one goes in or out. Can you inform your cast and crew that I will oversee interviews and security checks of all in attendance when I return ?"

Moreau was about to leave, but Philippe drew him back. "The officer mentioned Raoul. Is he part of this investigation?"

"I will tell you when I find out more. " Moreau turned and shared a brief word with his wife before leaving the crowded room. All occupants now engaged in conjecture about what had occurred, except one. Madame Giraud stood alone, looking directly at Philippe with a penetrating, accusing gaze.

Erik could not get the image of Carlotta out of his mind. He wanted to be with her to explain the incidents that now swirled around the Garnier. His life had come full circle, returning him to the underground lair, trapped it seemed by the curse of the Opera Ghost. "Stop playing and kill me now!" he cried into the darkness, hearing only his echo bounce back across the lake, taunting him.

He could never return, for he knew Capo would not rest until he got his revenge. His life would become little more than a silhouette of the life he sought and it had to remain so if the two divas he cared for were to live. His cocooned existence of extreme radio silence would endure as Moreau's investigation sought the criminals who'd wrapped their tentacles around Paris opera. Even Bernard had to disappear, leaving him one last contact to the outside world.

CHAPTER TWENTY-EIGHT

THE NEW OPERA GHOST

Several eventful weeks passed before some normalcy returned to the Garnier. Erik had directed letters to and forth to Madame Giraud, educating her about the bad actors who'd infiltrated the Garnier. They never met in person, only risking verbal contact from the secret compartment beside Box Five like a repentant sinner seeking absolution from a high priestess.

"Inspector Moreau and his team have spent the last fortnight interviewing everyone and there have been teams scaling the Garnier for hidden channels to the underground, without luck, it seems," said Madame Giraud.

Erik concurred. "All but one way through was destroyed and they haven't been anywhere near that. Are they still searching for me?"

"They believe you fled to Italy and have gone into

hiding. So investigations have been handed to local police."

There was silence as Erik took in the news before he asked about those he sought to help. "Is Carlotta safe?"

"She is very much in control, now Philippe has been taken into custody. It's likely he'll take the fall for Capo's work. She—"

Erik cut her short. "Is she well?"

Madame Giraud gazed at the wall that divided them, seemingly seeing through it to read his mind. "She is still upset with you but I know deep down she worries for your safety. It's Christine I worry about more. She is distraught over Raoul's death. At first, she withdrew from everyone, but following the funeral her sadness has turned to bitterness. She follows every detail of Philippe's case and often calls Inspector Moreau with information. She didn't rest until Viola was indicted for partnering Philippe in this crime."

"Viola probably knew little. Her only crime was to love Philippe. Can you do anything?"

"I don't think so. They were caught in a powerful web of players with large wallets. It's always the little fish that pay the biggest price. I believe the court cases commence next month, ironically at the same time *La Traviata* re-commences. The only good thing to come from all this is the notoriety has attracted increased ticket sales. They will be performing to full houses for the next twelve months."

"The music must win," Erik said, drawing approval from Madame Giraud.

"The walls that speak to us will always ensure victory. The Opera Ghost must live on in this generation and those to come," she concurred, waiting for a reply, but Erik had left without a sound. He floated through the hidden corridors of the Garnier, phantom-like, the music all that remained to quench a fallen soul.

CHAPTER TWENTY-NINE

CLOSING NIGHT

I returned through the portal back to where Flynn remained in the infinite chandeliers exhibition. "Are you ready for Diva's final performance?"

Raoul's death remained painfully raw in my mind. "She lost everyone she loved either through deception, sacrifice or fate."

"Diva sought and achieved fame and paid the price," said Flynn.

"I'm trying to help her. I'll make her see she still has much to live for."

"You can try, Benny, but her grief is profound. Help Diva perform her last and most difficult performance."

"Of course."

"Then you are ready. Finish the lyrics Diva requested. Then prepare for the performance and join her on stage this evening," Flynn said, extending his hand to me. We shook hands as if for the last time, making me even more determined to pull Diva from her grief.

Drawn curtains blocked the view of the patrons as they shuffled into the Garnier, the noise of the crowd rising as they gradually filled to the total capacity. Diva was on stage in a strapless red Valentino gown and Tiffany diamond necklace. She sat on the piano stool behind closed curtains, reading the notes and lyrics of my final composition, seemingly so enthralled with the work she didn't notice my approach.

I sat beside her and waited for her to finish. "You have captured all of them," she said, nodding with delight. "I'd kiss you, but this face took an hour for a makeup specialist to complete!"

Her beauty shone as bright as the diamond jewellery she wore. Her happiness was even more colourful. I wanted that moment never to change. "You are stunning."

Diva studied my choice of tuxedo. "You will draw some admiring eyes, but not too many. You should know by now that a Diva must have all the attention!"

We laughed, enjoying a private moment before they drew the curtains, announcing us to the eyes of the opera world. "I'm so sorry for everything that happened to you, Diva, especially opening night."

"Dark forces fell heavily on many that night. I lost my true love, as did Carlotta. She never spoke of him after that fateful evening, but I knew she loved Erik."

"She never knew of his fate?"

"No. Erik would never risk drawing Capo back into Carlotta's life. I found out from Madame Giraud only after Carlotta passed away."

"Erik died in the Garnier underground?"

"I believe so, but if Madame Giraud knew, she took it to her grave. I sometimes felt his presence when I struggled to return to opera."

I stroked Diva's arm. "He loved you every bit as much as Raoul?"

"No. Erik loved Carlotta. But he loved the music more. That was his final lesson for me. So I returned to opera, but not before I did many things I regret. Tonight, I want to right those wrongs, and your music will help me do just that."

She spoke with such hope. I dared to believe she'd be with me always. "Perhaps then you'll be ready to perform again. Then, I can write new music for you."

Diva fought back the tears, genuinely touched. "You have produced the final performance I asked of you. It will be remembered for an eternity if you follow my lead. Will you do that, Benny?"

I remembered Flynn's words of advice. "This is what my program...I mean, my purpose is."

Diva stood, youthful excitement in her movement, as she walked to her position on the other side of the piano. "Then we are ready."

I played some scales to check the grand piano was perfectly tuned. Then Diva signalled for the MC to introduce us, providing a review of the Diva's illustrious life before the curtains were opened to a mix of patrons, mainly humans, ranging from lifelong fans to the curious post-humans.

The spotlight fell on me as I played a montage of the Diva's memorable performances, from Verdi's famous operas to an overture into my arrangement. A second spotlight on Diva drew warm applause. She shone in her rose gown and received hushed appreciation as she began her accompaniment.

She sang "Chandelier" with genuine emotion, knowing it to be her last performance. The lyrics told of her life, love, and loss, effortlessly captivating her spellbound audience, quickly drawing standing ovations and multiple 'encores'.

Touched by her fan's response, Diva stepped to the front of the stage to share a last intimate moment. "Thank you, everyone. Did you like my new song?" Frantic applause.

"It's beautiful. My extraordinary friend wrote it. He happens to be sitting right behind me!" She turned to me, as did the spotlight. Again generous applause. "I love you dearly, Benny. Can we hear it again?" She asked, not demanding. I responded by playing a piece from it. "Isn't he a special musician, folks?" Extended applause.

The spotlight faded from me back to Diva. "Half tempo, darling," she whispered, and I played a mellow rendition so Diva could say more heartfelt words.

"Thank you for coming to see me tonight. My career peaked a long time ago, and I'm so grateful to all of you who remembered me. Everything I achieved was due, in part, to hard work, but mainly I was lucky. Lucky enough to meet talented people every step of the way to becoming a diva, from talented and patient mentors in my youth to a whole range of people who helped me overcome the many barriers to becoming a performer. The song you just heard was a tribute to all of them, most of whom have long passed away. Only one other still lives. So this encore song is not only for you, my most loyal of fans, but for the one remaining member of the *La Traviata* cast."

The Diva turned to me, and I again played "Chandelier" amidst rapturous applause, all the while wondering who had survived those tumultuous years.

The Diva sang with even more passion, believing this

to be her last performance. She held the audience in her hand as the spotlight slowly dimmed in time with the final verse, not a dry eye to be seen. Behind us, the background curtain slowly opened, revealing a group of musicians. I knew nothing of this surprise act and wondered if this was part of another encore. By the song's end, Diva signalled me to join her and take the final bow for the audience, who were pleading for more.

"Thank you. That was my final performance," Diva insisted to a chorus of disappointed fans wanting more. "Thank you. I have one last surprise. I have arranged a surprise guest to perform for you. Jazz fans may know her, but what they may not know is that she once graced this very stage, performing *La Traviata* on opening night."

Diva glanced my way as if to gain strength. "Viola?" I whispered, drawing a wry smile from her.

She turned back to the audience. "At the time, she was a promising performer, but events were to take that away from her, events I'm ashamed to say I contributed to, much to my lifelong regret. So tonight, with great pride, I introduce a true shining light of the music world, backed by her band. Please welcome Viola."

Diva and I walked from the stage to a porter who escorted us to reserved seats among the excited crowd to watch Viola's surprise performance. "Do you like my surprise?" She asked.

I nodded, excited to hear her performance. "She never performed opera again after her debut in *La Traviata*?"

Diva didn't respond immediately, more eager to see Viola's introduction. The spotlight turned back to the stage. Viola wore a shimmering black dress, and like Diva, had aged little from post-human implants.

"I wronged her, Benny. Once Philippe was convicted, I took further retribution on Viola, blaming her for everything Philippe did to me."

"What happened to her?"

"I saw to it that Carlotta removed her from the Garnier. Ultimately, she was convicted for being an accessory to Philippe's misdemeanours and served jail time. She didn't deserve that."

Viola looked out across the theatre, allowing her band to warm up, seemingly enjoying the bittersweet moment. Where her face showed no signs of ageing, her eyes, like the Diva's, were filled with melancholy, offering a glimpse of the life she'd led since that fateful night when she was the toast of Paris opera.

The band ready, Viola spoke. "It's been a long time since I stood on these famous boards. Too long," she said, looking directly to Diva. "At one stage, I vowed never to return, but I have you, Christine, to thank for convincing me otherwise. In many ways, I have you to thank for giving me the life I led. There were some awful lows, but ultimately I regained my love for music," she said, blowing a kiss to her husband, the bass guitarist in the band. "Christine and I met in troubled times, the opening of *La Traviata* a century ago. Some attributed the darkness of those times to the Phantom who ruled these hidden halls. Some say he still does. I dedicate this song to the many who were touched deeply by the experience, particularly two brothers. One paid with his life. The other lost his freedom."

The bright spotlight gave way to subdued background lighting. Viola and her band performed "Wayfaring Stranger", her haunting tribute to another time. It was mainly appreciated by the humans in the audience, ironically entertained by two post-human performers whose lives were prolonged by technological advances.

Diva sat spellbound by Viola's performance, seemingly wondering what may have been if not for her vengeful actions after Raoul's death. Viola's performance ended to a standing ovation that we joined, the applause not stopping until the curtains were drawn. The theatre lights remained off, hinting at a possible encore, until a light flashed high above, attracting the crowds' attention. Sparks flashed above the theatre chandelier. Smoke followed, then alarm sirens.

Theatre crew promptly appeared from the surrounding exits, overseeing an evacuation of the disbelieving crowds. Then, small fires consumed the chandelier and its structures, causing the great light to sway precariously. Frantic energy engulfed the group as they scrambled for safety; the intimacy of the earlier encore turned into a chaotic climate of fear and flight.

Frenetic movement cascaded out from the centre of the theatre until only two braved the peril of a swaying eight-tonne chandelier twenty metres high.

"It's about to fall!" I held my hand out to Diva to take her from the threat.

She took my hand but pulled me back, seemingly resolved to her fate. "I told you this was my last performance. If the Garnier wishes to take me now, so be it."

I shook my head. "Don't force me to carry you out, Christine."

"That's the first time you called me Christine. Stay with me, and I will reveal more secrets. You'll learn of what your life is and what it will be."

I could easily have carried her to safety, but her expression was intense, gesturing to an inevitability of our perilous yet momentous juncture. Yet, there was also serenity in her demeanour despite the threat. She'd planned this.

"We could share much more in the future. I won't let you do this, Christine."

"Would you want to continue to live, knowing you killed the one person who truly loved you?"

"Philippe's actions brought about Raoul's death. You couldn't know."

"I took his devotion for granted, too consumed by Philippe's slight. I was selfish. Raoul's reported death from a heart attack was a lie. I want the truth of his life to be told and never forgotten. Not the distortions recorded in history. I owe him that."

Flames spread across the theatre's ceiling, spewing a thick fog of smoke in its wake. Theatre crew frantically gestured to the last of the crowd, now more a mob desperately forcing its way forward through clogged exits. Visibility quickly deteriorated as my view of desperate faces fleeing disappeared, leaving only the high pitched sound of fear.

One attendant called out to Diva, drawing her attention to the escape route, before the fleeing crowds pushed him through the safety exit. Deadly plumes of smoke cast a black shadow over the beautiful theatre, hiding us from the rapidly emptying cathedral, leaving us to face the lethal circumstance alone.

So engrossed in her scheme, Diva appeared hardly

to notice the looming calamity. "I'm tired, Benny. I've lived longer than a human should." She held my hand and looked out to the stage as if there was no danger, and opera was being performed. "I spent most of my life feeling regret for what I did. To have Viola perform..." Diva's words faltered with a fit of coughing as the smoke besieged her. "She deserved better," she said, covering her face with her coat. She brushed away tears of smoke and sorrow before managing a smile in-between incessant coughing. "Viola's had a good life, Benny. It turned out well for her."

"The same could be for you," I said, offering my coat as a second protection from the fumes.

She leaned in close to me, gaining some comfort from the advancing smoke. "I tired of this life long ago. I long to meet Raoul again and live the life we should have had."

"You may never see Raoul again?"

An ominous rumbling sounded out as the fire claimed the chandelier's structure. The chandelier began spinning uncontrollably. Long cracks opened across Chagall's masterpiece, as the painting of angels melted away.

"Dear Benny, I only loved Raoul. You understand I can never show you how that felt, but together we can show others, many generations."

"I failed you, Christine. I brought no more than a

flirtation. But, please, let me take you from here. If not for me, for your fans. Think of the joy you bring them."

"You promised to do everything I asked of you," Diva replied, looking up to the fractured ceiling, "I'm just a shell of my true self, more like you than you realise. The end will be a blessing. Let Flynn have what's left of us, our digital imprints."

"They're just digital memories. Your human life will be lost. That's precious. I would give a hundred of my digital lives to have that. Please, Christine, we still have time!"

Diva defiantly lifted her gaze up to the famous chandelier, ignoring my protection, choking from lack of air, willing the glittering light to claim her. "After all this time, the Phantom still rules the dark corridors. He has come to claim us. Do you see him?"

Diva pointed to the light patterns traversing across the blazing fumes. I followed her gaze, searching for the Phantom, but the lights were no more than chaotic patterns shaped by the looming destruction. Then as the cracks began to widen, I did see a design I recognised, but not of the Phantom's making. Instead, the light emanated from a source far more potent than the supposed opera ghost.

I looked away from the devastation. "You planned this with Flynn, didn't you?"

Diva ignored me as if already lost to this world, determined to use the last of her strength to speak her truth. "Do you not see Erik?"

"The lights come from an infinitely more powerful source than the Phantom."

"Then we'll find answers in our next reincarnation."

"Why the theatrics? Flynn could have easily ended your suffering long ago."

"To my last breath, I remain a diva. Our story will be retold around the world for generations."

A large cracking sound roared from above, signalling the chandelier's imminent plunge. The Diva looked up for the last time. "I want this, Benny. Let Flynn and his kind retrieve our memories and retell a story of enduring love," she whispered, her last words.

Rather than carry her to safety, I comforted and protected Diva in a futile attempt to save her. Time left me only a glancing sight of a hundred globes encircling their massive gold frame, plummeting and shattering into a hundred-hundred light orbs flashing intermittently in my final memory, a volcanic plume of devastation. The famous chandelier fell for a second time in its illustrious history, continuing a legend that would outlast the renowned home of opera itself.

DIGITAL KARMA

A colourless bedroom came into view. A man in a white coat appraised me.

"How are you feeling today, Benny?"

I didn't respond immediately, taking the time to consider unfamiliar surroundings. "Yes, yes I..." I stumbled to register my predicament, wondering only if my name was Benny.

The stranger appeared to understand my confusion. "You drifted off to sleep again. Christine called. Do you feel well enough to see her now?"

Who was Christine? In trying to recall, I discovered my mind contained a vast library of memories to draw from, but the magnitude of choice confused me further. "Yes. Christine. Perhaps tomorrow, Doctor...?"

"Flynn. Doctor Flynn. I'll call her and let her know."

He took my pulse and wrote notes on a com positioned

at the end of my bed. I studied him as he drew the curtains to aid my rest. "Try to sleep some more," said Flynn, smiling before he left.

I returned his smile. "I will."

There was a familiarity about him I couldn't place. I nodded appreciatively, pretending drowsiness. Once he left the room I sat up and studied the room looking for clues about who and where I was, needing anything but rest. I walked around the room, stopping at a vase of flowers left on the bedside table with an open card from Christine. Straining to remember anything led only to failure and frustration, but then a scene from a popular 21st-century movie, *The Wife*, popped in my head. Glen Close comforted her husband, a writer, who'd collapsed from a heart attack.

The scene sparked a response. I remember. I tell stories of life and love. I've started a new story that I need to finish, a consuming passion, one I share with a partner. It had to be Christine?

Day turned to deep night, and I lay in the silence, slowly pinning more memories together, surprisingly with no trace of fatigue. Then a powerful new realisation snapped into my self-awareness. I don't sleep.

I never sleep.

TO BE CONTINUED...

The third and final instalment of
the Phantoms trilogy will be released in 2023

www.ingramcontent.com/pod-product-compliance
Lightning Source LLC
Chambersburg PA
CBHW020256120726
47904CB00001B/224